Fan

‘Spin[illegible] of Stephen King’s *Misery* will love Abby Davies.’
Sarah Linley, *The Trip*

‘Completely unputdownable! Disturbing, thrilling and absolutely fizzing with tension!’
Paula Johnston, *The Lies She Told*

‘Thrilling and equally frightful, Her No1 Fan had me on the edge of my seat.’
Sophia Spiers, *The Call of Cassandra Rose*

‘Really gripping and pacy. I loved the plot, so clever.’
Rebecca De Winter, *Best Friends*

‘I don't think I breathed during the last 30% of this book. The tension and creep factor were brilliant! Unputdownable!’
Jessica Huntley, *The Darkness Series*

'Her No.1 Fan is sooooo utterly gripping. I flew hrough the pages and I can't wait for more from this author.’
Mikayla Davids, *Her Daughter’s Lies*

‘This was so fast-paced and relentless that after reading it in two sittings, my head was spinning.”
Veronika Jordan, Book Reviewer

By Abby Davies

Mother Loves Me

The Cult

Arrietty

Her No.1 Fan!

HER NO.1 FAN

Abby Davies

Apple Loft Press

HER NO.1 FAN

Published worldwide by Apple Loft Press.
This edition published in 2023.

www.abbydavies.com

For Matt, Harry, Tabby and Immy

Chapter 1

NOW

I opened my eyes to a room I had never seen.

Through a fuzzy mist, I saw crimson walls and a standing lamp with a red shade.

To my right hung green curtains printed with elves.

I blinked and snatched a breath. *Breathe, Rachel, breathe.*

In the corner of the room stood a fully decked Christmas tree; on the wardrobe, a ceramic Santa Claus with a cracked hat; above my head, a naked bulb, unlit. Damp crawled across the ceiling like a mouldy network of varicose veins.

It's not Christmas. It's only September.

The air smelled of charity shop and dirty carpet.

Something deep inside me shivered. I listened hard. All was silent apart from a weird squalling in my head.

I was on a double bed. The mattress was bumpy, the duvet covered with snowmen, the room cold.

I'm still in my pyjamas.

My chest spasmed. A scream clawed at my throat. I craned my neck around and stared at my left wrist, which was handcuffed to an iron bed frame. I was abruptly aware of an intense ache in my arm, a burn in my wrist. Tears trickled down my cheeks and I began to shake uncontrollably. The handcuff clattered, and I begged my wrist to stay still, frightened he would hear, but the shakes wouldn't stop. I couldn't make them stop. My body wouldn't obey my brain.

Oh, God. Please let Jacob be OK.

Please let him be alive.

Jacob's dead.
NO. *He can't be. I can't lose him too.*
I looked at the door.
Someone was coming.

Chapter 2

Twelve Hours Earlier

'I'm sorry to tell you this, Rachel, but we discovered a structural problem, which can prevent women from becoming pregnant, and this is what is happening in your case...'

I took the leaflet without seeing it. 'What did you say about the chances of me being able to have a baby if I have surgery?'

Doctor Somerton smiled sympathetically. 'About twenty percent of women can conceive post-surgery.'

'Twenty percent? That's not very much, is it?'

'If you're not successful after that, there are other options of course such as surrogacy and adoption. But I expect you'll want to discuss everything with your partner first, have a good think about how you'd like to move ahead.'

I don't want to move ahead. I want to rewind time and go back to the way things were when I thought I was just unlucky - that life stress was stopping me from getting pregnant. I don't want this version of reality. I want the old one back.

Fighting tears, I stood up and left Doctor Somerton's room.

I drifted along the corridors of the hospital out into rain and the scent of wet tarmac. Above me the sky was bruised, almost black. Lightless and luckless – like us. Jacob and I had been trying and failing to get pregnant for over two years. To other people who weren't failing to get pregnant, it might not have sounded a lot, but that amounted to over two dozen failures – twenty-plus times your heart rose and sunk when that little blue mark didn't show its face. A thousand or more times you thought and worried and dreamed about it, all while trying to keep your chin up, put on a brave face, and stay positive. So many platitudes, so many clichés, so little luck. I should have known the problem lay with me; that I was the broken one, not him, but I'd spoken to friends who'd reassured me that it took time and not to stress about it, that fixating on the problem would only make it worse. But none of my friends had taken this long to fall pregnant, and deep down I think I'd known there was something wrong with me, I just hadn't wanted to admit it.

With no umbrella and no coat, I wrapped my arms around myself, bowed my head, and hurried out of the car park. Our three-bed on Sycamore Drive was only a five-minute walk from the hospital. When I'd arrived earlier, the sun had been smiling, the forecast dry, but now the skies were oppressive, the air bitter, nipping at my cheeks and hands like savage mice, trying to whistle up my legs towards my broken body through the tears in my jeans.

I have a structural defect. Why me?

Shivering and drenched, I halted at the traffic lights. Rain pelted off the concrete splattering my ankles. To my left stood a woman with four children. They were clearly hers because they shared her auburn hair. The littlest one slipped her hand into mine then jumped back in fright when she realised I wasn't her mummy.

The mother laughed and rolled her eyes at me, 'Sorry, love.'

I tried to smile but my lips were frozen. Why did some people get to have four perfect babies when I couldn't even have one?

The lights turned red, the walking man green. Someone hovered beyond my periphery waiting to cross.

Rain hammered down darkening the world in front of me. I trailed after the family up the hill, watching as the two youngest jumped and danced in puddles having a wonderful time – just as they should.

On instinct, I glanced back. A tall figure trudged up the hill a few paces behind me, his hands shoved in the pockets of a bright blue anorak, hood up, face down. If the red-haired family hadn't been five steps ahead of me, I would've felt nervous. Apart from me, the man behind, and the group ahead, the street was abandoned, the darkness and pouring rain limiting activity.

I checked my watch, surprised to see how late it was. Dread scudded up my throat. Jacob would be home soon, and I'd have to let him know the news. Picturing his hurt face, I shook my head against the idea of telling him. I couldn't bear his misery too. He was always positive, always smiling – to strip that away would be unbearable. My husband had always wanted a large family; he'd grown up with three brothers and dreamed of our children enjoying the same companionship he had as a child. I was an only child, and for that reason had always told myself I would give my first child a sibling, as I'd sometimes felt lonely growing up, envious of the rapport I'd seen between my best friends and their siblings. But now we'd be lucky if we got to have one, let alone two or more.

The family crossed the road and headed for Juniper Avenue. I watched them disappear into the gloom and listened to their fading voices. Such happiness, such energy. Children were everything. There was nothing I wanted more than a baby. Every part of me throbbed with longing and had done for some time. It was strange because I was happy, but something was missing. A hollow ache pulsed in my heart as though some part had been siphoned off. Only having a baby to love and nurture would fill this aching void. I knew I ought to count myself lucky because although my parents and I were estranged, I had Jacob, a nice house and my dream job, but I didn't care about any of that. I wanted a baby.

Twenty percent of women go on to get pregnant.

But eighty percent don't.

My shoulders tensed at the sound of the man in the anorak coughing behind me.

I hurried up the incline sploshing through puddles, socks wet-through, and turned left onto Sycamore Drive, focusing on my house. In less than fifteen seconds, I'd be inside, warm, safe, and drying off. I'd make myself a cup of tea, slip into something comfy and try to work out the gentlest way to break the news to my husband.

*

I sat on the bed drying my hair and avoiding my reflection in the mirror above the dressing table. Despite having sipped hot tea and dousing myself in near-scolding water, I couldn't stop shivering. I left the room and ramped up the heating, padded downstairs and grabbed the blanket from the ottoman then curled up on the sofa and waited. Jacob ought to be home any minute. Soon, I'd have to tell him and endure his shock and pain. Pain that would mirror mine and make everything feel that much more real.

I swiped at my eyes and stared around the room, which seemed strangely unfamiliar. This was our home of three years, my haven, yet it felt alien right now, its soft accents of pastel blues and pinks a hollow comfort. I'd taken such delight in choosing accessories, adoring the fact that Jacob and I had enough money to buy lovely sofas, walnut coffee tables and plush velvet cushions. We visited a couple of galleries together and spent ages debating over an expensive painting of an elephant with her calf, so good it looked like a photograph. I'd always loved the Disney film *Dumbo* and had collected elephant figurines and cuddly toys as a child. I still had a handful in our bedroom. Despite our estrangement, I'd kept the cuddly Dumbo my father had brought me back from the States. Just thinking about the scene where Dumbo's mother swung him in her trunk through the bars of her cage made me tear up. Now, that painting hung above the fireplace mocking me. Elephants could have babies. I couldn't.

Childhood nostalgia mingled with the terrible present. Even if I did manage to conceive, Mum and Dad would never get to meet their grandchild. I wouldn't let them. Not after all they'd said and done.

You won't be able to conceive anyway.

You might be able to. Don't be so negative.

I need to prepare myself for the worst. We both do.

What about surrogacy then? Or adoption?

My stomach tightened. It was too soon to consider those options. Too early to give up, I knew that, but pessimism had captured my mind spreading its blackness through every thought and feeling like an oil spill.

Where's Jacob? He ought to be back by now.

I frowned. Now and then he did this. Promised he'd be home at a certain time then turned up late, drunk off his head, slurring excuses about forgetting the time, having too much fun catching up with his mates. To be fair, he hadn't known about my examination. I should have told him, but he was already worrying about his dad, who had recently been diagnosed with type two diabetes. Jacob's parents were amazing, the kindest, least judgemental people I knew. Sometimes I envied his relationship with them, wished I had that, but I'd made my bed when I'd done the 'unforgivable' in my father's words. There was nothing I could do to change that, and I wouldn't change it even if I could. I didn't need my parents in my life. Didn't want them.

I glanced at the living room doorway, certain for a moment that I'd heard something coming from outside in the direction of the front door. A scuff. A moan. I listened harder. Nothing.

My mobile rang, making me jump. I grabbed it and

looked at the caller ID. My heart stilled. It was my mum. How strange when I'd just been thinking about her.

Not that strange at all. You think about them all the time.

I frowned as a hectic whirlwind of emotions flew through me, piercing, pinching and ripping. I hadn't spoken to them for years. But they were the ones in the wrong, not me. Jacob had tried to persuade me to forgive them, but I couldn't. The things they'd said and done were unforgivable – far more inexcusable than what I'd done. Jacob said I was being stubborn, and that nothing mattered more than family, but I disagreed. If they loved me unconditionally, they'd never have said those hateful words or acted out the way they did.

The funny thing was that they still sent me a birthday card every year and one at Christmas. I didn't do the same.

Yet, as I looked at their number on my screen, a lump thickened my throat. Hope, anger and fear constricted my airway as I stared at the word *Mum.* My finger darted to 'Accept', then hovered a milimetre above the green icon. There was nothing more in the world I wanted than to see my mum, to feel her arms around me, have her hold me, and tell her what I'd just learned about my chances of conceiving, but the ugly past reared up in my mind like Marley's ghost. I remembered the shame they'd made me feel; the way they'd looked at me, the way they'd treated Jacob, blaming him for influencing my decision. Mum had tried to call me last year on my birthday, but I'd ignored the call and not even considered answering it. But tonight, my finger twitched above the green symbol on my mobile.

Jacob always said life was too short. I swallowed. I wanted to answer but something held me back.

I let the call go to voicemail.

A spark of satisfaction burned but the spark died when I saw that Mum was leaving a voice message. She'd not done that before.

Fears darted through my mind – *she's calling to say Dad's*

ill – or she's ill – or -

Should I ring back?

No. They don't deserve it.

Another thump sounded from the front of the house. Jacob had a key, so the thump was odd. Uncalled for.

I crossed the hallway, grabbed my keys, unlocked the door.

Jacob lay on the porch in the foetal position.

My hand flew to my mouth, and I dropped to my knees.

He moaned something incoherent and stabbed a finger toward the driveway.

I glanced up and saw a figure running away into the darkness. A large figure in a bright blue anorak.

Chapter 3

'Oh my God – what happened?'

I moved his hair off his forehead. He had a swollen eye which was already turning black, a cut lip, and a bruised cheek. I had never seen him hurt before. Not like this.

'Inside. We need to get inside. In case he comes back,' Jacob muttered.

I helped him to his feet and into the house, constantly glancing behind in case whoever had done this had returned. Once Jacob was inside, I slammed and locked the door, and we went into the living room. He collapsed onto the sofa with a groan.

'I'll go grab the first aid kit. Hang on.' I dashed out of the room, my heart slamming against my ribs.

I found the kit and hurried back through the house. The rain had stopped. The world felt oddly quiet. Jacob lay on the sofa, his beaten eye almost swollen shut, the other staring at me, wide and alert with adrenaline. I handed him painkillers, grabbed the blanket, and laid it over his trembling body.

'I'll clean you up a bit then I'll call an ambulance. And the police.'

'No. It's not that bad. He kicked me in the stomach but missed my ribs. I'll be fine.'

'You don't look fine,' I said, dabbing his split lip with a wet flannel.

'It's probably worse than it looks.'

I sat back. 'The police then. I'll call them.'

'No. I will.'

'OK,' I said, a little taken aback by the harshness of his tone.

He pushed himself into a sitting position with a pained grimace. His face was deathly pale, lips shivery. 'He was outside the house, hovering by the window. I asked what he was doing, and he ran at me. Punched me three times in the face then kicked me in the stomach. I didn't have time to react.' Jacob paused, swallowed, frowned hard. 'I think…I think he was watching you.'

A blast of ice chilled my veins. I glanced up at the window, launched myself off the sofa and ripped the curtains closed. 'Are you sure? Did you see his face? Did he say anything?'

Jacob stared hard at me. 'Has someone been messaging you again? Is there something you haven't told me?'

'No.'

'Really? That creepy guy who says he has a wife and two kids and that he just admires your work hasn't been in touch again?'

I shook my head. There were a few similar men who'd messaged me on Instagram telling me how talented I was, how beautiful. They were harmless – or at least, I'd thought so before now. I'd messaged them back a bit. Not wanting to give them anything nasty to say about me, I'd kept my messages brief, but polite and grateful. None of them had threatened me in any way or said anything inappropriate, but when I'd told Jacob about one of them, he'd told me to ignore the man's messages, warned that replying would encourage him – 'give him ideas'. But I was small-time in my field. I was new to this world of low-grade fame, and I was flattered. I didn't want to appear aloof or as though I thought I was too good to engage with people. These men had, after all, taken the time to send me nice messages, congratulate me on my success and offer praise that, if I was completely honest, stroked my ego and made me feel good.

I sighed and glanced worriedly at the drawn curtains.

When Jacob had warned me, I'd snorted and told him he was overreacting, but now, looking at his battered face, I wondered if he was right. Had the man who'd hurt my husband been one of those men who'd messaged me? There were three of them – I'd only told Jacob about the first one, keeping the others secret because I didn't want him to rail at me again about it.

'Rach? Has that wanker messaged you again recently?'

I bit my lip. 'He hasn't, but…'

'But what?'

'Another one has. Another two actually.'

Jacob's jaw clenched. 'I told you to make it impossible for them to DM you.'

'I know, but I like getting messages from fans. Most of them are women anyway and they say such lovely things -'

'It doesn't matter. None of that's important. Safety is. Look, what did these guys say?'

'Honestly, it was just praise. Saying they think I'm an excellent doctor, that kind of thing.'

'Nothing weird at all?'

I could tell he didn't believe me. Despite everything, I felt my cheeks flush with anger. 'No, Jacob. I'm telling the truth.'

'OK, OK, just checking. Sorry.'

He took my hands in his and held my gaze. 'We need to report this and tell the police about those men who've been contacting you.'

I frowned, uncomfortable with the idea. Those men seemed fine. If the police tracked them down and interrogated them over something like this when they were innocent, it could affect their lives, and there was nothing whatsoever in those messages to suggest any of them wanted to do Jacob – or me – harm.

Before I could voice my thoughts, Jacob called the police.

I looked down at my flat stomach. Gazed at my best

friend's intense brown eyes, and his sore, puffy lip. I probably couldn't give him a child and now this. Maybe he was right. If he'd been attacked because of me, I'd never forgive myself.

*

Two police officers came to the house to take Jacob's statement.

Having them in the house made the whole thing more surreal and even scarier. In their uniforms, they seemed large and imposing, like actors rather than real-life law enforcement. Both officers were men with serious faces. I kept darting glances at the curtains, wondering if the man who'd beaten up my husband stood outside in the dark not far away watching the house, waiting for another opportunity to approach. Or attack.

The taller man said, 'I'm Constable Hirst and I'll be taking your statement today. I'll also oversee your case, so if you wish to contact me here are my details.' He passed Jacob a card.

I listened as PC Hirst asked my husband what had happened. Both officers leaned forward on the sofa. It was clear they were taking this seriously.

Shivers prickled my spine as Jacob described again what he'd witnessed before being attacked.

'He had his face against the window, really close. That one.' Jacob indicated the bay window, one of the features that had attracted us to this house.

My skin crawled. If that was where he'd stood, he'd have had a great view of me. With the living room lights on and the night black, I'd have been on full display. At least – thank God – I'd had the good sense to lock the front door. Jacob had drilled that into me when we'd moved in together. I used to be so blasé about that sort of thing, never locking my door unless I went out, but Jacob had seen an article about a woman who was stabbed to death in her own home by a disturbed man who'd simply walked in the front door and grabbed a kitchen knife. Now I always locked the front door when I was in the house alone.

'Can you describe what he looked like?' Hirst said.

'Tall. At least six feet. And big. Broad – not fat. He didn't have a belly on him.'

'Hair? Any distinctive features?'

Jacob sighed and dragged a hand down his face, wincing as his fingers connected with his sore cheek. 'He came at me too fast. I didn't see his face. One second, I was staring at his back then his fist was coming towards me. I know he was wearing a blue coat. That's about it.'

'It was a bright blue anorak,' I said.

Jacob looked at me in surprise.

'I saw him running away, and…I think he followed me back from the hospital.'

'The hospital? What were you doing there?' Jacob said, eyes wide with alarm.

'It's nothing to worry about,' I lied. 'I'll tell you later.'

'Did you notice any other details about his appearance, Mrs Brown?' Hirst said.

I shook my head. 'Just that he was big.'

'When did you first notice he was following you?'

'I first felt someone behind me when I was at the traffic lights on Fern Road. It was only when I turned onto Sycamore Drive that I glanced around and saw him behind me. I wasn't sure he was following me, but I felt uncomfortable. I practically sprinted to the front door.'

'Good job you did,' Jacob said, squeezing my hand. 'I can't bear to think what could have happened if I hadn't come home when I did.'

'I'd locked the door,' I said, trying to reassure him and myself, but thinking that if someone was determined enough, they'd have probably found a way to break in and get to me.

Jacob opened his mouth to say something then seemed to think better of it. His thumb stroked the back of my hand, easing my stress a little.

Hirst and Jacob spoke about the attack. I didn't want to hear it all over again, but of course, I couldn't make myself go deaf. Imagining some stranger hitting Jacob made me feel sick with rage. I thumbed a tear from my cheek and sipped cold tea, wishing I had something stronger.

'Finally, did your assailant say anything at all? Did you hear his voice?'

Jacob glanced at me then quickly away. Reluctantly, he said, 'Yes.'

Hirst and his colleague leaned further forward. I watched my husband's stressed face and wondered why he wasn't elaborating.

'Mr Brown. What did he say?'

Jacob looked at me and forced a smile. 'Can I have another cup of tea?'

I fought the impulse to argue, nodded and rose to my feet. Taking the empty cups from the officers, I offered them another cup too, but Hirst shook his head, eyes never leaving my husband.

Feeling unsteady on my feet, I left the room quickly and headed for the kitchen, but curiosity and fear had me in their toxic grip, and I crept back down the hallway and hovered just out of sight behind the living room door.

'What did he say, Mr Brown?' Hirst repeated.

I heard Jacob clear his throat and leaned closer to the door.

'Mr Brown?'

There was a long, tense silence.

'After he kicked me, just before he left, he said,' Jacob swallowed, 'he said, I need her. You don't.'

Chapter 4

I listened from the kitchen as Jacob saw the police officers to the door.

'Don't hesitate to get in contact with me. Anything odd, you give me a call,' Hirst said.

Jacob thanked him and locked the door.

I slumped against the counter.

My husband trudged into the room grey-faced. 'You heard, didn't you?'

'Yes. What do you think he meant by *I need her*?'

'I don't know. But we need to be extra careful. I don't want you walking anywhere by yourself, especially not after dark like tonight – oh yeah - why were you at the hospital?'

I turned my back on him and busied about loading the dishwasher. 'Why don't I pour us a glass of wine and we can go and sit down in the lounge? You look awful.'

'I'm feeling a lot better now. The painkillers have kicked in, and that arsehole punches like a little old granny. Just tell me. Please.'

He wrapped his arms around my waist and held me against his body. I could feel his heart beating against my back, still pacing too fast after the trauma of being attacked, despite what he said. I stared at his muscular forearms, at the mole on the back of his right wrist, allowing myself to take comfort from him for a few seconds, then pulled away, and turned to face him, eyes welling up.

'I had a scan and they've discovered I have a structural problem which explains why we can't get pregnant, but -'

Jacob's lips parted slightly. He opened his mouth to ask a question, but I held up my hand and forced a smile.

'There's good news. I can have an operation that -'

He exhaled and smiled, 'Phew - for a second, I thought you were going to say you had cancer or something. So, the operation will mean you can conceive?'

I nodded weakly, unable to correct him when he seemed so relieved.

'Is it a big operation or small?'

'It's not very invasive at all, luckily.'

He pulled me into a tight cuddle and kissed my forehead. 'First, you get that news then you find me beaten up on the doorstep!' He laughed a little hysterically, 'Whatever next?'

I buried myself in his arms, eyes hidden, wide open. I needed to tell him that the surgery would only increase the chance by twenty percent, but the words were glued to my tongue.

'I'm sure this bastard will go away. He must know we'd report him to the police. He's probably shit-scared about what he's done. Hirst doesn't think he'll bother us again. I don't think he will either,' Jacob said. I heard the worry in his voice, knew he was trying to be positive, lying to himself and to me to make everything seem less depressing and stressful.

'I hope so,' I said into his shirt, inhaling his warm, familiar smell.

'But,' he said sharply, pulling my face away from his chest, 'being extra cautious still stands. Promise Rach. Promise me you won't go anywhere on your own, especially not without your phone.'

I nodded. I was awful for forgetting my mobile. I was bad at forgetting everything. Hell, the other day I left the house without my keys.

'There is something else actually,' I said, wrinkling my nose.

'What?'

I rolled my eyes. 'It's my mum.'

Jacob went very still.

'She called me.'

'Did you answer?'

'No. Of course not.' My voice sounded defensive. I stared at him, daring him to tell me I'd done the wrong thing.

He frowned and drew back. 'What if she's calling to apologise?'

I shook my head. 'I don't care. It's too late for that.'

'Rach -'

I stood up. 'I don't want to talk about this. Not now.'

He nodded and looked toward the window.

I wondered about telling him the whole truth about the operation, but he'd just been attacked by a stranger who was probably stalking me. I'd tell him in a few days when he was feeling better.

Quashing the voice telling me I was bad to keep it from him, I followed my husband upstairs, brushed my teeth, changed into my pyjamas, and slid into bed.

Outside, the night was still and silent. No owls, no breeze, no people. It was cold for September. Gone midnight. No one was out there anymore. My stalker was long gone. Police officers coming to the house had made sure of that.

Jacob popped his head into the bedroom, toothbrush in his mouth. 'Going to put the bins out. Nearly forgot.'

'Sure you feel up to it?'

He nodded and flicked off the light for me, plunging the room into darkness.

I felt for my phone on the bedside table and thought about listening to my mum's voicemail.

No. She's dug her own grave.

So I wouldn't be tempted, I picked up my phone and felt my way blindly toward my bag. After a hesitation, I switched it off and dropped it inside.

I reversed my steps, climbed into bed, turned onto my side, and closed my eyes.

Within seconds, I felt fatigue tugging my mind into stillness. Worries still stirred but they were vibrations rather than quakes. In a distant part of my psyche, I heard the bedroom door open and close, felt the mattress compress as Jacob climbed into bed beside me.

But there was something different. Something wrong.

The hairs on my cheeks tingled.

A hard body pressed against my back.

My eyes shot open as a hand clamped over my mouth and something pierced my neck.

Chapter 5

NOW

I grabbed the duvet cover with my uncuffed hand and yanked it up to my shoulders, jerking into a sitting position and drawing my knees into my chest. Outside the room, a floorboard creaked. The keyhole rattled, the door opened, and a man appeared in the doorway smiling at me. He was tall, young and lean with shoulder-length orange hair and a hunch to his shoulders.

He entered the room, closed the door, locked it and replaced the key inside the neck of his jumper. It was attached to a black lanyard. He paused in front of the locked exit and stared at me, still smiling, mouth wide.

With long strides, he closed the space between the door and the bed and perched on the mattress less than a foot away, legs jigging. He wore brown socks.

I tensed every muscle, expecting him to touch me but he smiled and did nothing. He smelled of BO and his eyes were the palest shade of green I'd ever seen. More lizard-like than human. They held a manic gleam, like that of a child on Christmas morning. I glanced at his chest, at his Rudolph the Reindeer jumper. My heart thumped harder, faster. *It's September...oh God...*

Everything was suddenly too vivid, too vibrant, too real.

I shrank inside myself and looked down at my hands, struggling to get to grips with what was happening, my brain contorting itself into knots as it attempted to catch up to reality.

PC Hirst assured us that the man who attacked Jacob was unlikely to strike again…but he was wrong...this man returned less than an hour after the police left our house...

I tried to swallow and failed. My heartbeat drummed a crazy beat and my head pounded like a battering ram.

'Hi. I'm Mikey,' he said. He had a fast, nasally voice, 'Mikey James Bell. Welcome to my home.'

He beamed around the room. There wasn't a wrinkle on his face.

'As you can probably tell, I really like Christmas,' he said with a boyish giggle.

I followed his gaze to the fake Christmas tree in the corner. I never understood how people could choose fake over real. Jacob and I always got the real thing. The smell of natural pine needles was too good to miss out on. But on this occasion, I could understand why this man had opted for pretence. The tree was paler than it should have been due to the amount of dust it had gathered; this tree wasn't just for Christmas - like a puppy. It was a year-round feature, just like the mounds of tinsel draped across the headboard.

And the evil-looking Santa.

I screamed, 'HELP!'

Mikey put a finger to his lips and smiled wider. 'Don't do that.'

I closed my mouth. Licked my lips. Tried to still the thrashing panic.

His eyes drifted to the curtains. 'Anyway, we're three miles from the nearest road and the windows are double-glazed. Strong and sturdy. Isn't that great?'

He wiped his palms on his jeans then darted out a hand and touched my cuffed wrist. His fingertips were clammy and hot. I flinched; suppressed a shudder. He had piano fingers. Long, slim, dexterous. Surgeon's fingers, some people called them. I fought the urge to bat away his fingers and glanced down at the handcuff.

His gaze followed mine. He popped a hand over his mouth and giggled again. 'Oh, yeah, tricky to shake hands with your right one cuffed like that. What's say we shake like this instead?'

He whipped back his palm, wiped his hand on his thigh and held it out.

'Left to left. How's that?' he said, voice abruptly hard, still smiling.

I made no move to shake his hand. The thought of touching those long white eels brought bile to my throat.

'Why am I here?'

My voice shook like a scared child's. I raised my chin an inch, forced myself to meet his pale eyes.

Mikey grinned and lowered his hand. Both lips disappeared into his face. Ignoring my question, he gestured to the Christmas tree. 'What d'you think?'

I looked at the tree. At its flashing lights and plastic needles. It was monstrous. Hideous enough to make eyes bleed.

His eyes darted from mine to the fake thing he called a tree, waiting, expectant.

Waiting for what? A round of applause?

'It's...nice,' I said.

He looked away and sighed, a small, satisfied smile tugging at his mouth. Opening his eyes, he darted his face closer to mine. His irises were pale, speckled with black dots. 'I'm so glad you like it. I knew you would.'

I jerked my head back and it connected with the headboard with a dull thud. Behind him, the Christmas tree leered at me, and the whole room wobbled.

'Oops. Careful now, Doc,' he said merrily.

Doc. He's calling me Doc. Does that mean...oh God...

He reached out, licking his lips, eager-eyed, like a little boy reaching for his favourite sweet. I flinched and jerked away, smashing my head again.

Hurt flashed in his eyes and he folded his arms and

pouted. 'That's not very nice. I was only trying to help.'

'I'm sorry,' I said, battling a searing throb of panic.

He held the pout for another few seconds, eyes drilling into mine, hard but flat, then expelled foul breath into my face and smiled that thin-lipped smile. 'Never mind! I know we've only just met properly, so it must feel a bit weird to you, but - but I feel like I've known you forever. I mean...I guess I have been watching you at the weekends and following you quite a lot. Learning what I can. So funny how you never saw me, even when I was *this* close. It's a shame about your mummy and daddy though. You ought to make up with them. Not everyone has parents, you know.'

A lead weight plummeted through me, Freud's famous words ringing like death bells, *Mental patients are split and broken structures. Mental patients are split and broken structures. Mental patients are split and broken structures.* Like shattered crystals. Each crystal was unique; when it shattered into a million pieces, it shattered in a different way to any other because it had come from its own individual structure, a form moulded by nature and nurture, utterly unique, utterly original.

Utterly screwed up.

My stomach heaved.

I lurched forward and threw up. Regurgitated pea and ham soup splattered his thighs.

I looked up. He wasn't smiling anymore.

Chapter 6

Mikey turned his unsmiling face to the ceiling, and I followed his gaze, not knowing whether he saw the bulb above his head or only his own warped thoughts.

For a while, he was still. As still as a mannequin and equally freakish.

The smell of sick filled the room. I didn't dare move. I tried not to focus on the vein throbbing in his forehead or the Christmas decorations. My thoughts flashed to Jacob. I closed them down. Tried to stop myself from thinking about Mum and Dad. Thought about her anyway. Pain wrenched at my chest. Would I ever see them again? Was Jacob alive? Mikey must have sneaked into the house when Jacob went to put out the bins. Had Mikey attacked him again and then come inside to take me, or had he managed to sneak in unnoticed? Would I ever find out?

Mikey pushed himself backward off the bed, spun around and strode towards the door.

'I'm sorry,' I bleated, hating the begging tone in my voice, the way it shook.

His head snapped around and he gave me a thin-lipped smile. 'Don't worry. Don't worry. Don't worry. It's not a big problem. You didn't do it on purpose. Oh no. You wouldn't do that to me, would you Doc?'

I shook my head.

'Great. Back in a jiffy!'

His hand dipped inside the neck of his Christmas jumper and retrieved the black lanyard. He found the right key and slotted it into the door, then slipped out of the room. I listened to the key crunch on the other side of the door and flopped back onto the pillow.

So far, he hadn't touched me. I didn't know what that meant. It was good – obviously – but it didn't mean he wasn't going to try soon. A vision of him walking back into the room naked made my throat close.

Maybe it's not a sexual thing. Maybe he just wants to torture you then kill you.

Oh God.

I jerked upright and whipped my head around, eyes on my cuffed wrist. My wrists were small. The silver bangle jangled around my skin, looser than it ought to be. I'd been dieting, hence a measly portion of pea and ham soup for dinner, so maybe, if I made my hand as tiny as possible, I could slide it out of the cuff. What I'd do then was another question but extricating myself from the chain was a start. Biting my lip, I tucked my thumb into my palm as far as it would go and squeezed my fingers together making my hand look like a pterodactyl's skull. My hand looked smaller than ever.

With my left hand, I gripped the metal ring and began to pull it backward. The cuff reached as far as my knuckles then refused to go further. Shit.

Floorboards outside the room creaked, and I released the handcuff and turned around to face the door, heart pounding.

Mikey marched into the room, placed a bucket on the carpet and locked the door, popped the lanyard back inside his jumper, picked up his pail and strode over to me. His strides were jerky, eyes trained on the small puddle of vomit I'd produced. He now wore a clean pair of jeans. Bleach pervaded the charity shop scent of the bedroom as he slipped on a marigold and dunked the cloth into the steaming water, movements choppy, verging on aggressive.

I inched away, frightened he was going to upend the bucket of hot bleach over my head, but it was as if he was in a world of his own as if he'd forgotten I was there. For ages, he scrubbed and scrubbed.

I breathed as quietly as I could and stayed as still as possible, unable to stop staring at the lump under his jumper: his keys.

His breathing was heavy, eyes down, gloved hand thrusting back and forth, back and forth, grinding into the duvet cover so forcefully that the mattress descended half a foot. He was a well-built man; lean and strong. He was over six feet. I was five foot four. I worked out to stay toned, but I didn't do weights.

As far as physiology was concerned, I didn't stand a chance.

That doesn't mean you don't have to try.

I found myself staring at his eyelids. If I stabbed my fingernails into them hard enough, maybe…

His face snapped up. For a second, he seemed confused, in a distant place, cheeks flushed, forehead furrowed - then he shook his head, grinned, and said, 'There you go, Doc. Good as new.'

He seemed happy again.

'Thank you for cleaning it up,' I said, forcing a smile.

He waved away my gratitude. The corner of his mouth tipped up. 'Nah. That's nothing, not compared to what you're going to do for me.'

My blood, already cold, dipped into the minuses. The desire to lean back and smash my heels into his jaw fought with the notion that I ought to stay subservient, thankful, appeasing.

'And,' I swallowed, 'what am I going to do for you?'

'What do you think?' he said, clasping his hands together under his chin, eyes dancing.

Is this a game to you, Mikey? A bloody game?

'I don't know. That's why I'm asking.'

'There's no need to get snappy,' he said in a sing-song voice.

Behind the levity, I sensed annoyance. I could've been wrong. I was tempted to feed that irritation, see where it led; if it made him storm off again, I could recommence my attack on the handcuff.

My eyes must have betrayed me, glancing down at the metal tethering me to the bed, because Mikey said, 'Oh yes. That's just a precautionary measure.'

I hesitated. Made my voice soft. 'Against what?'

'I don't know. Um…'

He slipped his thumbnail between his teeth and started nibbling.

I waited, watched him work from the tip to the soft nail bed, which was already red raw. He teased away a cuticle then ripped it clean off. Blood collected and he slipped his whole thumb in between his lips and sucked noisily like a baby. His eyes refocused on mine and widened in shock as if surprised to find me here watching him. I tried to smile as he yanked his thumb out of his mouth, tucked his chin into his neck, and shook his head violently, muttering under his breath.

I considered lying and telling him that I sometimes sucked my thumb too, but instinct told me not to remind him of what he'd just done. If he felt ashamed of doing it, me telling him I did it too might not condone his actions but backfire and make him think I was being patronising which might make him angry. I knew nothing about this man. Couldn't predict anything.

He raised his hand and reached out tentatively to me. 'You need to acclimatise to your new surroundings. You can begin tomorrow,' he said with a firm nod.

'Begin what, Mikey?' I asked, terrified but desperate to know, to have this rotten uncertainly wiped from existence.

His fingers continued to hover in the air. I couldn't peel my gaze away. Chills crawled down my arms.

'Begin what exactly?' I repeated.

He jumped up from the bed and said, 'Hungry? I have pizza! Ham and pineapple, your favourite! Back in a mo.'

He collected the bucket, glove and cloth and hurried

out of the bedroom.

I listened to the door lock then turned my attention to the handcuffs, wondering how on earth he knew what my favourite pizza was. Had I done a post on Instagram about pizza? I didn't think so. No. I was certain I hadn't. My posts were usually about books or work. How long had he been stalking me? Weeks? Months?

I glanced around the room, realising I hadn't yet scanned every surface and item, and continued to pull the cuff, gritting my teeth against the pain of metal slicing skin. On either side of the bed were two pine tables, one topped with a small snow globe containing Father Christmas in his sleigh. Santa was just as trapped as me, but at least he could see through his cage.

The other table was topped with a cheap-looking lamp that had a dark green shade. Both had one drawer.

I stopped working on my bind and yanked open the snow globe drawer to find a stack of porn magazines that had clearly been used a lot and a bottle of KY Jelly. The top magazine was called Beautiful Brunettes. It was covered with a topless woman, who couldn't have been much older than eighteen, with huge breasts and bright green eyes. Just like me. Except for the breast part. Mine were smaller than that.

He's clearly interested in women then. And he likes brunettes.

He hasn't touched you yet. Maybe he won't.

Don't be so naïve. What else could he want you for?

Focus Rach! Focus!

I slid the drawer closed, shutting off dark thoughts, the horror of what might happen to me tomorrow.

Leaning across the bed, I opened the other drawer to see *Tom's Midnight Garden*, a children's story. I'd read it at school in Year 7. Liked it. Looking at it now, thinking about Mikey's slippery eel fingers turning those pages, I felt like tearing the whole thing to pieces, but I had work to do; wasting time destroying his book wouldn't achieve anything.

I returned my attention to the cuff and I licked my hand to lubricate the skin. I pulled and pulled. Blood seeped through the skin around my knuckles. I licked again, tried again, scanned the bedroom.

Opposite the bed was a pine desk and chair.

Hanging on the chair was my handbag! The orange, leather one Jacob had given me for Christmas. I couldn't believe I hadn't noticed it before. The drugs and hideous Christmas decorations must have muddied my focus. But there it was, my bag, the holy grail.

Why did Mikey bring your bag?

Don't worry about that now. If your phone's in there and you can reach it…

I wrestled harder, my left arm burning with the effort of pulling, but still, it wouldn't come off. Exasperated tears blurred my vision, my bag morphing into a puddle of blood, a mirage mocking me – then another idea popped up. I could almost see the emoji lightbulb hovering in front of my nose; if I stretched out fully, maybe, just maybe, I could hook the bag with my foot and drag it up here.

I thought I heard a sound outside and froze. How long had Mikey been gone? How long did it take to cook a pizza? If he was making it from scratch, he might be a while –

Who makes pizza from scratch?

Some people do…

No, they don't. The only people who do that are MasterChef wannabes and does Mikey strike you as one of those? His breath smells like rotten meat for God's sake, not Michelin star lamb cutlets with mint sauce.

Jacob loved fine dining. I did too. Now that we were earning decent salaries, we could afford to treat ourselves. For our third wedding anniversary, Jacob had gone all out, taking me to Heston's restaurant.

That was only three months ago.

I needed to stop thinking about Jacob. The thought I might never see him again was a knife in my spleen.

Stop torturing yourself. Do something. Now.

I moved onto my back and stretched out my arms and legs, making my body as long as possible. My Achilles' heels now sat atop the iron railing, which hurt. I pointed my toes, stretched harder. The big toe of my right leg – which must have been slightly longer than my left – brushed against the supple leather of my bag and I bit my lip, pulled back my left leg, bent it, planted my foot flat under my bottom and pushed up, arching my back, and forming a half-bridge with my body. Yoga had stood me in good stead because my body held firm and my right foot jutted out another inch.

Trapped inside its cuff, my right wrist burned. I clamped my teeth together and focused on the strap of my handbag. Moving my foot to the right, with my big toe I touched the strap looped over the back of the chair and managed to slide my first three toes between the wood and leather. With painstaking slowness, I crept my foot upwards. At the top of the chair back, I attempted to lift the bag. My foot quivered with the strain. My first three toes were the only ones long enough to tuck under the strap, so they had to take the whole weight of the bag, fighting against gravity and the assortment of rubbish I had inside. The top arch of my foot began to ache, my toes trembled, and my supporting leg shook. I didn't know how much longer I could hold the position. In yoga, we usually held the one-legged bridge for about 30 seconds before swapping to the other leg, but this time I didn't have the luxury of swapping and trying to remove the bag with my left leg because it wasn't long enough or close enough. I could feel my buttocks quivering, the muscles burning. Great for those bums, ladies! I heard Maria's powerful voice enthusing. Maria, my yoga instructor, who had dated Jacob a handful of times before I'd met him, my Jacob, my person, who I might never see again if I couldn't get my bloody bag onto this bed with me.

Don't think about Jacob.

I managed to lift the bag a centimetre, but it was a centimetre too much, and I gasped as the shakes took over, rendering my body useless for the job at hand, my toes powerless. My left foot slid out from under me, and I dropped onto the bed and gritted my teeth in frustration. I'd been so close. If I could just stretch a teeny-tiny bit further and try again, I thought I could do it.

I gave myself a minute or so to recover then shuffled my bottom slightly further down the bed, trying to pretend my arms weren't screaming - that I was tied to a torture rack - and reformed the position. My toes slipped under the strap. I braced myself and stretched my leg as far as it would possibly go. One, two, three, LIFT. Though trembling, my toes raised the bag. The strap was halfway down the length of my three toes, weighing down the central knuckle joints. For a second, I thought my toes were going to break backward under the weight. The pain was intense, a bruising bark that travelled up my foot, stretching my tendons to their limit, but somehow my toes held strong, raising the strap up and over the top of the chair. Free of its captor, the bag hung on my shaking toes. I tried to push my toes upwards to encourage the strap to slip down over the back of my foot, making it more secure as I tried to move it backward towards the bed, but my toes wouldn't rise any further and they were weakening, trembling, screaming against the weight.

'No, no, no, no -'

My toes flopped downwards, and the strap slipped off. The bag thudded to the carpet, horribly loud and final. My body hit the mattress again.

I ground my teeth and squeezed my eyes shut, furious with myself for failing and ruining such a brilliant opportunity to get help. I couldn't even see the bag now because it was on the floor at the end of the bed.

Floorboards creaked. The door clicked.

I frantically hauled myself into a sitting position and tried to look like I hadn't moved.

A horrifying thought pierced all else.

What if he notices my bag's moved?

Chapter 7

Mikey entered the room carrying a tray topped with a plate of pizza and a yellow cup. He kicked the door closed behind him and didn't bother to lock it. I stared at the door, wishing I'd focused on getting the handcuff off rather than making a mess of the bag situation.

His eyes latched onto mine and a grin transformed him into a parody of normal; a happy, twenty-something man bringing pizza to his girlfriend.

He perched on the bed and placed the tray tenderly on my lap. 'There you go, Doc. You must be famished.'

I still had the taste of sick on my tongue, but I wasn't going to complain. This might be the only food I got for days.

'Thank you, Mikey.'

'My pleasure.'

I picked up the yellow cup and raised it to my lips, scared it might contain more drugs. My head still felt sluggish from whatever he'd injected me with. But I was thirsty, my tongue a dried sponge, so I took a small sip. It was orange juice minus the bits. It tasted normal.

'I like it smooth,' he purred, eyes bright.

Something about the way he said the word smooth made my skin crawl.

Keeping my eyes lowered, I picked up a slice of pizza and took a small bite. For a terrifying second, I was worried it wasn't going to go down. I felt him watching me, breath held, that crazy smile pinned on his face.

With difficulty, I swallowed, and he sighed with pleasure.

I downed the rest of the juice and ate two slices of

pizza. It wasn't handmade. I wondered where he'd bought it, where the nearest shop was. How could we be three miles from the nearest road? Was he lying or were we in a very remote location I'd never imagined existed in this day and age? My instinct was that he was telling the truth. He hadn't seemed at all worried when I'd screamed before, and the room didn't appear to be sound-proofed.

'May I?' he said, eyeing the plate.

I nodded.

He licked his lips and reached for the biggest slice.

I was desperate for a wee so what I said next wasn't a lie. 'I need to use the bathroom. Please.'

A frown fell, but it lasted less than a second. He jumped off the bed, 'Oh yes, of course you do. We were in the car for seven hours so you must be bursting. I've been twice since I picked you up.'

Seven hours? Where the hell are we?

If I was seven hours from Flitwick, where on earth could I be?

I tried to picture the UK in my head. My geography was rubbish. How far was Wales by car from Bedfordshire? Far. As far as seven hours? Parts of Wales were remote, I knew that much. At university, before I'd met Jacob, I'd dated a guy from Elan Valley.

Scotland has remote areas too.

Panic burbled in my chest. I looked at Mikey, made sure I sounded innocent, 'Where are we?' I smiled. Behind my lips, my teeth chattered. If we were seven hours from home in a remote area three miles from the nearest road, how would anyone ever find me?

Mikey didn't hesitate. 'Skiddaw Mountain.'

'Where's that?'

He put one finger to his lips and backed away from the bed carrying the tray, then he turned and headed for the desk. My muscles clenched as he approached the now-bagless chair.

Please don't realise. Please don't realise.

A memory of wishing the same thing years ago echoed in my brain. I hadn't wanted Mum and Dad to know what I'd done – had tried so hard to hide it from them, cover my tracks - but they didn't have slush for brains, and it hadn't taken them long to figure out my deceit, and when they had, almost everything had fallen apart. Did Mikey have slush for brains?

God, I hope so.

He stopped abruptly, a foot away from the chair. He pivoted to face me.

'What happened here?' Confusion clouded his eyes.

I didn't know what to say; hoped he wasn't referring to my handbag and its altered position but knew better.

'Doc, is there something you need to tell me?' He placed the tray on the end of the bed and put his hands on his hips. His tone had dipped into a flatline.

Goosebumps prickled my arms.

'No,' I said, 'I don't think so. Please may I go to the toilet now?'

He rolled his tongue around his gums. His hands dropped to his sides and hung limply. 'Yes,' he murmured, eyes unreadable, 'let's go.'

He picked up the tray from the mattress, jerked around and placed it on the desk. In one fluid motion, he bent over and picked up my orange bag. He glanced at me and said, 'I brought this with us so that if things don't go to plan, I can put your bag in a ditch far away from here to lead the police off my scent. Also, I like the colour.'

I watched as he slung it back over the chair and then, with another glance at me, pushed the chair in an inch.

My heart sank.

Mikey James Bell wasn't as stupid as I'd hoped.

Chapter 8

Mikey withdrew his lanyard from beneath the red wool of his Christmas jumper, bent over and slotted the key into the cuff.

I stared at my free wrist, unable to believe he'd released me as he didn't have a gun or any other weapon as far as I could tell, but on getting off the bed and standing opposite him less than a metre apart, I realised how big he was. To him, I was weak. And he was right. Trying to fight him now would end badly, possibly with my blood all over the bed.

Mikey backed away to allow me space to walk ahead of him toward the door. All the time I was aware of his presence at my back, his breath on the top of my head, footsteps in time with mine yet heavier, surer of themselves. This was his territory. His playground.

Ideas flew around my head like sick birds, none of them good enough, fluttering upwards on baby-weak wings then spiralling down to the ground and shattering; if I made a run for it, he'd catch me; if I turned around and shoved him in the chest, he'd barely move. His body was steel while mine was clay. No, I wasn't going to win a physical battle. I had to be smarter than that, smarter than him.

But how? I could feel the clock ticking, picture Mikey digging my grave. After he was done, he wouldn't release me. He'd bury me in this wilderness he called home and never look back.

Chills smothered my skin, the inside of my throat. For a few seconds, I thought I was going to pass out, but the danger passed, and I stayed on my feet, stomach churning, mind blitzing idea after idea, destroying concepts before they fully formed.

At the door, he reached past me, brushing my arm with his – please don't let that have been intentional - and opened the door, then gestured for me to leave the room in front of him.

Leaving my prison felt like a giant leap, but it wasn't. I wasn't cuffed or on a leash, but I had a predator at my back, and he wasn't going to let me go until he'd gotten what he wanted. According to Mikey, I was going to discover what that was tomorrow.

I can't be here tomorrow to find that out. I have to be gone. Somehow, I need to find a way.

I stepped onto a gloomy landing. To my right stood a closed door.

'It's down there,' Mikey said in my ear.

I headed left along the hallway. On the right rose stairs covered in a beige carpet that had seen better days. Out here there weren't any Christmas decorations. The walls were papered in an archaic design of pink roses on a cream background. A banister soared up the far wall like a headless snake. I wondered how many hands had touched that snake. How many women Mikey's eel fingers had touched. Was I the first woman he'd brought here or the third, fifth, tenth?

How many people has he hurt?

I began to shake uncontrollably. Mikey's hand landed on my shoulder. I jumped.

'You OK, Doc? You're not sick, are you?'

I shook my head; thought about the life he'd made me leave behind. About Jacob. I had to fight this fear and keep going.

'Great stuff!'

He guided me past an open door. I glanced to the left and saw a simply furnished room with a single bed. Walking on, we passed two more rooms whose doors were shut. At the end of the landing, we reached another door, which stood ajar to reveal a small bathroom.

'Here it is. Take your time,' Mikey trilled, 'I'm sure you want to freshen up. Brush those sicky teeth. I got you a new toothbrush. It's blue, your favourite colour.'

How the hell does he know that?

He opened the door for me, reached inside and flicked on the light.

I stepped into the room, turned, and stared at him as he closed the door. I couldn't stop shaking but forced myself to meet his eyes. In my head, I still had a modicum of freedom. He couldn't read my thoughts.

Chapter 9

He hadn't locked me in the bathroom, but I knew he was outside, waiting like a giant cockroach, scuttling backward and forwards, excited for me to emerge once more and for his sick game to continue – whatever game that was. My mind wandered to black places. The problem with having a good imagination was that everything you conjured was so vivid.

Nausea swam in my throat; would he tie each of my limbs to the bedposts? What was he going to do to me tomorrow?

I flushed the chain and scanned the room. There was no cabinet on the wall, just a bath, bin, sink with a rust-flecked mirror above, grey tiles, and rusty taps. I bent over and checked the bin in case there was a discarded razor in there, or anything else I could use as a weapon, but it contained nothing save for soiled tissues.

'Everything OK in there, Doc?'

'Yes. I'll be out in a minute.'

'Don't forget to brush your teeth.'

Trying not to imagine him forcing his lips onto mine, I brushed my teeth and splashed cold water on my face. I looked a mess, worse even than I'd thought. Tension pincered my jaw and my eyes were puffy. I did up the top two buttons of my shirt, thought about making myself sick then smearing vomit all over me in the hope that it would put him off coming anywhere near, but a host of visions swooped down like vultures stabbing at my brain with their carrion-stinking beaks; *he'll strip me down, hose me off…then climb in the shower with me and…*

I met my own eyes in the mirror and stared at the green

of my irises until my face blurred black. I was changing, losing myself already. I was becoming a terrified little girl; a person I didn't recognise - but I couldn't let that happen - I was Rachel Brown, tough, stubborn, successful, a woman who made her own luck, pursued her dreams no matter the personal cost. And yet…

A rat-a-tat-tat on the door made me flinch.

'Doc?'

'Coming.'

I opened the door and forced myself to look up into his smiling face.

'Better?' he said.

'Yes. What time is it?' Conversation would make me seem more human.

He seemed surprised by the question but checked his watch. He wore a Spider-Man one, the sort an eight-year-old might wear.

Infantilisation. Could that be part of his problem?

The term flashed up behind my eyes like a siren; I remembered more than I thought from my psychology degree. Even though my aspirations had lain elsewhere, I'd found the subject interesting and must have absorbed more into my subconsciousness than I'd realised. Infantilisation was when an adult was treated like a child. But, as Mikey was alone, it seemed more like self-infantilisation - was that even a thing? And what did any of it mean anyway? He was just a geek obsessed not only with Christmas but superheroes. Maybe this was more a case of nerdiness rather than psychosis.

Given that he's kidnapped you, I'd be inclined to disagree with that one.

He was talking. I tuned back in. His eyes were narrow, smile tremulous. He poked my shoulder. 'Hey, Doc, did you hear what I said? It's rude not to listen.'

'Oh, sorry, no.'

Mikey tutted. 'I said it's midnight. Well past my bedtime,

which means we had better go to bed now.'

I looked up at him in the gloom, but he was staring straight ahead, at the bedroom door, chest rising and falling fast.

He gestured for me to go in front of him and I moved as if through a quagmire, dread adding ten-tonne weights to my feet.

'Mikey, please, think about what you're doing. Once you do this you can't take it back. You -'

He seemed not to hear me. He reached past me and opened the bedroom door.

I stared up at him, shaking my head. 'No. I don't want to go in there. I'm not ready to sleep yet. I'm not tired.'

'You'll need your rest for tomorrow,' Mikey said, pushing me gently into the room.

A blur of red, green, silver and gold attacked my senses. Christmas overload, a mad canvas that reflected the madness inside this man's head.

'Get back on the bed, Doc', he said, 'I'm sorry I have to cuff you again, but once trust is built, we won't have to worry about such things.'

'Please,' I whispered, struggling to speak, 'please don't.'

'On the bed now young lady,' he said, voice firm, gruffer.

I got on the bed and brought my knees up to my chest.

'Good.' Mikey slipped the cuff around my wrist, nodded, and patted my head. 'Work starts tomorrow. I'm so glad you're here.'

With a giggle, he skipped out of the room humming *Rocking Around the Christmas Tree*. It used to be my favourite Christmas song.

Not anymore.

Chapter 10

My body rattled like a baby's toy, the key twisting the only sound apart from my drumming heart. I felt certain he was going to change his mind and come back, slip under the covers with me, do dreadful things. I was sure of it. So sure that I wrapped myself in the duvet like a caterpillar in its cocoon, tucking the cover under my bottom and legs and feet, trying to create some kind of shield against the monster that was Mikey James Bell. He was all smiles and lightness. Letting me go to the toilet, feeding me pizza, buying me a toothbrush – my favourite colour no less – but he was insane.

Wrapped in my duvet shield, I dragged my gaze from the door – which, unbelievably, remained locked – and eyed my bag. Mikey had placed it back on the chair, then pushed the chair in an inch. He was playing with me. Making it just out of reach, toying with me like a greyhound with a lure.

I glanced at the door once more, worried he was poised outside the bedroom on the landing listening, waiting for me to make a move. If I tried for my bag again and it thudded to the carpet or I knocked over the chair and he was hovering out there, he'd hear it, unlock the door, burst in and…

But if I sat here and did nothing, I'd stand no chance of escaping.

I glared at the elf curtains. They beamed back like tiny versions of Mikey. I wanted to rip them to shreds.

It was a nightmarish decision to make, far harder than ignoring my parents and pursuing my dream career. In that instance, my relationship with them had hung in the balance so it had been terribly difficult. I'd felt guilty and selfish, like I was betraying them. I'd felt cowardly for hiding the truth, and had worried they were right - that I was making a mistake, that I'd never make it - but my mortality hadn't hung in the balance that time. Right now, I was in a life-or-death situation. I was choosing between swimming in a sea of sharks or remaining in a sinking ship waiting for a lifeboat to come; a lifeboat that probably never would.

According to Mikey, I might as well be in the Bermuda Triangle with no radio contact. My orange bag was a buoy I could cling onto though; if my phone was still inside, I could use it to alert the authorities. If Mikey was telling the truth and I was somewhere near this Skiddaw Mountain, I could tell someone where I was; they'd send help and the nightmare that loomed on the horizon might never come. There couldn't be many houses in such a remote place. Satellite would find me. It had to.

My heart skipped: I'd made my decision. I'd never been a static person anyway. Spontaneity was my go-to. Action over inaction won every time. And I was as stubborn as a donkey.

I exhaled, inhaled. Before I made my move, I had to be sure he wasn't out there. I'd already learned that there was a creaky board in the floor right outside the room; a dead giveaway, and there'd been no creaks so far.

I listened for a while. Minutes ticked by. They felt like hours.

Nothing.

Outside, the night was silent. Nothing stirred.

'Twas the night before Christmas, when all through the house; Not a creature was stirring, not even a mouse; The stockings were hung by the chimney with care, In hopes that St. Nicholas soon would be there; The children were nestled all snug in their beds; While visions of Mikey danced in her head.

I listened again. It was hard to shut out the poem. I knew the words so well because as a little girl, my dad had said it to me every Christmas Eve when he'd tucked me into bed. I used to get shivers of excitement when he said those precious words. I imagined I was the mouse sniffing about the presents under the tree – which was stupid because that wasn't what the poem said - but I'd pictured that anyway. Now though, like the very idea of Christmas, it was destroyed. If I ever got out of here, I didn't know that I'd be able to celebrate Christmas ever again.

I thought about my parents. About the phone call I'd ignored.

Focus, Rachel. Focus.

Wondering if I was in shock, I switched my attention to the chair.

The bag dangled temptingly, like a treasure chest at the end of a rainbow.

As quietly as possible, I unbound myself from the duvet and stretched out.

Again, I formed the half-bridge, thrusting my hips up and extending my right leg as far as it would go, toes already trembling. My three longest toes brushed against the leather. I bit my lip, dug deeper, pushed further. My armpits wanted to detach themselves from my body. Tears stung my eyes and dribbled down my cheeks.

Come on, come on, just a little bit further…

The pain in my hand was unbearable. I glanced up to see blood soaking into the bed, dripping down my skin. My gorge rose; I was so squeamish I couldn't even watch the fake operations in *Emergency*. Jacob, on the other hand, delighted in it. He found my squeamishness hilarious. Just last week he'd wobbled fish guts in my face. But this blood was real. I could smell its coppery tang.

With a whimper, I slumped back onto the bed.

After a few deep breaths, I reset. Alongside the other pain, my spine seemed to be complaining now too, but I gritted my teeth and stretched further, so far that my toes hooked under the strap.

Hope bounced yoyo-like as I managed to lift the bag off the chair back. Into the air it went, suspended on my quivering foot, closer, closer, closer still to the bed, and then – there it was! On the end of the bed, on the mattress, safe and sound.

I released the strap then got my heel behind the bag and pulled it backwards. When it was reachable, I used my left hand to grab it. Unable to believe my success, I stared for one glorious moment at my bag, brought the leather to my nose and inhaled. The smell took me back to the moment Jacob had given it to me, to his pleasure at how much I loved it. I wanted to bury my face in it for longer, savour the memory, but there was no time.

I scrambled into a sitting position to take the strain off my wrist – feeling immense relief as the sear reduced to a throb - and, using my mouth to hold the bag still and my free hand to unzip, tore open the bag.

Thumps of excitement filled my head as I tipped the contents onto my lap and searched for my phone. My hand found it.

The door rattled.

Chapter 11

Mikey stood in the doorway holding my mobile. 'Looking for this?'

He wore a smile that wasn't a smile and didn't extend to his eyes.

I looked down at the phone in my hand. It wasn't mine. He'd played a mean trick – put another phone in there. Got my hopes up then dashed them. I tried to turn it on anyway, but it was dead. I dropped the useless mobile back in the bag, every muscle in my body coiled like barbed wire, heart pounding.

Mikey loitered in the doorway. He wore red and white Christmas pyjamas covered with pugs in Santa hats. He flipped my phone up in the air and caught it. 'You won't get any reception up here anyway,' he said simply, continuing to throw and catch.

'Then why take it out of my bag?' I blurted, blinking out tears of frustration.

Mikey looked confused. He entered the room leaving the door wide open. I looked behind him desperately.

'You first,' he said, stopping beside the bedside table and splaying his fingers over the snow globe, 'Why did you want your phone? Aren't you comfortable? Haven't I taken good care of you?'

He was wounded now; hurt puppy eyes, fingers scratching his head. His free hand tightened on the glass globe. It was a small piece, but rock-solid. Hard enough to do serious damage.

'I just wanted to let people know I'm not hurt,' I said, 'I'm sure you'd do the same if you were me.'

'If I was you, I'd be grateful and polite.'

He perched on the bed and hitched his knee up. It almost touched mine. Removing his hand from the globe, he hovered it above my calf and whispered, 'I've already let everyone know you're OK. Want to see?'

'What do you mean?'

'I sent a text to your husband pretending to be you so that he knows you're okay.' He unlocked my phone as if he'd done it a thousand times then tapped the messages icon and held up the screen.

'Hey Jacee-Joo, gone to visit an old friend who needs a shoulder to cry on. There's no reception where she is, so I'll be out of touch for a while. Love ya, Rachee-Roo xxx'

He quickly turned off the phone and slipped it into his pocket.

I could feel the colour leeching from my face. Even though his message to Jacob didn't make any sense at all and there was no chance Jacob would believe it, the fact that he'd pretended to be me and used my phone felt invasive, and the way he'd used our private nicknames for one another was unnecessary and mean. 'How do you know my pin?'

He puffed out his chest. 'I'm good at following people without them latching on. I always used to pretend I was invisible and follow Nana around when we lived in the old house. She never guessed I was there – except one time that is, and she gave me what for, so I never did it again.'

His face crumpled. He slid my phone back into his pocket.

Eyes vicious slits, he darted his face into mine. 'You're a wicked, sick boy, Mikey,' he said in the voice of an old woman, 'wicked, sick boys need to be punished.' He was panting now, fists clenched on his thighs, digging in.

'No. I'm not. I'm a good boy. I want to be a good boy. Show me how.' It was a little boy's voice.

Mikey shook his head violently, darted off the bed, and scurried away into the furthest corner of the room. He stared at the carpet, rocking back and forth on his heels, arms wrapped around his body. The temptation to say something tugged at my vocal cords but I stayed quiet.

Clearing his throat, he looked up, darted glances at me and murmured, 'That's why, that's why.'

'Why what?' I said, unable to look away as he began to pace back and forth, hands shoved in his pyjama pockets.

'No, no. She's good. No. I can. She just needs time,' Mikey muttered, head down, pacing faster, making the floorboards quake and snowflakes flutter upwards in the globe.

'I'm sorry,' I said, gathering the stuff on my lap, 'here, I don't need it. Any of it. Take it. I'm tired. I just want to go to bed.'

Mikey stopped and stared at me. His face was blank. Vacant. A vein in his forehead throbbed.

After a long time, his eyes brightened. 'Yes! You're right. Tomorrow's a big day for you. For both of us. Time to prove yourself. And you must be exhausted. I am too. Yes, I'll leave you now.'

He strode away, ignoring – or not seeing – the proffered goods in my hand. At the door, he whirled around, 'Oh, one more thing.'

I waited, pulse hammering.

'Sleep well, sleep tight, don't let the bed bugs bite. If they do, take a shoe, beat them 'til they're black and blue!'. After a low bow, he left the room and locked the door.

You, Rachee-Roo, are completely and utterly screwed.

I looked down at the useless contents of my bag, watched tears plummet onto a packet of Kleenex. As if commanded by an alien host, my hand picked up a tissue and pressed it to my eyes.

Chapter 12

I couldn't help but wonder if I was being punished. I probably couldn't have children and now I was being held prisoner by a psychopath. Was my dad right; was I selfish and spoiled - 'rotten to my core'? Did I deserve these terrible turns of fate?

Staring at the red-tinged room, the past whirled around my head like a tornado.

When I was eleven, my dad, a neurosurgeon, and all-round genius, had argued for private school. He'd studied at Eton then done medicine at Cambridge and claimed nothing compared to independent education. Mum was a teacher who'd also attended private school then completed her teaching qualifications at Oxford. She wasn't one to argue and had enjoyed her time at school so she gave in but wouldn't agree to boarding – couldn't bear the thought of me being away any longer than necessary.

I knew then, at the tender age of eleven, that Mum loved me more than him; that what mattered most in his head was that I reflected his accomplishments, made him proud through academic success. And I strove to do just that. I knuckled down and studied hard. Got straight As in my GCSEs. Four As at A Level: Psychology, French, English Literature, and, because I begged for months, Drama. According to my dad, Drama wasn't a real subject. Mum had been on the fence, but I'd always wanted a dog and they'd never got me one – something my mum felt bad about – so she'd finally joined my side and argued that I only needed three A Levels anyway; what would one more hurt?

As a result, Dad hadn't spoken to me for six weeks. Six

whole weeks of being ignored. Six whole weeks of wanting to hurt myself to make the pain go away.

The tension had been stifling, my guilt a gnawing parasite, but drama was my passion and Mum was on my side - just. Deep down, I'd known it for years, but never allowed myself to embrace the idea, knowing the scorn it would trigger.

In my final year of sixth form, we'd been to see Macbeth and I'd known the second Lady Macbeth walked on stage that that was what I wanted. I wanted to act. Be on stage or screen. Hear the audience roar.

The realisation was terrifying and thrilling. I knew I couldn't tell my parents, knew I had no choice but to do my psychology degree, as decided, but a plan started to grow in my head. Against their wishes – again – I got a job before university and started saving. My parents were generous with their money, and I knew they'd cover all necessary expenses at university, but they wouldn't give me money for what I really wanted: acting classes.

A sound yanked me out of my head. It was a harsh bark – human-sounding - a person's voice. It didn't sound like Mikey.

I listened intently, heart thwacking.

Nothing stirred. Not even a shiver of wind.

I wondered if I'd imagined it. Surely Mikey lived alone. There couldn't be another insane person living in this house.

I swallowed thickly and closed my eyes. The house was silent. My mind was the opposite.

Chapter 13

Morning came with the twitter of birds. I stared at the dark green curtains, at the grinning elves, and tried to picture what lay beyond. I wished I was one of those birds. Free. Outside. Away from Mikey's home. Away from this madness.

But I wasn't. I was in hell.

My hand throbbed. It looked bad. Apart from hitting my head on a radiator when I was ten, I'd never hurt myself badly. Never broken a bone or needed stitches. I'd been stung, bruised, scraped, scratched, and burned by the iron, but I'd never experienced this type of wound; one inflicted by another via handcuffs. Of course, if I hadn't tried so hard to escape, the damage wouldn't have been as bad. One good thing was that he hadn't actively hurt me, but he had said tomorrow was when I got to work, and it was tomorrow today. What 'work' meant was a mystery. A mystery that poisoned my thoughts like radiation. My instinct was to ask Jacob what he thought Mikey meant. When I was stuck, Jacee was my go-to. My rock. I was clever when it came to studying but he was the logical one.

A hot tear rolled down my cheek. The thought that Jacob was in pain – or worse – was too much; a sea urchin lodged in my chest. Just yesterday, all I'd cared about was the fact that I might never be able to have a baby, but now that didn't matter at all. All that mattered was Jacob being OK.

I had to find out if Mikey had hurt him, but even if I asked, I doubted he'd tell me the truth. The Mikey I'd met was troubled. Incredibly troubled. He'd not used violence on me, but it was clear he wasn't in complete control of his actions and thoughts. I tried to remember what he'd said when he'd talked to himself. It was like he'd been attempting to convince someone that I was OK, and he'd mentioned something about trusting me – that trust would come with time.

I chewed my lip and thought back to my degree, straining hard to remember one of the lectures I'd attended. Phrases jumped up and down in my brain like yoyos and I grabbed onto them, trying to weave the fragments into something meaningful…survivors of chronic abuse…powerful delusion that perpetrator is present in the room…continues to control…

Was Mikey a survivor of abuse? Could I somehow tap into that, find out why he was so damaged and use it to my advantage? Maybe, if I could get inside his head, I could persuade him to release me.

Feeling slightly bolstered, I pushed my mind backward to my course. I'd taken a module on trauma, psychosis, and dissociation. It had been fascinating but nowhere near as fun as acting. I remembered trying to concentrate during seminars and lectures but finding it hard because I was buzzing with excitement and nerves about the auditions that were coming up. Still, my brain managed to open a crack; nuggets of knowledge tunneled upwards. I squeezed my eyes closed, scanning memories, trying to remember something that might be useful.

The creak made me jump.

Chapter 14

I shot down into a lying position, curled my free hand into a fist and stared at the door. It clicked and swung inwards, revealing Mikey, smile wide, eyes bright. He looked rested. Clean and fresh-faced in a blue Christmas jumper covered with penguins. Jeans again. No shoes, just brown socks.

Whistling *Santa Claus is Coming to Town*, he loped into the room, stopped by the bed and grinned down at me, hands everywhere, too excited to be still. 'Wakey wakey sleepyhead, time to get you out of bed!'

I briefly considered launching myself upwards and punching him in the stomach, but I was still tied to the bed.

'Sleep well, Doc?' he said, leaning down to unlock the cuff.

I grunted.

'There you go. Free as a bird. Ready to begin work?'

I cupped my bloody hand in my left and managed a nod.

'Great. Don't look so worried – we don't bite.'

'We?'

He giggled and beckoned for me to stand and go ahead of him towards the door.

My arm felt strange, heavier than normal. I got off the bed and did as he wanted wondering what he meant by 'we'. Was he referring to a real-life person or the voice in his head? I didn't know which was worse.

As I passed the desk, the idea of grabbing the chair and smashing it into his groin came but it was crushed by the pressure of his hand on my shoulder.

'Trust is so important, don't you agree?' he breathed in my ear.

Shivers rippled down my neck. 'Yes, trust is really important. Who do you trust, Mikey?' I made myself glance round at him.

His smile wavered. He seemed lost for a moment, pale eyes clouding.

The silence felt too loud, then it was broken by a patting sound. I looked down to see his free hand tapping his thigh.

I stepped onto the landing. 'I trust my mum. I really miss her. I hope I get to see her soon.' I paused, fought the feeling that I was broaching dark territory. 'Where's your mum, Mikey?'

His hand tightened on my shoulder. The tapping got faster.

'Dead.' His voice was so quiet I barely heard it.

'Oh. I'm sorry.' My mind raced. 'Was she – er - what was she like?'

'She left when I was six. She left me alone in the house. I was alone for three days before they found me.'

'Who found you? The police?'

He slipped his thumb into his mouth. His jaw jutted back and forth as he scraped the enamel off his nail with his teeth. Abruptly, his eyes refocused on mine, and he whipped his thumb out of his mouth and hid his hand behind his back guiltily.

'There was no food in the house apart from stale cornflakes. Once I finished those, I ate her lipstick.'

'That must have been awful. I'm so sorry Mikey.'

His smile returned, wider than ever. 'That's all in the past. Now is perfect because now I have you.'

I looked away and suppressed a shudder.

The tapping stopped. He steered me towards the bathroom with a light touch that made my skin prickle, breath minty but sour at the same time, hot on the back of my head.

'Do your business then get dressed. There're fresh

clothes in there for you. I chose them specially.'

He winked and closed the door behind me.

I exhaled a long-held breath and dashed to the toilet, fearing I was going to be sick.

After a minute or so the moment passed. I turned slowly and noticed clothes draped over the side of the bath. He'd provided knickers but no bra. I tried not to wonder why.

Knowing Mikey could walk in at any moment, I yanked off my pyjama top and pulled on a fluffy pink jumper that looked like it had been sheared off an Easter bunny. I glanced at the door. I could hear him whistling another Christmas song. I ripped off my pyjama trousers and knickers in one go, grabbed the fresh pair and pulled them on so fast I scratched my leg. I reached for a pair of jeans and pulled them on. Next a pink pair of socks. One item remained. I frowned, wondering what the white, sheet-like garment was, and picked it up, and then everything clicked, and a horrid idea surfaced; he kept calling me Doc, and now he wanted me to wear a white doctor's coat. There was even a stethoscope under the coat, hanging over the edge of the bath like a long black worm. Was this all about some sick fantasy? I play doctor, he plays patient?

His whistling stopped.

I pulled on the lab coat and put the stethoscope around my neck, hands shaking.

'Hurry up, Doc. We need to get this show started.'

Hurriedly, I used the toilet, brushed my teeth, and gently cleaned my sore hand. There was a small window just big enough for me to squeeze through, but we were upstairs; if, somehow, I managed to squeeze through, what then?

I turned to see the door swinging open.

'Ready?' he said, eyes darting around the room.

I left the bathroom and hovered at the top of the stairs.

It was the pathway to Hell. The staircase was unlit, but

the bottom glowed like fire. Behind me stood the devil.

Chapter 15

At the bottom of the staircase hung a watercolour portrait of a pale-eyed woman with strawberry-blonde hair. Her nose was sharp, lips pencil-thin, and she wore a stiff white blouse that choked her neck. Her long, spindly hands rested on a black skirt. The resemblance between the painted woman and Mikey was striking. The picture's colouration was wishy-washy, as if the artist had painted through a depressive lens; the golden frame that held the painting cheap and tacky – not real gold or wood, but a plastic type of material adorned with swirls and twirls trying to pretend it was the real deal.

'Who's that?' I said, stopping halfway down the stairs.

'That's Nana,' Mikey said.

I looked back. In the half-light he looked like a ventriloquist dummy, skin waxy, smile too wide, eyes vacant.

'I can see the similarity between you,' I said.

His eyes found mine. For a second, his gaze hardened. He smiled again and the spell was broken. He prodded my shoulder blade and I carried on walking down, unable to stop thinking that I was walking to my death bed, the stethoscope a noose around my neck soon to be drawn tight.

The further down we went, the thicker the air became.

On the bottom step, I looked at what appeared to be the front door. Heavy oak. Bolted and windowless. A scraggy doormat announced WELCOME in faded black letters. Leaves and crumbs dirtied the hallway floorboards, which were faded and scraped. A transparent shade hung from the centre of the hallway. The walls were papered and peeling; yellow roses on a moss-green background. Specks of mould despoiled the wall behind the wallpaper in the uppermost corners alongside cobwebs. A pile of shoes lay messily. Coats and scarves hung above, including Mikey's bright blue anorak.

I swallowed dryly.

'That door,' Mikey said excitedly.

I glanced around to see him beaming at the door to the right. It was closed but did not appear to be locked. I hesitated, glancing to the right up the hallway where another door stood slightly ajar.

'Kitchen,' he explained.

'So we're going into -'

'The living room,' Mikey said. I could hear his breath quickening.

I wrapped my uninjured hand around the bronze doorknob, braced myself, then twisted and pulled the door towards me slowly. Inch by inch a section of the room appeared. On the left side, beneath a pair of stained crimson curtains sat a vine-patterned sofa.

I trailed my gaze across the room, inching the door forward, afraid of what I might see, half-expecting to see more freaky Christmas stuff. Scratched and scraped floorboards made up the floor, another vine-patterned sofa lined the back wall, behind which lay yellowing wallpaper peeling like sunburnt skin, and a huge faux-gold framed photograph of the woman from before and a little boy with pale green eyes and orange hair.

There was something arresting and disturbing about the photograph. Neither woman nor boy smiled. The woman was stone-faced, her eyes as hard and cold as lead, lips pursed tighter than an oyster shell. Something akin to fear hovered in the small boy's eyes, and his body language screamed of tension and discomfort. I shivered involuntarily. The photograph reminded me of one of those after-death photos that Victorians used to take to commemorate the dead.

I stepped into the room. Mikey pulled the door closed shutting us in. The smell was awful; manure, tobacco smoke, unwashed bodies and urine blended with the medicinal tang of hospitals and bleach. I stared at the rocking chair on the far side of the room. A shriveled old woman who looked barely human sat in the chair knitting furiously. A brown blanket covered her lap and she wore a purple dressing gown that had seen better days. Behind her on a pine cabinet sat an ancient-looking television and a dead plant in a white vase.

'Doc, meet Nana,' Mikey yipped, gesturing to the old lady.

I stared at her curtain-length, grey hair. It was thinning so much that parts of her scalp were visible, so insubstantial it resembled the cobwebs on the ceiling.

A glass ashtray piled high with cigarette stubs stood on a pine coffee table, within easy reach of the old lady.

'Nana, she's here! I've finally done it! Look, Nana, look!'

Mikey grabbed my arm and pulled me up to the rocking chair. The stench of urine drifted upwards from the old woman, who remained focused on the pale-yellow wool that she was knitting. I watched her nicotine-stained fingers work and fought a wave of pity. This poor old lady lived here and was being cared for by Mikey. It was a wonder she was still alive, and no wonder she looked like she was rotting from the inside out.

The chair rocked ever-so-slightly, but she displayed no sign of hearing him.

'Nana?' he said, less sure now. 'Nana, look. Haven't I done a good job?'

'Juice,' she said, 'Ciggy.'

I jumped at the harshness of her voice.

Mikey flinched and nodded. 'Yes, Nana. Sorry, Nana. Right away, Nana.'

He grabbed my arm and pulled me over to the radiator. To my horror, he withdrew a second pair of handcuffs from his pocket, slapped the ring around my sore wrist and secured it to the top of the radiator.

'Back in a jiffy,' he said. He dashed out of the room.

My skin tingled and I looked down at the old woman, but her head was bowed, needles clicking. Now and then she stabbed a finger at her glasses to push them back up her pointed nose.

Chills ran down my spine as I looked at the red velvet curtains. Beyond iron-latticed windows lay the dreariest, deadest landscape I'd ever seen. Craggy rocks and yellow-green moss fuzzed and spiked the terrain like huge scabs. Where there was grass, it was short and rough-looking, and no trees or bushes punctuated the area to give it a more wholesome, woody feel. It was barren and deserted. Utterly remote and unwelcoming, the ashen sky bleak and empty. The sort of place I'd never choose to visit.

As a child, we'd ventured to the south coast for our summer holidays. In my teens, my parents had taken me to Venice and Rome. Our destinations had always been full of people. Mum and Dad hadn't taken me on walking trips or mountain treks. They liked good food, culture, and the hubbub of popular destinations. Preferred sunny weather so traveled to warmer places. They'd never been on holiday to Wales, Ireland or Scotland. Neither had Jacob or I. Cold, miserable weather never appealed to either of us. This place felt like it belonged to the UK, a colder, more barren landscape devoid of sun, sand or sea.

It's too far from anything here for anyone to think of looking for you.

I rubbed my temple. Tried to control a rush of panic.

Stomach churning, I scanned the terrain for any sign of human life but there was none: no houses, no dog walkers, no cars, no roads…

Just miles and miles of nothing.

Chapter 16

'Pretty girl.'

I turned around. 'What?'

'Prettier in the flesh.'

The old woman stared at me. Her glasses had slipped down her nose again. Above them, her pale eyes were sharp.

'Er – thank you.' I lowered my voice, leaned over and said, 'Please, you have to help me. Mikey's not well. He's taken me and -'

She tutted and looked back down at her knitting.

'Please, Mrs – Miss -'

'Bell. Mrs Ethel Bell. You may call me Ethel,' she said without looking up.

'Ethel, do you need help? Is he keeping you here against your will too? Maybe if we work together -'

She burst into a coughing fit. Tears leaked out of the corners of her eyes and her breath crackled. She raised her chin, snapped her head around and shrieked, 'JUICE!'

Another coughing fit took hold. Mikey rushed into the room holding a Christmas mug that said 'Ho, ho, ho', and a pack of Marlboro Bright King Size. He was flushed and sweaty, and seemed in a panic.

'Here you are Nana,' he said tenderly, holding the mug to her lips.

She snatched it from him and glugged blackcurrant juice noisily. Liquid spilled down the sides of her mouth and dripped onto her purple dressing gown. She slammed the mug on the coffee table then hooked a finger at him, 'Ciggy.'

With frantic fingers, he pulled one out of the packet

then slipped it between her shriveled lips. He withdrew a lighter from his pocket and lit the cigarette, seeming to sag with relief when she grasped the butt between her fingers and inhaled its poison. She exhaled smoke into the room, hacked out another cough, then took another pull. I watched Mikey watch her. He seemed to be waiting for something.

Finally, he smiled and moved to perch on the sofa at the back of the room, knees jigging.

'Nana? Are you pleased with me? I've done well this time, haven't I?'

She continued to suck and cough, suck and cough. The air grew murky, and my eyes began to sting. I forced down a cough and glanced back and forth between Ethel and Mikey.

'Nana?'

Mikey's eyes turned glassy. I realised with a jolt of something close to pity that he was trying not to cry.

'Nana?'

'Oh, will you just shut your trap!' The old woman's nostrils flared as she glared up at Mikey, who swallowed and looked down at his knees.

'Sorry Nana.'

'But yes, you've done well. She's perfect.'

Mikey's eyes flickered upwards. Though tears shone in his pale irises, pride glimmered there too. He nodded fervently then looked at me. 'Time for you to get to work.'

'What do you mean?' I stammered.

Nana focused on her knitting, but I could tell her ears were pricked; she was listening to every word that passed between us.

Mikey grinned and stood up. He loped across the small room and bent over Ethel. 'May I?'

She nodded sharply.

He glanced up at me. 'This is what you're here for.'

I watched, heart hammering, as he lifted her long grey

hair away from the right side of her neck to reveal a huge growth. I held back a grimace and looked at him. 'What is it?'

'A tumour. You ought to know that,' Mikey said, giving me a weird look.

'And, er, why are you showing it to me?' Alarm bells belted in my ears as the cogs started to turn, slowly at first and then faster and faster – he calls me Doc – he thinks I should know what that hideous lump is – he brought me here to do a job –

'You're going to remove it. The doctors at the hospital won't do it.'

'What? Why?'

Ethel's face jerked up. Scorn twisted her lips. 'They want to make me do chemotherapy. But they won't remove it. They want to reduce its size first. But that's a load of rubbish. I just want rid of it. Cut off the bastard. Cut it off and blitz it in the blender for all I care.'

Mikey was nodding. 'Yes, Nana's right. She's always right. Chemotherapy will kill her, but if you remove it, it'll go away and -'

'I don't think it works like that. If the doctors say -'

'Fuck those cunts!'

I recoiled at the viciousness in the woman's voice and the madness in her eyes. With a spasm of fear, I realised that nothing I said would make her change her mind.

I stared at the ugly bulge and tried to imagine myself cutting into the old woman's flesh. Just the thought of it made me feel sick. I shook my head. 'No. I'm not a real doctor. I could really hurt you. I could kill you.'

Mikey rolled his eyes. 'Yes, you are. We watch you every week on Emergency. We've seen your work. Only last month you removed a tumour from a plumber and saved his life!'

Ethel's fingers worked at her knitting. I wondered what she was thinking. Wondered if they were as deluded as each other.

Again, I shook my head. This time, I softened my voice, aiming for sympathy. And I was sorry, sorry that they were blind to reality, sorry they'd targeted me. 'I'm sorry this has happened to your nana, Mikey, but *Emergency* isn't a real documentary about real-life doctors. It's fiction. I'm not a real doctor and I never have been. The closest I ever got to being a doctor was studying psychology at university. I'm sorry to tell you both this, but I'm an actor. I've never operated on anyone for real and I wouldn't know where to start.'

Mikey frowned hard and looked from me to her. 'Nana? What does she mean? Why's she saying that?'

Ethel held out her hand for another cigarette, eyes on me. A cold tingle shivered across my back. She took the cigarette and slipped it between her lips. Mikey lit it and Nana darted forward with reptilian speed and stabbed the burning end onto my arm. I gasped and darted as far away as I could, smashing my hip against the radiator.

'Liar,' she hissed.

'I'm not lying. I promise. I'm telling the truth. I -'

She looked away.

'Well,' she said softly.

Fear flitted across Mikey's face. He glanced at me then back at Ethel. 'Are you sure? Don't we want to get the operation started though? Get it over and done with?'

He shrank at the look she gave him then darted towards me, uncuffing my wrist and gripping my upper arms. His hands were cold but firm.

'For how long?' he said.

'As long as I deem fit,' she snapped before pushing her glasses up her nose and resuming her knitting.

Chapter 17

Mikey manhandled me out of the living room into the hallway and told me to take off the lab coat and stethoscope, which I did gladly. He hung both items on the banister and closed the door softly, never letting go of my arm, his nails digging in like needles. He gripped my other arm then pushed me down the narrow path towards another door. My head spun with questions but none of them would leave my lips. What did 'well' mean? Why had that single word frightened Mikey?

Mikey released one of my arms and twisted the doorknob, kicked open the door, then cursed and turned back. Still clenching my arm, he opened a door under the stairs and retrieved a pair of brown boots, which he slipped on. Was he taking me outside? Why? Was he going to bury me alive on this mountain? Suffocate me with earth?

'Please,' I said as he righted himself, grabbed my arm and pushed me through the doorway, 'Please don't do this. I haven't done anything wrong. I just want to go home. I'm sorry I've upset your nana, Mikey, but I was telling the truth. I'm not a d-'

He whirled me around. 'Why are you lying to us? We need your help. You're an amazing doctor. We've been watching you for months and months. You always do the right thing. You're honest and clever and incredible. Why are you doing this? Why are you lying?' Tears welled in his eyes and for a second he looked like a terrified little boy. 'I can't lose Nana. I won't. You need to start telling the truth and get on board or you're going to regret it.'

He sniffed and let go of me to smear his hand across his nose. He wiped the side of his Christmas jumper and spun me around. Through a blur of panic, I took in gloomy kitchen units, a refrigerator, and a table and chairs. Mikey pushed me past the table towards another door. Before he opened it, he picked me up and slung me over his shoulder in a fireman's lift. His shoulder dug into my tummy, and I battered his back with my fists and screamed, but he only tightened his grip on my legs, opened the door and stepped outside. From my upside-down position, I could make out nothing more than overgrown grass and weeds. A cold breeze whipped my hair across my face, and I pushed it away, desperate to try and see where he was taking me. His breathing became laboured as he trudged through the grass.

'Mikey, stop! Please. Put me down. You need to listen to me!' I cried, but it was as if he'd gone deaf.

My arms grew weak, and I stopped hitting him. Instead, I sunk my teeth into his right buttock and bit as hard as I could. He gasped and let go of my legs. I fell onto my side and rolled away, winded and bruised, desperate to get to my feet.

'You bit me,' he shouted.

I scrabbled to my hands and knees, but he was already on top of me, his weight pressing me facedown into the grass. My arms and legs came out from under me and he lay on my back, pinning me down. His breathing quickened and I heard him grunt, 'Do it. Do it now.' A second later, his voice returned to normal, and he said, 'No. No. That's not right. She's good.'

He stayed there for a while, crushing me against the ground.

After a while, his breathing steadied. He sighed heavily and turned me over to face him. Behind his head the sky was ashen. His cheeks were flushed, eyes confused and hurt. 'You shouldn't have done that, Doc.'

'I know,' I said, 'I'm sorry.' I begged with my eyes, trying to look as genuine as possible. 'I am a doctor. You and your nana are right. I was scared to tell the truth. It's just that I'm used to operating in a hospital where I have all my equipment and nurses on hand to help me.'

His eyebrows shot up and relief brightened his face. 'Of course! I knew there would be a good reason for you to lie. I'll go tell Nana right away then you won't need to be punished. She'll understand. I'm sure she will.'

He pulled me to my feet and dusted me down with a gentle hand then led me to a beech tree. 'I just need you to stay here a minute so I can check.' He pulled the cuffs out of his pocket and gestured for me to put my arms around the tree trunk. I did as I was told, hoping he was right; if Nana bought my story, she'd put a stop to the punishment she'd decreed. Mikey cuffed my wrists together and grinned. 'Back in a jiffy! Don't go anywhere.' He laughed at his own joke then ran back towards the house.

I stared after him, legs trembling. When we'd been on the ground, had he been about to – no, I wouldn't complete the thought. Any punishment would be better than that.

Chapter 18

I waited and waited and waited. The back garden was about one hundred feet long, enclosed by a rickety fence with a few trees whispering in the wind. The grass was unkempt as if no one had mown it for a decade and a rusty lawnmower that looked broken lay on its side a few feet away from me. Beyond the fence lay nothing except for barren ground; not a single house stood in view, decrepit or otherwise, making me feel I may as well have been on the moon. At the very end of the garden stood a cluster of trees and I wondered what lay behind. They looked as though they had been planted there intentionally to form a barrier. Maybe something lay beyond them out of sight, a house I couldn't see. To my right, stood a rusted climbing frame, its blue paint almost gone. I imagined Mikey climbing those bars as a little boy, his orange hair bright against the dull sky. In my vision he fell off and hit his head and never got back up. It was a horrible thing to imagine, but if that had happened, I wouldn't be here right now. I'd be at home with Jacob. His face flashed into my mind, and I shook my head; I had to focus on what was happening. Try to understand these two strangers, get inside their brains. They were both unstable. Ethel seemed to control Mikey. He was utterly under her spell yet scared of her too. I wondered if there was a way I could turn him against her, but I understood so little about them, didn't know the extent of their madness or the complex nature of their relationship. Perhaps if I went along with this insane idea and removed the old woman's tumour, they'd let me go. I could promise them I wouldn't say a word. They could dump me back home, blindfold me so I wouldn't be able to remember how to get to their house. If I performed this task for them and the lady somehow survived, they might be so grateful that they'd go along with my suggestion.

I stared at the goosebumps on the back of my hand. I felt sick, bruised, and tired. And cold. Despite it being September, the wind was like ice against my skin. All I wanted was to go home and throw myself into my husband's arms. Tears stung my eyes. I blinked rapidly and glanced at the cigarette burn on my wrist. Ethel was a vicious person. If Mikey feared her, she must have done things to make him feel that way. Maybe she'd burned him too. She might have done worse things than that. People weren't born crazy. They were turned crazy. Despite my father being distant throughout my childhood, he'd never laid a hand on me. Neither had my mum. She'd been affectionate and kind; the sort of mother I'd always wanted to be. For a second, I dipped my chin to look down at my flat stomach, thanking God I wasn't pregnant. Just the thought of bringing a baby into this hell brought bile to the back of my throat. Maybe my inability to conceive was a blessing rather than a curse. The hand fate had dealt me was too brutal for a baby's involvement. I was probably going to die here. If I was pregnant, my baby would die here too, never knowing its daddy or grandma.

No. Don't give up hope. They might let you go. You just need to do what they say. Play along. Act.

I looked up at the grey sky, head ringing with the word 'act'. I was an actor, and I was good, really good. I'd been nominated for best supporting actor at the TV Awards in the summer. Jacob had been so proud. Though he was the main lead in Emergency and played my husband in the series, he hadn't been nominated for any awards, but he'd not minded at all. To celebrate he'd booked us a romantic getaway in Bath, my favourite English city. We'd wined and dined at a restaurant then partied the night away at a cool bar. Jacob had said I was the best actress in the world, that one day I'd be in a James Bond film, which was a super-unrealistic but fun ambition of mine, one I'd told only him. I knew Jacob was biased but it was true to a certain extent: I was a good actress. If I could play a role in front of a whole camera crew, I could play a role in front of two insane people. Being able to slice into someone's flesh was a whole other story of course.

I heard a bang and looked at the back of the house at Mikey, who was loping towards me. I tried to read his expression, but his face was blank, eyes vacant.

'What did she say? Are you taking me back inside?'

He unlocked the cuffs, slipped them into his pocket and seized my upper arms.

I craned my neck around to look up at him. 'Mikey?'

Whistling *Let It Snow* he steered me away from the tree towards the back of the garden and the cluster of oak trees.

'Mikey! Please, tell me what's going on. Where're you taking me?'

A cold sweat slicked my armpits, and my heartbeat went berserk.

'Mikey! Stop. Please. It's not too late to take me back inside.'

'Liars need to be punished,' he said simply.

He pushed me through a narrow gap between the fence and an oak tree and hustled me toward a stone well. A thick rope ran from around the base of a tree stump into the black cavity.

I shook my head and tried to pull away from him, but his grip tightened, and he crushed me against the well. With one arm across my shoulder blades and his body pressing against my back, he held me still while he yanked on a rope with his free hand. I struggled to no avail, watching in horror as a large wooden bucket emerged out of the darkness.

'Get in,' he said, grabbing my arm and pulling me towards the bucket.

I screamed up at him, 'Are you insane? No!'

'Get in or I'll put you in,' he said. He was avoiding eye contact, but his mouth was set, jaw locked. 'I must do it. She told me to.'

'And if she told you to jump off a cliff?' I said.

A slight frown wrinkled the space between his eyebrows, but he moved quickly, picking me up like a baby and heaving me into the bucket. I kicked and punched and managed to catch him on the shoulder. He grunted but didn't back off. I tried to climb out of the bucket, and he shoved me back down again and again. I rose to try once more but he held up his fist and said, in a hard dangerous voice, 'Don't.'

I froze, and whispered, 'Please don't do this, Mikey.'

'I have to,' he said firmly.

Without another word, he grabbed the rope and lowered me into the mouth of hell.

Chapter 19

Everyone was afraid of something. Jacob's greatest fear was heights; Mum's was spiders; Dad's was snakes; mine was small spaces.

The bucket hit the bottom of the well with a thud, jarring my spine. Mikey's face appeared in the circle of grey sky so high above me that he became a thumbprint on a blank canvas. I didn't know how far down I was, but I couldn't make out his face. From this distance, his head was a button with no stitches. His words drifted down to me like a demonic melody, singsong yet distant, the voice of a man in a trance.

'Nana says punishment is good for the soul. When she's decided you've served your time, I'll be back. Don't worry. It's not as bad down there as you might think. You'll get used to it in a bit. I know I did.'

He disappeared.

I was alone in my worst nightmare.

With shaking fingers, I touched the cold, dank stone wall. The surface was dark grey, rough in some places, slimy with algae-like moss in others. An ancient blend of mould and dampness circled me, creeping into my pores, up my nose and down my throat. Years-old grime oozed from the stone, and thickened the air. It was syrupy and unnatural. Breathing became an issue. I could see little and my head swam with fear. The grey wall blurred into a ghostly portal. A tunneled grave. Darkness closed in, insistent and oppressive, an invisible beast intent on my suffering.

Panic exploded in my brain, transmitting shock waves through my body. My breaths became gasps. I tried to breathe in and out slowly. I closed my eyes against the pressing walls. I pictured myself on a sunny beach with Jacob lying by my side, blue sky open above me, fresh, sea-salted air around us, but reality had me in its hideous grasp, and the tiny space pushing in from all sides asserted itself, crushing my lungs and warping my senses.

I told myself the attack would subside; I just had to wait it out, breathe through it; it wouldn't kill me, but I felt like I was dying. Darkness and death swamped all logic, sucking me down into a dark, terrifying void. I was all alone. So desperately, hopelessly alone.

'Breathe, breathe…' I whispered.

In that moment, all I wanted was my mum. I heard her voice urging me to fight, to look up, look out, find the pathway to light. I felt her breath on my hair, smelled her vanilla-rose perfume, her Olay face cream. She was smiling, encouraging me, holding me tight, wiping my tears, just like she had when I'd fallen off my bike and scraped my knee all those years ago...

I opened my eyes and looked upwards at the tiny circle of sky. A bird soared across the opening. It was only a speck of life against pale grey, but it broke the terror; pulling me out of the hopeless fear, and giving me space to think and breathe.

I put my head between my knees and gave myself time. Finally, my breathing slowed, and my heart rate evened out. My cheeks were wet from crying, my ears pounding, mouth dirt-dry, but my mind took control once more. Almost without realising it, I was holding the rope, pulling it down until it was taut. It was tied around a thick tree stump, so should hold my weight without breaking. I would climb out of here if it was the last thing I did. Now was my chance. Mikey would be in the house tending to Ethel's needs no doubt, which meant I had an opening.

The rope was coarse and thick. I pulled myself to a standing position in the bucket. My knees were as wobbly as jelly, but I didn't collapse. With gritted teeth, I reached up the rope and pulled my feet onto it, wrapping my legs around and gripping with my knees. In seconds, I realised how hard the climb was going to be. The last time I'd climbed a rope like this was when I was about ten in gymnastics at school, and it had seemed easy, but climbing was much easier at that age than mine. Already, I was struggling to hold my weight.

I peered skywards. At a guess, I was twenty feet below ground level. At a little over five feet, that meant I needed to pull my body up fifteen feet.

Not for the first time since arriving at this awful place I wished I'd invested time and effort in weightlifting classes and cursed myself for my laziness. My agent had even suggested I try to build more muscle, arguing that these days female actors were more desirable if they were muscular and toned rather than thin. Stupidly, I'd ignored her. Yoga was enough for me. I used to think it made me strong, and it did in a way, but it wasn't the same as doing weight-bearing exercise. If I'd built my upper body strength, this task would be a lot more achievable. Another thing I would change – if I ever got away – was to take up self-defense classes, maybe even kickboxing. One of my colleagues did kickboxing and she had abs of steel.

I reached up and heaved. Though I'd only pulled myself up twice, my arms were starting to ache. Gravity was my enemy, an invisible foe I must battle against if I was to climb this mountain.

The one thing I had at my disposal was determination. And pig-headed stubborness – according to my dad. I shifted my body up a little further and winced; my hands were starting to burn. Trying to ignore the pain, I continued my slow ascent.

I was about halfway up when I felt the walls closing in again. My vision danced and I clung on to the rope for dear life and repeated *red sky at night, shepherd's delight* over and over. There was no rhyme or reason for that saying to pop into my head, but it did, and I focused on those words as if they were my lifeline.

After a while, the stifling blackness receded and the burning in my palms took precedence. I still had about seven feet to go. It seemed an eternity. Soaked in sweat, I reached up and shimmied my knees and ankles up the rope. My arms quivered in protest. They were growing weaker by the moment. Glancing down, I realised that if I fell now, I might break my leg – or worse.

I couldn't give up now.

Biting my lip, I pulled and reached, pulled and reached, pulled and reached, and at long last, I dragged myself over the top of the well and rolled onto the long grass. Wispy clouds smothered the sky like smoke.

I was breathless from exertion yet elated; I had made it. I was out.

Rolling onto all fours, I staggered to my feet and looked back at the row of oak trees that obscured the cottage, listening intently. My chest spasmed at the sound of whistling. Mikey was coming.

Chapter 20

For a moment I was paralysed. The whistling grew louder. He was on the other side of the trees.

I turned and ran through the long grass towards the fence at the very end of Ethel's land. Seizing the top plank with sore palms, I stepped onto the bottom plank and climbed over, then ran as fast as my trembling legs would allow. I wore only socks, and the deserted expanse was dotted with craggy rocks, the ground damp and cold beneath my feet. As I ran, I tried to avoid the worst of the jagged ground, looking up then down, scanning the terrain for any sign of manmade objects or people.

My heart dropped; there were no trees and therefore nowhere to hide. The land spewed out before and all around me like an unending desert, offering nothing and no one, no refuge, no hope. It was a no man's land. An alien plain. Even the air smelled wrong. Fresher than inside that awful hovel, but as damp and earthy as a disinterred grave.

I glanced behind me. There was no sign of Mikey. I imagined him staring down into the well, his eyes widening when he realised I wasn't there. Then again, from the top of the well, he probably wouldn't be able to see me. Would he notice the rope pulled tight and work out what had happened or would it only be after a couple of minutes of trying to speak to me and getting no response that he worked out where I'd gone?

Latching onto the latter idea, hope floated upwards, buoying me on. I ran faster, adrenaline giving me speed. How high up this mountain was I? Was it the sort of mountain that attracted scramblers or climbers? If it was, there was a chance I might see someone who could help me. And Mikey had said we were three miles from the nearest road – if I could keep running for three miles and get to a road there might be somewhere I could hide. Then I could wait for a car to come.

I imagined the relief I would feel when I saw a car. I'd run out of my hiding place waving my hands and screaming for help. In this fluffy pink jumper, I wouldn't be hard to miss. Only a complete bastard would continue driving on sighting a young woman in distress in the middle of nowhere.

Yes. I would make it. I would keep going until I was crawling, my body out of control with the shakes like marathon runners who pushed themselves too hard. I remembered watching the London Marathon a couple of years ago with Jacob. Two elite female runners had crawled to the finish line, their bodies jerking and spasming as if they had shellshock. The look of determination combined with the pain on their faces had me thinking how stupid they were to force their bodies to such extremes. They weren't running for survival. They were running for glory. But when I'd voiced this, Jacob had surprised me by saying that they probably lived for moments like this; that those women had put in years and years of gruelling training, dedication and sacrifice, and that therefore, in a sense, running was their purpose in life; their reason for living.

What was my reason for living?

The answer was easy: Jacob. He was my everything. My absolute.

My mind turned again to the possibility that Mikey had hurt him, but I reminded myself that although Mikey had punched Jacob before, he could have done far worse. To take me, he hadn't needed to kill my husband. He'd only needed to make sure Jacob couldn't get in his way.

My legs were heavy now, my thighs burning. A stitch tore into my side. I was struggling to draw breath.

Don't stop.

I repeated the mantra over and over again, but it didn't take long for 'don't' to fade and 'stop' to scream. The pain was all-encompassing: poison liquifying my muscles, scorching my insides like boiling treacle. The urge to stop screamed louder and a devilish voice whispered that I could stop running and walk for a few seconds, give myself time to get my breath back then start running again.

Those marathon runners; if they could do it, so could I. I had to do it, for Jacob.

I set my jaw and continued running.

Quivering with the effort of putting one foot in front of the other and aware I was slowing down, I glanced back. For one horrific second, my heart stopped. I thought Mikey was coming after me, but it was a only figment of my harried imagination, a shadow of a haunted mind. Energy leeched from my bones in the aftermath of the sudden burst of terror, but I carried on running across the barren land, and then the terrain was changing, sloping downwards with uncanny suddenness, and suddenly I was stumbling over a ridge and down a slope covered with loose stones. I slid and fell. My right palm hit rubble; little stones cut into my skin, and I gasped, my wrist a block of pain. I allowed myself to drop onto my bottom. Through a fresh well of tears, I examined my raw wrist and palm. Beads of blood dotted the heel of my hand, and my wrist was tender – sprained or twisted I couldn't be sure. Another weakness. Another hindrance. At least it wasn't broken.

The quietness was shattered as my name rang in one long, hideous syllable, drawn out by desperation and rage, the voice of my pursuer far, far too close. It was him - Mikey Bell - shouting my name across the mountain.

The fact that he wasn't worried about being heard by a passing stranger made my stomach drop another foot; there was no one in the area to hear me scream.

Chapter 21

I scrambled to my feet, found my footing, and hurried downwards. The mountainside wasn't too steep, thank God, but the ground was slippery and unforgiving, slowing me down. My socks made my descent quiet, but my feet were on fire, my calves hot coals laced with acid. Every breath was torture, every step a battle. My thighs were concrete slabs. Gravity was my friend and my enemy: she pulled me down and I went with her and against her. I stumbled, tripped, fell. Got up. Carried on. Fell again.

'DOC!'

I looked back. No Mikey. But he was close. Close enough to reach my ears, his voice a bullet to my heart.

I reached another ridge, this one more challenging. I climbed down, wincing against the pain in my wrist. I landed on steeper ground, continued my descent. His voice punctured the air again, stole my breath.

I glanced back. No sign. Had he gone a different way?

The slope turned into a death slide, too steep to continue facing forwards. I pivoted to face the mountainside and climbed down as quickly as I could, terrified I was going to lose my footing and fall to my death – or worse – if Mikey found me incapacitated he would carry me back to that hellhole and then what? Kill me? Force me to operate on Ethel then let me die of my injuries? Or would he leave me to rot? Soon I would be carrion for the crows, a devil's feast. It would be a long time before anyone found me. When they did, the headline would read something like 'Rising Star Plummets to Death'. Jacob –

Stop it. Stop torturing yourself.

Stones were rolling down, hitting my head. I looked up. Held myself still against the mountain, limbs trembling. Rubble continued to rain down on me. Scuffs and heavy breathing pierced my ears.

No.

Mikey's head poked out over the ridge. His eyes centred in on mine. A wicked grin twitched his lips and he panted, 'Found you!'

I glanced down. It wasn't far to the bottom now. Not far at all. I hurried down. My foot slipped and then I was falling, hands scrabbling for purchase and finding none, stomach scraping against stone. I landed hard and crumpled. Adrenaline blitzed the pain. I looked up. Mikey was crawling down the side of the mountain with inhuman speed – a mountain lion in a Christmas jumper. It was almost laughable. But of course it wasn't. He was like Spiderman made real. He must have grown up here; had climbed his whole life. His arms and legs moved in perfect harmony; he and the mountain were one.

Somehow, I got up. The land was flat again. I glanced right and left; there was no sign of a road. Once again, the land ahead and to both sides stretched out into nothingness. But there – what was that? I began running towards it; a speeding glimmer on the horizon. A car. Salvation. Far but not unreachable. I just had to keep going. Mikey wasn't off the mountain yet. There was still a chance I could make it. That car would be gone by the time I reached the road, but another was bound to come soon. It had to.

Sweat dripped into my eyes, and I blinked frantically, chest heaving, every muscle dying to melt into the ground, to blend with the earth, to cave to gravity. I imagined I was on the moon, and my legs found a little resistance and propelled me on, every step a giant leap. Though everything ached, desperation won out; I needed to beat Mikey. If it was the last thing I did, I'd reach that road. I'd never set foot in that terrible cottage again. Never.

The road came into view at last, blurry as a mirage in the desert. I tripped and fell onto all fours; looked back – Mikey was coming. He was off the mountain only ten steps behind.

A silver Land Rover was coming from the left. I got up, stumbled forward, waved my arms, tried to scream and only managed a croak. I threw myself forward into the road, waving and waving, trying to cry out and the car slowed and then a red-haired man was poking his head out.

I tried to speak, but there was no air left.

I looked back, Mikey was grinning from ear to ear, out of breath but upright, jogging towards me. 'Simon! Hi there. How goes it, friend?'

Simon climbed out of the car and straightened. He was a head shorter than Mikey with a thick beard.

I backed away but Mikey lunged forward and wrapped his arm around me, hugging me tightly against his side. I opened my mouth to speak and felt something sharp puncture my back.

'This is my cousin,' Mikey said, 'She's visiting for a few weeks. We were playing a game of cat and mouse.'

Simon raised one bushy eyebrow. His eyes clocked my bloodied wrist.

Clouds fogged my head. My mouth wouldn't work.

'Oh dear,' Mikey said, his voice fading, 'Are you okay?'

I tried to focus, tried to plead for help with my eyes, but Simon dissolved into mist.

Chapter 22

For the second time in less than twenty-four hours I woke up in an alien place, groggy, head pounding, mouth dry, heart slamming against my ribs. I jerked upright and immediately regretted it, my head splitting with pain. A coppery smell tainted the air. I processed it quickly, my eyes widening as I realised that it was the smell of blood. Where was it coming from? Was it me? I looked down to see myself covered in a soft grey blanket. I was lying on a sofa in a living room decorated in grey and sage. Modern. Clean. Expensive-looking. Bronze figurines on shelves. Books. Photos on the wall of the man who'd pulled up in his car...Simon, that was it, with a Chinese woman. There were two doors. Both closed. One to my right and one to my left. I looked down at the soft grey carpet. Swallowed a scream. A puddle of blood darkened the floor. A dark stain travelled from the puddle to the door to my right. I pushed myself to my feet, wobbled and knocked a coffee table. A vase of lilies thudded to the floor. I stumbled towards the door, taking a wide berth of the blood trail, and tried the door handle, but it was locked. Where the hell was I? Where was Mikey? And Simon?

I swallowed a wave of sick. I didn't want to think of the horror that must have taken place while I was unconscious.

My gaze landed on the coffee table. I hurried over to it, dizzy from whatever Mikey had given me, only just able to see straight. I picked it up and heaved it across the room to a pair of sage curtains pulled tight, then placed the table on the ground. I could use it to break the window.

I whipped open the curtains and stared in dismay as Mikey stared back at me. He stood directly outside the window beside Simon's Land Rover. Blood spattered Mikey's face. His eyes were bloodshot, skin whiter than I'd ever seen it.

He frowned at me, shook his head and slipped some keys into his pocket. I backed away from the window, turned and ran straight through the puddle of blood heading for the other door, away from the front of the house.

The front door slammed open a split second before I slammed the door shut behind me. There was no lock. I was in a large dining room. I flew past the table, opened another door. I was in a study of sorts. I ran through the room and yanked open another door – this house was huge, like a maze. A set of carpeted stairs led off a wide hallway. Another closed door stood across the way. I hesitated, looked back at the study floor – a trail of bloody footprints lay behind me. Mikey stormed after me, doors banging as he flew through each room.

Which way should I go?

Up. Higher ground will give you an advantage.

Will it?

Yes.

No.

Yes.

GO.

I tore off my blood-damp socks and threw them towards the blood trail, then grabbed the banister and hurled myself up the stairs, praying the blood hadn't gone through to the soles of my feet.

I reached the top of the stairs and looked right. Three closed doors. I ran to the middle one, opened the door, slipped inside, closed it behind me. There was no lock. Mikey was already on the stairs, boots like horses' hooves thundering after me.

With a sickening jolt I realised he was going to find me. My only hope was to find a weapon, hide, hope I could take him by surprise. I imagined attacking him and felt a weird sort of thrill-come-horror. I could hit him if I had to, but I didn't want to kill him. I didn't know if I could kill a person, even someone who had taken me against my will. I thought about Jacob. Knew what he'd tell me to do: do whatever it takes to stay alive.

I was in a white double bedroom. A scan told me there were only two hiding places – under the bed and in the wardrobe - and nothing I could use as a weapon. My eyes landed on the dressing table. Spotted a makeup bag. Mikey was crashing around in the room next to mine.

I lunged for the bag, frantically unzipped it, grabbed a lipstick, ripped off the lid. Wrote on the mirror. The door swung open; I tossed the lipstick and stepped in front of the mirror to hide it. Mikey stared at me from the doorway. He was panting and red-faced. Sweat dampened his hair, slicked his upper lip. A smile broke out that met his eyes; it was full of relief and excitement and victory, as if we'd been playing a game he'd won. 'Gotcha.'

I sagged against the wall. 'Please let me go, Mikey. Please.'

'No can do, Doc. We need you. Nana needs you. If you don't remove that lump, she'll die, you know that.'

'What did you do to Simon?'

Mikey's eyes darted to the window. His gaze lost focus and he slipped his thumb into his mouth. A frown pinched his forehead. His face paled. Spots of blood dotted his cheeks.

'Mikey? Where's Simon?'

'I had to do it. He didn't give me a choice,' Mikey whispered, voice distorted by his thumb.

'Do what?'

'He attacked me. I told him all about you. About our plan to save Nana but he wouldn't listen. He, he, he -'

He looked at me, eyes watery, pleading. 'I didn't mean to do it.'

'I'm sure you didn't. But if he's hurt, we should call 999. Get an ambulance here.'

Mikey shook his head. 'It's too late for that. He's gone. In the boot of his car. I…I need to get rid of the body.'

'What?'

'And besides, if there was a chance of bringing him back, you'd do it, wouldn't you, Doc?'

I couldn't speak. Simon was dead. Mikey had actually killed him.

He drifted to the bed and perched on the edge, legs jigging. He sucked his thumb noisily, eyes darting everywhere but focusing on nothing. Abruptly, he started smashing his fist into his temple. 'Stupid, stupid, stupid!'

'Mikey, stop. You're hurting yourself,' I gasped.

I looked at the door, terrified he was going to turn his rage on me. I thought about making a run for it.

To my surprise he stopped hitting himself and looked at me, pure despair in his eyes. 'Nana's going to be so angry.'

'Then we won't tell her,' I said, inching away from the mirror towards the doorway.

Mikey hung his head and rocked back and forth. I took another small step. He looked up. 'We won't?'

I froze. Shook my head.

'But lying is bad,' he said.

'What she doesn't know won't hurt her.'

Then I had a thought. I turned to face him. Looked deep in his eyes. 'Mikey, you don't have to go back there. You can leave. Start fresh. Get away from her. She's horrible to you. She's controlling you, bullying you. You'll be so much happier if you leave and it's not right, living with -'

'NO.' He stood up and darted forward, making me jump.

He towered over me, frown heavy, fists clenched. 'No. Don't say that. Nana's good. She looked after me when no-one else would. I could never leave her. How can you say something like that?'

'Because it's true,' I said.

He shook his head. 'No.'

'She's not well. She -'

'NO.'

He grabbed my arm and dragged me out of the room. 'We need to go back right away. Nana needs me. She can't be alone for too long.'

'Please, Mikey, please let me go.'

He ignored me and pulled me through the house in silence. He took a wide berth of the blood in the living room and yanked me out of the front door towards Simon's car. I tried to twist out of his grip but his hand was an iron clamp on my arm.

He opened the boot and told me to get in. I stared in horror at Simon's body. His head had been cracked open by something. Beside him lay a bloodied bronze figurine of a Labrador.

'Please, God, no –'

'I'm sorry. I know it's not nice, but I can't trust you yet,' Mikey mumbled, unable to look at the body.

I shook my head. 'You can trust me. I promise. I'll sit in the front next to you and I won't move a muscle.'

Mikey frowned and swallowed hard, thinking.

I held my breath. Prayed he wouldn't make me get in the boot with Simon's corpse.

He dragged a hand through his hair. It stuck up at odd angles. He looked confused and lost.

'Please,' I whispered, placing my hand on his arm.

He looked down at my hand in surprise. His face softened. His eyes searched mine. I held his gaze, gave him a small smile.

At last, he nodded. 'Okay. Passenger seat. But don't move.'

Feeling absurdly grateful, I did as I was told. Once we

were strapped in, Mikey drove away from Simon's house. Silent tears dribbled down his cheeks the entire way back to the cottage.

Chapter 23

Mikey held one finger to his lips. 'Don't make a sound.'

I nodded and allowed him to shepherd me inside the front door. He turned and locked the door, using one of the keys on his lanyard then guided me towards the stairs.

On the landing, he opened the airing cupboard door and handed me a towel then steered me into another room. There were no Christmas decorations in this room, only a single bed, a small wardrobe and a chest of drawers. Nothing adorned the walls except for flowery wallpaper. In the corner stood a creepy old rocking horse. It was more of a prison cell than the Christmas room.

Mikey opened the middle drawer and pulled out a pair of women's jeans, socks and another pink jumper identical to the first one he'd given me to wear. He thrust them into my hands and told me to have a shower, that he'd be waiting just outside the door. He never spoke above a whisper and kept glancing at the floor and swallowing nervously.

I did as I was told.

My tears blended with the shower water. I was drained and sore, my wrist a throbbing abscess. I didn't even have the energy to care about Mikey coming into the room. Still, I made it quick, got dressed and hesitated at the doorway, dreading whatever lay ahead.

Mikey opened the door. He handed me the lab coat and stethoscope. I pulled on the coat and looped the stethoscope around my neck.

I fingered the piece of medical equipment, an idea tugging on my mind. 'Where did you get this from?'

'Ebay. There's an internet café I use sometimes when I

go food shopping. You can get anything on Ebay. It's great.' He seemed to perk up a little.

'I know,' I said trying to inject energy into my tone, 'just last week I ordered this hair curler. It was a lot cheaper than getting one from Boots.'

Mikey grinned.

'Nana doesn't understand things like Ebay,' he whispered wrinkling his nose. 'She doesn't understand a few things I understand.'

'I bet that can be a little lonely?'

Mikey looked at his feet. Shrugged. 'Not really. I'm used to it.' His head snapped up. 'Anyway, you need to get to work.'

He pushed me back into the bathroom and told me to sit on the toilet seat. For a second I thought he was going to attack me, but he simply shut the door, turned to the sink and proceeded to wash the blood off his face. He washed his hands for a very long time in water so hot it turned his skin red.

'Doesn't that hurt?' I said, feigning more concern than I felt.

Mikey stared at his reflection and murmured, 'Punishment is good for the soul.'

Not for the first time, I blessed my lucky stars that he wasn't blaming me for what he did to Simon. I thought about the body in the boot. Wondered what Mikey planned to do with it. Simon's car was parked out the front of the cottage right beside his. It wasn't exactly inconspicuous. Soon, Mikey would have to move it. Get rid of the body.

Inwardly I shivered, shocked that I was thinking such things.

'Please can I have some painkillers?' I said.

Mikey nodded and retrieved a packet from the medicine cabinet. He popped out two pills then beckoned me over to the sink. I took them quickly; conscious he was standing right behind me while I leaned over. I could smell his body odour; it seemed to fill the air around me.

'What's hurting?' he said.

'My wrist,' I said, holding it up and pushing back the sleeve of my jumper.

Mikey's eyes widened in horror at the red-raw, swollen mess that was my wrist. He frowned and bit his lip. 'I'm sorry, Doc.'

I was shocked by the sincerity in his voice. 'If you have to cuff me again, please can you cuff my other wrist?'

He nodded and gave me a tentative smile.

He led me out of the bathroom back into the bedroom and told me to sit on the bed. He stripped down to his boxers, discarding his dirty clothes by tossing them into the corner of the room. I looked away, but not before I saw the state of his back. I swallowed a gasp. His back was smothered with scars. Every single one was round and small, exactly like a cigarette burn.

Physical abuse, infantilisation…no wonder he's so messed up.

'Who did that to you, Mikey?'

He pulled on a clean pair of jeans, twisted around to look at me. 'Did what?'

'Hurt you?' I gestured to his upper body.

His chest was smothered with scars as well.

He glanced down at his body and frowned heavily as if only noticing his ruined skin for the first time. Without looking at me, he yanked on another Christmas jumper and mumbled, 'No one.'

Sensing the subject was closed, I allowed him to steer me out of the room and down the stairs, my trepidation mounting with each step.

Outside the living room door, Mikey paused and looked at me, eyes wide. 'Don't say anything about what happened. Okay?'

'I won't, but why? What are you so scared of?'

He ignored my question and pushed me into the room. My nose was immediately assaulted with stale cigarette smoke and urine.

'Where the hell have you been?' Ethel snapped. She hadn't moved from the rocking chair.

'After I pulled her out of the well, she was really, really sick so I had to let her get cleaned up so she could fix you properly. Sorry Nana. Are you okay? Do you need anything?'

I avoided Ethel's gaze. Her eyes flicked from me to Mikey, narrowing in suspicion. 'You're not lying, are you boy?'

'No. I would never lie to you Nana,' Mikey said. His voice wavered.

I chanced a glance at her. She was beckoning to him with a gnarled finger. 'Come here, boy.'

Mikey moved towards her, pulling me with him.

Chapter 24

'You stink,' Ethel said.

Mikey said nothing.

Despite everything, my heart went out to him. Ethel was a witch, a cruel, vicious harpy intent on bending Mikey to her will. But he was a grown man now; shouldn't he be able to stand up for himself? Then again if this monstrous woman was all he'd ever known…

It didn't bear thinking about. But I couldn't stop imagining what he must have endured; first, he'd been abandoned by his mother, then he'd been subjected to God knows what at the hands of this demonic crone for almost his entire life.

Ethel gestured for him to come closer.

'You'd never lie to me, would you boy?'

Mikey's Adam's apple bobbed as he struggled to swallow. His cheeks flushed. He lowered his eyes and said, 'No Nana. Never.'

'Tell me again what happened.'

Mikey glanced at me. His eyes welled.

I blurted, 'He's telling the truth. I was sick. I got it all over me. Mikey was really good. He cleaned me up, gave me a change of clothes.'

She ignored me and looked at Mikey. Leaning forward, she said, 'Show me.'

'Show you what, Nana?'

'Show me her clothes!'

Mikey's eyes widened. He nodded and backed away. 'Yes, Nana. Right away, Nana.'

He tugged me with him, and we hurried out of the room. Without speaking, he pulled me back up the stairs.

'Mikey,' I whispered, 'let's just leave. Go somewhere safe. You don't have to stay here with her.'

He let go of my arm and massaged his temples, muttering under his breath.

Sensing an opportunity, I placed my hand on his shoulder. 'Mikey, listen to me. If you leave here, you'll be happy. No one should have to live this way, controlled and bullied by someone like her.'

'No,' he mumbled, 'you don't know anything. I'm bad. I need to be kept in line.'

'That's not true. You're a good person.' He was distracted. I glanced at the stairs. Thought about making a run for it, but the door was locked. He had the key on his lanyard around his neck. I wouldn't get far.

'What am I going to do?' he said, more to himself than me.

'About what?'

'About the clothes – there's no sick on them! She'll know.'

An idea burst to life in my head like a flame. This was great. A chance to win him over. Get him moving to my side. If I could become his ally, maybe even his friend…

'Are your jeans still dirty?' I said.

He frowned, puzzled.

'The jeans I threw up on. Where are they?'

'In there.' He pointed to the single bedroom.

'Get them.'

Still frowning, he pulled me along into the room, dug around in the bottom of the wardrobe and retrieved the soiled jeans. 'I haven't washed them yet,' he admitted guiltily.

'That's good because I've got an idea. Rub them on my clothes.'

'MIKEY.' Ethel's voice screeched through the floor. Mikey jumped.

'But - but that's lying,' he whispered.

'Maybe, but what's the harm? If you don't tell this tiny lie, you'll have to tell her about Simon, and what then?'

His face paled. A faraway look glazed his eyes and he rocked back and forth on his heels.

'MIKEY!'

He jumped again. Nodded.

I watched him rub his jeans over the first pink jumper. Another idea hit me, and I stuck my fingers down my throat and brought up bile which I smeared over the jumper too.

'You'd better wash your hands,' he said, pulling a face.

I almost laughed. Instead, I agreed. We both washed our hands in the bathroom, then Mikey steered me downstairs. With every step, hope drifted up; if I could win him over, maybe he'd let me go.

'That took a long time,' Ethel snapped the second we entered the room. 'Give it here.'

Mikey hurried over and passed her the garment. She wrinkled her nose and said, 'I don't want to touch it, for Christ's sake. I can smell it from here. Take it away.'

Mikey deflated with relief. My heart fluttered with victory; one small step, one giant leap towards potential freedom. Maybe.

'Now,' she said, staring at me, 'you can get on with it and fix me.' There was a cold glint in her eye, almost as if she was enjoying my powerlessness.

'Okay,' I said slowly, thinking – if there was a chance I could get Mikey away from the house, maybe I could escape, 'but I'll need certain things first.'

She raised one eyebrow and pursed her lips.

'What do you need, Doctor Sparks?' Mikey said, excited.

I sent my mind back to the *Emergency* episode Mikey had mentioned before where I removed a tumour – what equipment did I need? What drugs did I request? I was good at memorising my lines but as soon as I'd said them in front of the camera for the last time, my brain had a way of making them fade with weird speed. Jacob was the opposite; if I asked him his first line for a specific episode six months ago, he'd remember it in a flash.

I needed to get into acting mode; play along, make them believe I was a real doctor. Another way of pleasing Mikey would be to get into character and be Doctor Elouise Sparks, surgeon extraordinaire. He was clearly obsessed with the programme and my character. If I could feed his delusion, it might be another way to win him over.

I took a deep breath; tried to sound confident and professional, adopting my Doctor Sparks voice – clipped and deeper than normal. 'I'll need latex gloves, antiseptic wipes, a scalpel, a suction device, plenty of cotton pads, wire and needle for stitching,' I swallowed, my gorge rising at the thought of cutting into someone's flesh – all that blood – 'and…hang on. Let me take a quick look at the tumour.'

Fighting a grimace, I leaned over, moved Ethel's wiry hair out of the way and inspected the lump on her neck. I stood up and nodded sharply, clasping my hands as Doctor Sparks would. 'Yes, I was right. I'll need an extra-large adhesive wound dressing and a syringe. Oh, and…' Shit, shit, how much morphine? Then an idea popped into my head, bright with possibility like a ruby at the bottom of the ocean, 'and…as much morphine as you can get your hands on.'

Chapter 25

I was handcuffed to the bed again inside Satan's grotto, fretting about whether I'd done the right thing and trying not to think about the corpse in the Land Rover and what Mikey may or may not be doing this very second. How long did it take for a body to start to smell? For it to begin decomposing? For rot to set in?

Hang on - Satan is a jumbled up version of Santa – how strange.

Why think that now? You're losing the plot.

I looked down at the cheese sandwich Mikey had given me. I'd managed to eat half of it, but knew I couldn't force any more down, not now my thoughts had veered to the body.

If only I'd stayed downstairs instead of running up…maybe I'd have got away.

At least you managed to leave a clue.

I put the plate on the bedside table and relived the moment I'd grabbed that lipstick and frantically scrawled what I could. Would it be enough? Had I written the right thing? Doubt gnawed at my insides. I chewed my lip.

Closing my eyes against the hideous one-handed Santa, I visualised the mirror, the letters and numbers I'd written on the glass. A frantic scribble that could mean everything.

JM 14 97 5. The first 7 units of my national insurance number. The last two were missing; I'd run out of time.

You should have written your name.

I shook my head. No. I'd done the right thing. If I'd written my name, I probably would have only managed to write my first name, and there were millions of Rachels in the world.

Not millions who've recently gone missing.

A sudden realisation occurred, and it felt like a spear to my heart: why hadn't I written Mikey's name? If I'd managed to write M. Bell, the police would've been able to find this address and –

I felt like smashing my head into the wall. Anger and self-hatred roared inside me.

You idiot. You ruined your only chance of getting found.

I tried to breathe through the anger and panic. Tried to think. I couldn't spiral downwards and allow myself to sink into self-pity and loathing. I needed to remain strong. Try to cling to the chance that my message might help the police find me. The fact that I wasn't far away from Simon's house was a plus surely. And maybe they'd find my DNA there. The police must have taken a hair from my hairbrush. And they must have lifted my fingerprints from our house. My fingerprints were on that lipstick, on the banister too, and the doors. Hopefully they'd find one in Simon's house, then they'd know for sure I'd been there – God, would they think I was the killer?

No. They'd find Mikey's DNA there too.

Only if they have it on the system.

Mikey was unstable, and violent when pushed, but that didn't mean he had ever been arrested. Mikey might not even be his real name. For all I knew, his entire identity could be a lie.

Panic pulsed. My whole body hurt. The painkillers had taken the edge off, but my right hand still throbbed.

I grabbed the cup of water Mikey had left and downed it in one.

The plastic tree mocked me. I wanted to tear it to pieces. I never wanted to see a Christmas decoration again.

Mikey had gone to the internet café to order the stuff I'd said I'd need. He was out of the house. Now would be an ideal time to escape, but I didn't want to wreck my left hand as well. If I got a chance to run or attack – a chance, that was, that didn't put my life at significant risk - I'd need at least one functioning hand to battle my way out. Luckily, I was left-handed, so I'd be able to wield a scalpel.

I imagined turning and plunging the scalpel into Mikey's neck, ripping the lanyard off his bleeding body, running to the front door, and unlocking it then driving away in Mikey's car. The old lady couldn't stop me; it was only Mikey who could do that. If I could disable him, I could escape. But he wasn't stupid. I doubted he would allow me to hold a scalpel willy-nilly. He would come up with a way of controlling me while I operated. After all, he'd learned from the best.

I thought about Mikey's scarred torso. Hatred for Ethel buzzed louder and louder in my head. She had turned him into a monster. If I had to hurt anyone, I'd rather it was her, but while she was mentally powerful, he possessed the physical power. Nothing Ethel could say would force me to stay in this rotten place, but if I couldn't bend Mikey to my will or find a way to catch him off-guard he could easily keep me prisoner by using his physical strength.

Get inside his head. Get to know him. Bond with him emotionally. And act the hell out of Doctor Sparks.

Much as I wanted to remove Ethel from the situation, Mikey had made it very clear that if I wanted to leave, I needed to make her better by Christmas Day. I didn't know why I had to keep her alive until then, but suspected it was because that day was so special to him. He seemed to be obsessed with it. There was a chance then, that if I somehow performed a miracle and managed to keep her alive and help her recover from my botch-job of an op, he'd stick to his word and let me go. But would he really? I'd seen his face. I knew where he lived. He'd killed Simon because Simon had tried to help me. He was a violent, unpredictable young man.

I tried to recall the look on Mikey's face when he'd said he'd let me go. There had been a sincerity there, I was sure of it, and yet…

A door slammed. He was back.

Chapter 26

A smoky, chemical smell entered the room along with Mikey. I frowned, trying to work out what the smell was.

Mikey was sweaty-faced, and edgy. He paced back and forth in front of the bed then sharply turned to face me. A strange, slightly crazed smile lifted the side of his mouth. 'I did it.' His voice was no more than a whisper. He came to perch on the bed beside me, bringing an unpleasant waft of BO.

'Did what?'

He fingered his lips. Moistened them with a flick of his tongue. 'Got rid of the evidence.'

Evidence. Simon.

A million horrors skittered through my mind. I kept my face blank. 'How?'

'Lighter fluid. I already had some, so I burned the house down. And hid the body where nobody will ever look.' His larynx bobbed. He licked his lips. Looked at me intensely. 'I've done the right thing, haven't I?'

I didn't know what to say. He'd destroyed all evidence of my presence in the house. My message on the mirror would be gone.

'Where did you hide Simon's body?'

He rubbed his nose. It was slick with sweat. 'That doesn't matter. Somewhere safe. I did right, didn't I, Doc?'

I forced myself to meet his eye.

How did you reason with a psychopath? This certainly wasn't the time to point out that no, he hadn't done the right thing. He'd done the opposite. He'd kidnapped me, murdered an innocent man then hid his corpse somewhere, and burned his house to the ground.

'There definitely wasn't anyone else in the house was there?'

'No way. I checked.'

'How did you check?'

'Looked through the windows. Knocked on the door. No answer. And Lori wasn't back yet. Her car wasn't there.'

'Lori?'

Mikey bit his lip. 'His wife. I've met her before. Had to borrow some sugar. And she gave me a Christmas card last year. She's nice.'

I felt myself pale. That poor woman.

Mikey was about to slip his thumb into his mouth.

Get inside his head. Bond with him.

'What about the car?' I said.

'Burned that too. That's why I'm so sweaty. I had to run home.' His hand flopped back onto his lap.

Had he left footprints? That was my only chance now. If the authorities got to the fire and noticed the footprints, they could follow them here.

'Doc, tell me I did the right thing.' His brow was furrowed. Tears threatened. He blinked rapidly. He needed my reassurance. This was good.

'Yes,' I said, 'You did the right thing.'

'And I shouldn't tell Nana?'

He looked so vulnerable suddenly, it almost made me reach out for him. Almost, but not quite. I'd have rather stuck my hand in a shark's mouth.

'Absolutely not. What's done is done. There's no point telling her anything. It'll only make her lash out at you.'

'You mean, punish me?'

'Yes. Punish you.'

'But don't I deserve to be punished?'

Yes. One hundred percent.

'No. Like you said, Mikey, it was an accident. Simon attacked you. You acted in self-defence.'

He sighed and tipped his face to the ceiling. He

remained in that pose for a weirdly long time, eyes vacant, lips parted.

I waited, trying to suppress the panic burbling in my chest.

'You didn't finish your sandwich,' he said.

'I was full.'

'You shouldn't waste food, you know. It's not nice. Do you mind?'

I shook my head.

He plucked it off the plate and shovelled the leftovers into his mouth.

'Mikey, when are you going to go to the internet café to order the things I need for the operation?'

He brightened and jumped off the bed. 'Oh yes! I'll go now. Oh no – it's too late to go now. It closes at five. I'll go first thing tomorrow.'

'Great.'

He beamed at me. 'I'll leave you in peace now, Doc. I need to tend to Nana. I've neglected her terribly today.' Fear flitted across his face.

Relief at the thought of him leaving the room made my entire body deflate. I watched him stride to the door.

At the door, he stopped and looked back at me. 'You need anything before I go?'

Freedom. A Knife.

I shook my head and faked a huge yawn. 'No. I'm fine thanks. I think I'll go to sleep now. I'm shattered.'

'Oh yes. Of course. You'll need plenty of rest to prepare yourself for the operation. If I order the stuff tomorrow, hopefully it will come in a few days' time, then you can operate.'

I nodded eagerly. 'Yes, please don't bother checking on me before you go to bed. I'm sure I'll be asleep, and I don't want to be disturbed. If I don't get enough sleep in the days leading up to the operation, I could make a mistake.'

'Oh gosh! Yes, I mean, no. I won't disturb you until the

morning. Making a mistake would be bad. Very bad. For Nana and for you.' He held my gaze for longer than necessary as if trying to force his words to sink in. Little did he know, they'd had the desired effect. Beneath my ribcage, my heartbeat rattled along like a freight train, carried by the fear of the unknown. What if I killed her by mistake? What would Mikey do?

'You'd never make a mistake though, Doc. You're the best surgeon in the world. That's why we chose you. Right?'

I sat up straighter, put on Doctor Sparks's voice. 'You're absolutely right, Mikey. I'm an excellent surgeon. The best.'

He nodded. His jaw softened. He smiled and turned to leave.

Realising I'd not made much headway with the bonding thing, I blurted, 'You're a good man, Mikey.'

His eyes widened. Doubt battled with the desire to believe me.

Before he could speak, I said, 'Your heart's in the right place. You're taking really good care of me. And of Ethel. You're a good person.'

His smile faded and a deep frown crushed his forehead. 'But I have these thoughts. These…' His gaze flashed to my chest then up to my mouth.

Every muscle in my body tensed.

He grew empty-eyed and seemed as though he wasn't quite in the room with me. It was as if someone had pressed pause on him, as if he were a remote-control robot that had just been switched off. He took a step towards the bed, then froze. Red-tinted light distorted his features. A panicked look took hold and he scurried back to the door and left without another word.

A moment later, rain pelted the windows, shattering the quiet.

I felt like screaming.

The footprint trail would soon be gone, and with it, my last trace of hope.

Chapter 27

A part of me died that dreadful night.

Lying on the bed inside the Christmas room, chills flared along my arms, the crimson lampshade and elf curtains fading and morphing into my parents' living room with its blisteringly white walls and Trompe-l'oeil, champagne drapes and pristine cream sofas. In place of the pine desk, stood the television, Christmas carols ringing in angelic peals, Mum clutching a glass of Baileys, a dreamy smile on her face, milk moustache above pearl-pink lips. Beside her, ankle on knee, arm stretched along the sofa back, sat Dad in his checked pyjamas, red-cheeked and purple-lipped from his fifth glass of Chateau Latour.

The lighting was subdued. Soft light shone from the Tiffany lamp on top of Dad's drink cabinet. The house smelled of oranges and pine needles. White fairy lights twinkled on the real, ultra co-ordinated Christmas tree. Pearlescent baubles shaped like teardrops, crystal snowflakes, and silver-beaded tinsel draped the verdant branches offering a tasteful display that struck me as rather contrived. In mine and Jacob's rented flat, our tree – half the size of this one – was bedecked with randomly arranged jewel-coloured baubles. On top, a gold star from Asda; atop my parents' tree, a porcelain angel from John Lewis. My dad had snorted when he'd seen our tree.

Jacob couldn't be here tonight; Grandma Nancy was ill. His entire family had rallied around her in her two-bed cottage in Dorset, which meant I was alone with my parents, heart pounding like a boxer's fist as I worked up the courage to confess.

'Is something wrong, darling?' Mum said.

I took a swig of wine. Dutch courage.

'How's the job hunt going?' Dad said.

It was now or never. 'It's not.'

'What's not?' Mum said, tearing her eyes from the TV.

'Um, job hunting.'

Dad angled his head. *Silent Night* crooned. His thick eyebrows rose into his hair. A warning edge crept into his gaze. 'How so?'

I cleared my throat. 'I, um, I'm not looking for a job as such. I'm auditioning.'

Mum frowned and looked at Dad. Realisation yanked his eyebrows into a heavy furrow. 'You can't be serious.'

I stared at my wine.

They exchanged a look. I waited, stomach clenched.

'Darling, we've talked about this -'

'And I suppose you've been using our money to keep you afloat while you chase this ridiculous dream?' Dad said, slamming his glass down. Wine sploshed onto the coffee table. Mum gasped as if blood had been spilled and dashed out of the room to fetch a cloth.

'Rachel. If you think we're going to let you throw your life away after everything we've done to help you get this far -'

'Dad. Just stop. Please. Jacob and I have spoken about it and we've agreed it's time I go for it. I've wanted to be an actress for as long as I can remember. If I put it off any longer, I won't stand a chance.'

'You don't stand a chance now,' he said.

I shook my head. Fought tears. 'I'm good. Jacob's good too.'

'But good isn't good enough in this industry. And you're too intelligent to do something so mindless. You have a brilliant mind. You'll make an excellent psychiatrist, and you've worked so hard - too hard to throw it all away.'

'But I love acting. I want to do what I love.'

'What about psychiatry? What about helping people? I

thought that's what you loved.'

Mum dashed into the room and started scrubbing. She was crying.

'Mum? What's wrong?' I said.

Dad's anger bloomed at the sight of Mum's tears.

'I'll tell you what's wrong,' he said, standing up and stabbing his finger at me, 'what's wrong is that we can't believe you're being so selfish. After all we've done for you, all the monetary support we've given you over the years...it's like a slap in the face. Throwing away your career for the sake of what? A pipe dream? A little girl's ambition? You need to grow up. And Jacob – I could throttle that idiot. His speech at your wedding last year made me think he's a bright spark, but he's just as stupid as you. I can't for the life of me understand his family supporting him in this ludicrous endeavour. They'll lead to his downfall, mark my words. He'll drag you along with him in this hopeless journey of his only to end up penniless and bitter when he inevitably fails. You'll fail too, not for want of trying or lack of talent, but because this industry is simply too competitive. There's too much luck involved. And there's no money, not unless you become a movie star. Honestly, Rachel. I thought you were brighter than this, but yet again, you're proving the opposite.'

Mum looked at me and shook her head. Disappointment glistened in her eyes. 'Shame on you Rachel. We've done everything in our power to support you, and all you've done is lie to us and throw everything back in our faces. And now Christmas is ruined.'

She burst into tears, threw the cloth at the TV and ran out of the room.

Dad pinched the bridge of his nose. When he looked up, there was a hateful curl to his lip I'd never seen before. 'There's nothing your mother or I can do or say to change your mind. You don't seem to realise that we want what's best for you. That we care so much, and that we know better than you do. Well, so be it. I'm wiping my hands of you. You can sod off and do whatever the hell you want, but there'll be no more money. No more helping pay the bills anymore. You're on your own. What you've done and what you're doing is unforgivable, Rachel. Please, just go home. I can't bear the sight of you. Go back to your precious Jacob and do whatever the hell you want. That's it. I'm done.'

He stormed out of the room. *Only Fools and Horses* was on TV now. We always watched it together on Christmas Day.

Through a fresh swell of tears, I turned off the television. I told myself they were both drunk, that they didn't mean what they'd said, but their words cut deep, deeper than steel.

No matter how many weeks and months passed, the wounds would not heal. Instead, they calcified.

Neither Mum or Dad got in touch to apologise. For my part, I knew I had nothing to apologise for. I had lied to them, but they had forced my hand. To my parents, the world of work was black and white; to Jacob and me, it was every colour of the rainbow. I wasn't ready to accept defeat and succumb to the black. I intended to fight for as long as it took to achieve my dream, even if it meant going against my parents' lifelong wishes, turning them against me and earning their disrespect.

The following year or so was hard. I worked as a waitress at the local pub and auditioned for everything under the sun. For a long time, I only managed to get little gigs, an extra here, an extra there.

But I never gave up. Jacob was a rock. My rock. He held me when I cried, and offered encouragement every time I was rejected. His family helped us pay for acting lessons, and lent us money for a car.

Three years later, when a talent agent spotted Jacob and me playing Demetrius and Hermia in *A Midsummer Night's*

Dream at Milton Keynes Theatre, we were put forward for the roles of Simon and Elouise in *Emergency*, and the rest, as they say, was history. My parents never rang to say well done.

Chapter 28

My stomach felt slushy and sore. I didn't know if it was from the greasy full English Mikey had cooked, or nerves, but thought it was probably a combination of the two. I avoided my reflection in the mirror above the bathroom sink and dressed as slowly as I could get away with. Pulling on the doctor's coat made my skin goose. Mikey banged on the door, eager to get going. His energy wasn't contagious - it was maddening. I scraped my hair behind my ears and looped the stethoscope around my neck, then entered my character. Doctor Elouise Sparks was a profoundly accomplished surgeon, experienced beyond her years, slick and cool under pressure. She boasted qualifications up to her eyeballs.

The opposite of me.

Mikey banged again. 'Time to go, Doc.' He sounded like a kid on Christmas Day. For a beat, I imagined throttling him, the relief that would come if he no longer breathed.

'I'm coming,' I said.

I wiped my clammy palms on the coat, exhaled a long, shaky breath and opened the door.

Mikey clapped his hands and stood back to let me go first. 'Looking sharp, Doc. Looking sharp.'

'How's our patient this morning?' I said, descending with my hand on the banister for support. I couldn't stop shaking, and it wouldn't be good if Mikey noticed that. Doctor Sparks didn't shake. Her hands were as steady as a laser, her skills beyond compare. Even her husband, Doctor Simon Sparks, who Jacob played in the show, was nothing compared to her. He worked in the obstetrics and gynaecology department dealing with pregnant women.

Last series, he'd almost had an affair with one of those pregnant women, but Elouise had caught him flirting with her and quickly put a stop to his antics. In real life, I trusted Jacob completely. Part of that trust came from the knowledge that his first long-term girlfriend had cheated on him and hurt him deeply. I'd never been cheated on, but it had always been a fear of mine.

Thinking about Jacob made the pain in my tummy worse; it was a cramp now gnawing away at my insides like a rat.

Will I ever see him again? Is he okay?

The worry was a demon, a thing possessed. A beast with pupil-less eyes and blood-laced teeth.

I stopped at the bottom of the stairs and turned. Mikey rested his hand on the crook of my elbow. I longed to shake it off but didn't.

'What is it, Doc?' he said, suddenly panicked, 'Is there something else you need? I've got everything you asked for. I'm sure I have, and Nana thinks you're going to do it now. If you don't…' Fear made his cheek twitch.

'I need to ask you something, Mikey, and it's really important that you tell me the truth.'

'Is it about the operation?'

'No. But I won't be able to concentrate if I don't ask you this.'

'Oh, okay. Sure. Fire away.'

I cleared my throat. 'You know when you, er, took me from my house?'

He frowned but nodded.

'Did you hurt Jacob again?'

He licked his lips. Seemed confused for a second, as if he didn't know what I was talking about.

I shifted my weight. Clamped my lips together knowing it wouldn't do to rush him.

Finally, he looked directly at me and shook his head. His eyes were wide, expression earnest. 'No. I promise I didn't. I crept in when he was busy. He was talking to someone out by the bins. A neighbour, I think. I considered doing something again so he wouldn't get in the way – because I knew he wouldn't understand why I needed to take you – but he was distracted so it was easy to slip in and out of the house. I carried you down the stairs then out of the back door and went round the side as soon as I heard the front door open.'

I scanned his face for any sign that he was lying. He seemed to be telling the truth. The pain in my stomach retreated an iota. Relief fluttered in my chest, bright and fast as a hummingbird's wings.

'I don't like hurting people, you know,' he murmured.

'I know.' I didn't know – not with one hundred percent certainty - but I wasn't going to admit that.

Mikey steered me into the living room. He closed the door behind us and nudged me forward when I didn't move.

Ethel lay on the two-seater sofa dressed in a white nightdress. The curtains were closed, and the lights were off, making the small space gloomy and claustrophobic. It was the first time I'd seen her in a week. Mikey had kept me upstairs, mainly in the Christmas room apart from daily bathroom visits. He'd delivered breakfast, lunch and dinner to me every day without fail and hadn't bothered me after nine pm, stating how important it was for me to rest up before the operation. I'd encouraged this line of thought, ever fearful he would change his mind and come to see me in the night. Now and then, he seemed to lose himself to a darker voice, and his eyes would trail up and down my body, lingering for too long on my chest. It was clear he had an evil spirit inside him, one that he fought to suppress every day. I couldn't help fearing there would come a time when he fought and failed. Desperate to avoid such a scenario, I'd been as polite as possible and gently tried to pry into his thoughts and feelings, build a bond of sorts, but it had been like pulling teeth. All Mikey cared about was collecting the items for the operation; he wasn't in the mood for talking about anything else. I'd done my best to stay in character, reassuring him that I knew what I was doing. He'd clung to my lies with pitiful desperation. He loved his nana. Despite how she treated him, he wanted to save her, and truly believed I had the ability to do so.

Mikey moved me to stand next to Ethel's makeshift hospital bed. Her face was the colour of an ashtray. The room smelled worse than last time; like body fluids and smoke and sickness rolled into one.

Mikey had covered the sofa with a black sheet of weed control membrane. His attempt, he'd told me, to create a sterile environment. He'd also hoovered the carpet – a rare occurrence apparently – and wiped down the surfaces.

It was laughable really. At that moment, Ethel had a cigarette between her lips. Ash scattered her nightgown like dead confetti. She reminded me of Frankenstein's bride. She fixed her pale eyes on me. A weird smile cracked her lips.

'Excellent timing, Doctor Sparks. I've just finished my ciggy. Mikey.'

He dashed over and took the cigarette then crushed it into the overflowing ashtray.

On the second coffee table on a flowery tray were the things I'd requested: antiseptic wipes, a scalpel, a suction device, wound dressings, cotton pads, wire and needle for stitching, a syringe, latex gloves and several bottles of morphine.

'Wonderful. Everything looks in order. How did you get hold of the morphine?' I said casually.

Mikey puffed out his chest. 'Stole it from the hospital. Remember, I'm really good at hiding and seeking.'

Hope sparked in my chest. Maybe the police were on their way here at this very moment. If anyone realised morphine had been stolen, they'd look at CCTV footage and spot Mikey. They'd track him down, come here and save me.

'My clever boy.' Ethel gave him a small nod.

Mikey glowed. He seemed lost for words and only able to grin stupidly at his nana.

I wondered if it was the first time she'd given him praise.

Ethel's eyes narrowed. 'Doctor Sparks, you're going to fix me today, aren't you?'

I nodded. 'Of course. Now, I'm going to inject you with 30 milligrams of morphine to help with the pain.'

It was a complete guess. I didn't want to kill her, but I couldn't have her going into shock and dying of a heart attack.

Ethel nodded. Mikey paced back and forth, unable to keep still. His excitement seemed to have morphed into anxiety and he kept bringing his thumb up to his mouth, then remembering where he was and shoving his hand into his pocket. He wore a Christmas jumper with lights on it. They flashed continuously. I wished he would turn them off; they were making me more nervous.

'Please can you turn the lights on Mikey,' I said instead.

He nodded and loped to the door, flicked on the switch. Immediately, the room brightened, and I glanced down at Ethel, shocked to see how pale she'd become. It seemed even she wasn't immune to fear.

'Turn off that stupid jumper,' she hissed. She gave me a nod, as if saying she'd known what I was thinking a moment ago.

Mikey scrabbled to find the light switch. He turned off the jumper and perched on the armchair then jerked to his feet a second later and paced again.

The veins on the old lady's arm were purple, easily visible through her papery skin, but not close enough to the surface for me to be sure I could get the needle into one of them. I didn't even know if the drug had to go in a specific vein, but there was a vein that went across the middle of the inner elbow that doctors always used; that was the one I was going to aim for.

'Mikey, please can you fetch a dressing gown cord or a belt. I need to restrict the blood flow so that the vein will become more prominent.' It felt like something Doctor Sparks would say. Despite everything, I felt a small stab of pride, and a surge of hope; maybe I could pull this off after all and Mikey would let me go.

Mikey returned with a dressing gown cord.

'Thank you. Oh, and you'll need to remove these.' I held out my cuffed wrists.

'Idiot,' Ethel hissed.

Mikey's face fell. He yanked out his lanyard and hurriedly uncuffed me. He stuffed the cuffs in his pocket and stood an inch behind, his breath hot and sour on my neck.

'Give her some space, for Christ's sake!'

Mikey leapt back a foot and wrung his hands.

He stood in front of the door, barring my exit.

I slipped on the latex gloves then dabbed her elbow with an antiseptic wipe and filled the syringe with 30mg of morphine, half-focusing on what I was doing, half-imagining plunging the needle into Mikey's eye.

I inhaled, exhaled, tried to stay calm, but I could feel my heartbeat escalating. My palms were already sweaty.

I placed the syringe on the tray and tied the furry cord around Ethel's upper arm. Her eyes never left my face. I could feel them burning into my brain like lasers. I felt certain she was trying to drill a hole into my mind. Trying to read me. She wanted to believe I was this Elouise Sparks character, but deep down perhaps she knew she was lying to herself. She knew that I was here against my will, yet I was – in her deranged psyche – her only chance of survival. She needed to put her trust in me, but couldn't quite let herself, so she watched me like a drone, scrutinising my every movement and decision, analysing and evaluating everything I did.

So far, my hands were playing ball. They were steady; I'd practised over and over in the privacy of the Christmas room, acting out the movements I imagined I'd need to make during the operation. I'd even rehearsed lines in my head. It seemed, so far, to be paying off. I couldn't afford to make a mistake. Mikey and Ethel were obsessed with *Emergency*. I'd heard them watching it last night. It was surreal hearing mine and Jacob's voices bleeding through the floor, muffled yet recognisable. We never watched ourselves anymore; it made both of us cringe, especially me. I'd always notice something embarrassing or unattractive about myself. Jacob over-analysed his performance. When it came to acting, he was even more of a perfectionist than me.

I glanced up at Ethel. Stole a glance at Mikey. They had seen me perform in countless shows. They had expectations, and I needed to rise to them. I had to pull off this final act.

The vein in her arm bulged. It was a purple worm. A worm filled with blood.

My heart crashed against my ribs.

I picked up the needle.

Chapter 29

Mikey stopped pacing to watch.

The needle went into Ethel's skeletal arm, straight into the vein. I knew it would but was still surprised by how easily the thin rod of metal entered her flesh. It made me feel powerful; in control. For a moment, I gripped the needle. My fingers sweated inside the latex gloves. Ideas spun and swirled. I looked around at Mikey. He was pale with worry, but so big and strong. Too strong to fight.

Don't risk it. Not yet.

You're being a coward.

No. I'm being sensible.

Coward.

Ethel winced as I removed the needle and placed it on the tray.

'I'll give it a couple of minutes to kick in,' I said.

Mikey was at my side bouncing on the balls of his feet.

I looked down at the needle. The metal glinted temptingly.

'Is it working?' he said.

Ethel grunted and closed her eyes. 'It is.' She sighed. Her breath rattled. The hardness in her jaw softened.

Please don't let me have given her too much. God, don't let her die.

Her chest continued to rise and fall. I watched, acutely aware of Mikey standing next to me, watching her too. Nervous energy emanated from him like radiation.

'Does this hurt?' I said, pinching her neck just below the tumour.

'A little.'

Mikey stuck his face in front of mine. Worry crushed

his brow. His breath was rotten. 'Is it meant to hurt still? I thought you were giving her enough drugs to get rid of the pain?'

'I've given her enough to ease the pain, but she's old, Mikey. If I give her too much, her heart won't be able to cope, and she'll die. That's why I'm not giving her any anaesthetic. Plus, I'd need an anaesthetist to administer that properly.'

'Oh.'

'Quit fussing, boy,' Ethel hissed, 'Doctor Sparks knows what she's doing.'

'Sorry, Nana. I just -'

'Shut up. Let her concentrate.'

Mikey's face fell. He retreated to the doorway and paced back and forth.

'He's distracting me,' I said.

'Sit down!'

'Yes Nana.'

Mikey perched on the edge of the armchair, legs jiggling, hands clasped so tightly his knuckles turned white.

'That's better,' I breathed.

Nana nodded. 'Now get on with it.'

I went to pick up the scalpel, then remembered I needed to clean the area first. I wiped the tumour gently with a few antibacterial wipes, hoping it was enough to prevent the wound from getting infected.

I looked around at Mikey. 'You've definitely disinfected this scalpel?'

'Yes. I promise. I put it in boiling water for ten minutes like you told me to.' His eyes flicked to Ethel, hope alight in them. He wanted more praise. He wasn't going to get it.

Through gritted teeth, Ethel said, 'You'd better have done what the good doctor told you.'

Mikey nodded frantically. 'I did, Nana, I really did. I promise.'

'You'd never lie to me, would you boy?'

'No, Nana. Never.' Guilt laced his eyes. He was probably thinking about what he'd done to poor Simon.

Luckily Ethel's eyes were closed, so she missed the guilty look he gave me.

The room suddenly felt too small and too hot. The huge, framed photograph of boy Mikey and Ethel loomed over me. Mikey's eyes bore into my back. Ethel opened her eyes and stared at me. Everyone was watching me. There were no cameras, but this was worse, because this was real.

I picked up the scalpel.

My stomach cramped as I moved it towards Ethel's neck.

My hand hovered in the air an inch above the lump. Should I spin around and try to plunge the scalpel into Mikey's neck?

No. He's too far away. Too risky.

I refocused on the tumour. Was there anything else to do first? Had I forgotten anything?

Do it. Do it or die.

Sweat beaded my hairline. I prayed Ethel wouldn't notice. The room was cool; there was no reason to sweat.

I closed my eyes briefly. Channelled my character. Imagined I was on set. Lights, camera, action.

'I'm going to make the first incision now,' I said, but it wasn't me speaking; it was Elouise Sparks. She sounded confident, and ready. Her hand was steady.

I inserted the small, fine blade into her neck, preparing myself for her to jerk away and scream, but she merely flinched and hissed between her teeth. Blood oozed from the cut – more blood than I'd expected for such a small incision. Panic blurred my vision.

'Mikey, are your hands clean?'

'What?'

'Are your hands clean?'

'Er – yes, I think so, I mean -'

'Grab a handful of cotton pads and get ready.'

He hurried over and did as he was told. His hands were shaking.

I cut around the outer edge of the tumour, trying to imagine I was cutting a potato rather than a lump of flesh. Ethel moaned but managed to stay still. Blood gushed from her neck.

'Press the pads here,' I said.

Mikey did so. Blood soaked through the pads almost immediately. It trickled between his fingers down her neck into her nightdress.

'Press harder,' I said.

Ethel moaned more loudly. Her hands became fists at her sides.

I tasted sick in my throat, felt my stomach heave. I breathed through my nose, imagined that potato.

Holding the tumour with my free hand, I cut away the rest of it as smoothly as possible then practically threw the lump into the black bin liner Mikey had put beside the sofa. Blood gushed from the wound. I grabbed the suction device, turned it on and held it to her neck. She screamed and tried to pull away.

'HOLD HER STILL.'

Mikey hesitated.

'DO IT NOW OR SHE WILL DIE.'

He clamped his hands around her upper arms and pinned her to the sofa. She thrashed and whipped her head about, screaming expletives at him.

'Keep her head still.'

Mikey lay on top of her, pinioning her with his body and holding her skull still in his large hands. 'No, Nana, no. Stay still now. You have to -'

She spat in his eye and continued to struggle, profanity after profanity hissing from her lips.

'Ethel, stay still. You're making it bleed more.'

She ignored me.

I discarded the suction device and stared at the wound,

suddenly aware that it would be impossible to stitch it together because the lump had been sawn clean off, leaving a wide gap that couldn't be bridged by skin.

How to stop the bleeding? What would a real doctor do?

I grabbed the adhesive dressing and stuck it over the wound. Blood immediately soaked through. I slapped on another one and another one, but the same thing happened.

Ethel stopped fighting. Her body went limp. Her eyelids drooped.

'Is she dead?' Mikey cried, 'Oh God. What's happening? Why's she not moving?'

I grabbed her wrist. There was a faint pulse. Relief swallowed me whole. 'She's passed out. Have you got a scarf?'

'A scarf? Uh, yeah.' He ran out of the room.

I kept pressure on the wound. My hands were shaking now, the gloves slippery with blood. Horror rose in a chokehold. My teeth chattered. I clamped them together as hard as I could. Swallowed a lump of sick. Sweat dripped into my eyes. If this didn't work, I was done for.

This has to work. It must.

Mikey handed me a tartan scarf. I didn't even bother to ask if it was clean. I tied it around Ethel's neck as tightly as I could without killing her. We both watched as blood soaked through the scarf.

'I need another one,' I said.

Mikey left. He returned with a thick, grey scarf. I tied that over the first one, held my breath. Blood seeped into the material but didn't soak it. We both watched for another minute. The second scarf had done the trick.

I unclenched my jaw and allowed myself to breathe. Knowing I had to stay in character, I turned, forced myself to smile up at him. 'Well done.'

Tears glittered on his cheeks. His breaths were heavy and rancid, eyes as cold as ice. Sounding exactly like Ethel he said, 'If she dies, you die too.'

Chapter 30

For the rest of the morning I remained by Ethel's side playing the dutiful doctor, a role I was beginning to hate. If I ever got out of this, I didn't think I'd be able to act Doctor Elouise Sparks again. She was a curse to me now, a name imprinted into my memory in blood.

Mikey spent most of the time pacing back and forth. He was pale and waxy, sweating buckets into his Christmas jumper. Now and then, when Ethel was conscious, he'd thrust a cigarette in her face, but she'd swipe his hand away with a look that said *don't be so stupid.*

'Can't you give her more pain relief?' he said.

The stench of blood seemed to have invaded my olfactory nerves, taking over so that I couldn't smell anything else. I looked at the bottles of morphine. The truth was that I didn't know if I could give her anymore. I wanted to. I wanted to give her so much she died, but if I did that Mikey might follow up on his threat and kill me. I had to keep her alive until Christmas Day.

'It's too dangerous to give her more now. I'll give her another shot at about six 'o clock.'

She was sleeping now, her chest rising and falling shallowly, but now and then, her eyelids fluttered, and she groaned and tossed as though she was on her deathbed. I couldn't help worrying that she was. The bleeding seemed to have stopped, but what if the first scarf had been dirty? What if the wound was already infected?

When I was a little girl, I'd slashed open my hand on a barbed wire fence. It had needed five stitches to close it. In the hospital, nurses had unwrapped and cleaned it out three times before stitching it up. I hadn't cleaned Ethel's wound at all yet. The truth was that I was too afraid to see the mess I'd made of her neck. Terrified I'd throw up the second I saw it. But Doctor Elouise Sparks wouldn't throw up, would she?

I looked at the white scar on my hand and stroked it with my index finger. When we watched TV together, Jacob smoothed his finger over that exact point.

A hollow ache rose in my throat followed swiftly by a beat of anger. If it wasn't for Ethel twisting Mikey's mind, none of this would be happening. I'd be safe and sound back where I belonged, back in our fight to conceive a baby. A fight I longed for more than anything at this moment; struggling to get pregnant was bliss compared to this horror show.

'I don't understand why you can't give her more now,' he said sulkily.

'How old is she?'

'Eighty-one. So?'

'That's why. When people get into their eighties, their bodies are a lot weaker, their immune systems a lot lower than people your age. How old are you Mikey?'

'Twenty-five.'

With the mental age of a ten-year-old.

He sighed heavily and began to pace once more. His face was twisted and grey. 'She can't die. You won't let her die, will you Doc?'

He stopped and stared me in the eye. There was a nasty edge to his voice. He dragged a shaky hand through his greasy hair. Abruptly, he said, 'I'm hungry.'

He stormed out of the living room leaving me alone with the old woman.

I thought about my chances of escape if I were to act now. My hands were cuffed again, but I wasn't bound to anything. I could roam where I pleased with relative ease. If need be, I could run.

You ran before and look where it got you.

I glanced at the morphine and the syringe. My heart thudded.

No. Don't risk it.

I took a small step towards the table. Clanging and clattering echoed from the kitchen.

I took another step.

A claw hooked into my thigh. I spun around to see Ethel eyeballing me. 'Water. Now.'

To my horror my eyes flicked towards the pillow under her head. I could suffocate her with it, grab the syringe and –

'Don't even think about it. I'll scream and he'll come. He'll beat you black and blue.'

I swallowed thickly and passed her the water.

'Mikey wouldn't do that to me,' I said, trying to convince myself more than her.

'He will because I'll tell him to.'

Her words sent ice into my veins. She looked so weak and pathetic, but her mind was lethal.

She held the cup with trembling hands. When she tried to lift it to her lips, water slopped onto the blanket. She glared at me. 'Are you going to help me or not?'

I hurried forward and helped her sit up cringing at the damp sickliness of her body.

'Thank you, dear,' she said with a slight smile.

She took small sips of the water and broke into a coughing fit. Sucking ragged breaths, she let it play out, face scrunched from pain. After the fit subsided, she extended her hand for me to take the cup. I took it, horribly conscious that she was watching me.

For a while, she stared, her eyes narrow, lips pursed. I couldn't help worrying what she was thinking – was she going to tell Mikey to kill me even if she made it to Christmas? Perhaps my death would be her Christmas present.

I let my gaze drift to the curtains, imagining what it

would feel like to be free. Wondering if I would ever be free again.

'Are you crying, Doctor?' she rasped, fake pity drenching her voice.

I forced back tears and shook my head. 'The operation has gone well, I think. Obviously, we won't be able to do a scan to see if the cancer has all gone, but -'

'Oh, cut the crap Rachel.'

I gaped at her, 'You called me Rachel, but I thought -'

She waved her hand and winced. 'I know you're not a real doctor. I'm not stupid! He's the idiot who believes all that nonsense.'

'Then why bring me here? Why not bring a real doctor to operate? Why not go to a proper hospital?'

'I despise hospitals, and Mikey wouldn't have brought you here for any other reason.'

'But the risk of me operating on you is so high – why would you do it?'

'The pain is a necessary evil. For my idea to work, Mikey needs to see you as a hero.'

'But…what? What's your real reason? Why me?'

'In time, you'll see. He already likes you; I can see it in his eyes. Do you know you're the first woman he's ever touched?'

There was a disturbing twinkle in her eyes.

Utterly confused, I went to ask another question, but Mikey strode into the room. When I looked down, Ethel's face was turned away and her eyes were closed in sleep – real or fake I couldn't tell.

Chapter 31

Mikey handcuffed me to the iron bed frame in Ethel's bedroom then stomped downstairs to fetch her.

Ethel's lair was small, and it smelled of attic, urine and ash. Unlike my room, there wasn't a Christmas bauble in sight. It contained a single bed covered with a patchwork blanket, a bedside table topped with a brown ashtray, a gold lighter and fringed lamp, putrid green in colour, an oak wardrobe and dressing table topped not with make up or jewellery but empty ashtrays. I eyed the trays. What a horrid thing to collect. There was a tray made of cut glass, a blue ceramic one, a swamp-green affair shaped like a cactus and a white porcelain tray with a painting of a mallard duck in the centre. Net curtains skimmed a windowsill lined with dusty miniature cacti, their spikes as sharp as their owner's tongue. The carpet was beige and threadbare, the flowery wallpaper smothered with framed photographs of a man I assumed must have been her husband. There were no pictures of Mikey in the room, and no pictures of Mikey's mother or any other children the Bells might have had. It was as if the room was a shrine to the woman's late husband – at least, I assumed he was dead. The oldest he seemed to be in the photographs was about fifty.

A shiver rippled down my back as I noticed something odd. In one image, a little hand was tucked inside the man's, but the child who owned the hand had been cut out of the photo. Who would cut a child out of a photograph like that?

Ethel. Who else?

I looked up as Mikey carried her into the room and tenderly lowered her to the bed. If circumstances had been different, I'd have felt sorry for them both, and I'd have admired Mikey's selfless commitment to her care, but instead, as he fussed over tucking her in to her precise specification, I dreamed of ways to hurt him – put him out of action so I could escape.

What would Jacob do?

He'd have escaped already. He's far cleverer than you. More logical, less emotional. He'd have found a way to overpower Mikey by now –

But you can't overpower him. You're too weak. You need to play the long game. Get inside his head.

Mikey hurried out of the room.

Ethel eyed me coldly from the bed.

In a thin hiss, she said, 'Don't bother telling Mikey what I told you. If, by some miracle, he pays any heed to your words, I'll tell him to put you in the well again.'

'Is that what you used to do to Mikey?'

'Wicked boys need to be punished.'

'He's terrified of you even now. Is that what you want? To isolate him and make him so scared of you he'll never leave? He needs to live his own life. Make friends -'

'He'll never leave me. He needs me too much.'

'And what about when you die? Where will that leave him then? He'll be alone with a complete inability to function in normal society. Has he even got any qualifications?'

'He'll be fine. He'll have Mr Bell's inheritance to live off. It's not much but it's enough and I've taught him everything he needs to know about managing money. Besides, all he cares about buying are his precious Christmas jumpers and decorations. And,' she added with a sly smile, 'don't forget, he'll have you.'

'Me? No he won't. I'm going to make sure you live to see Christmas. That's the deal. If you're alive and well on Christmas Day, he's going to let me go.'

Ethel snorted. She opened her mouth to reply, but

Mikey entered the room, uncuffed me, and handed me the morphine and syringe. 'Time for your bedtime medicine, Nana!'

Ethel ignored him and held out her arm. I wrapped the dressing gown cord around the shrivelled limb and waited for the vein to stick out. Conscious of Mikey standing close, I filled the syringe with 30ml and stabbed it in a fraction harder than necessary. Ethel's eyes narrowed giving me a beat of satisfaction, but she didn't say anything.

'Thank you, Doctor Sparks.'

I bit my lip and fought the urge to correct her. *Rachel. My name's Rachel and you know it. I'm an actress not a bloody doctor.*

Mikey bent over and kissed her forehead. 'Night night, Nana.'

She grunted and turned her face away.

With a hurt expression, Mikey took hold of my elbow and led me out of the room.

I paused and turned to look up at him. 'You are going to let me go on Christmas Day, aren't you Mikey?'

'If Nana's okay, yeah, course I am.'

He sounded sincere, but his eyes cast about oddly.

'Mikey, please don't lie to me.'

'I'm not.'

'When you let me go, I won't say anything to anyone. You know that don't you?'

He hesitated, then nodded. 'I can trust you, can't I Doc? You'll go back to your normal life and forget all this ever happened. You'll have done me and Nana such a big favour, so it's only fair I let you go. But,' he angled his neck strangely and scratched behind his ear, 'if you tell anyone anything, I'll have to come find you to shut you up.'

How he'd know I'd told anyone anything before the police arrested him was another story. It wasn't as if he was a tech-whiz or hacker who had bugged my house. But I knew that if he thought things through too deeply, he'd realise what Ethel had known all along: there was no way he could let me go. He would have to keep me here forever, or he would have to kill me. I'd seen their faces, I knew their identities, I knew where they lived. If I went free, they were done for.

And yet it seemed like Mikey planned to stay true to his word. As long as Ethel didn't get inside his head and twist him against the idea…

When has she ever not managed to control his decisions?

I gave him the warmest smile I could muster, and whispered, 'Let's keep our deal a secret. Nana doesn't need to know about it yet. Okay?'

Mikey looked back at her closed door. Guilt and confusion pinched his brow. He glanced at me. 'Like Simon?'

'Exactly. There's no need to tell her everything. What she doesn't know won't hurt her. Plus, she's just been through a serious operation, so the less you give her to think about at the moment, the better.'

He nodded slowly, then nudged me towards the Christmas room. We both froze as the sound of a car pierced the air.

'What the -' Mikey dragged me into the bedroom and dashed to the elf curtains. He moved the fabric a minute amount and stole a peek through the window.

'Oh God, oh God, oh God.' He let the curtain drop and whipped his face around. 'If you make a sound, I'll have to do something bad.'

He ran out of the room, closed the door and locked it.

I looked down in wonder at my uncuffed hands then ran to the window and yanked back the curtains.

I watched as a Chinese lady climbed out of a red Range Rover. She had parked beside Mikey's rusted white Ford Ranger. I recognised her immediately: it was Lori, Simon's wife – widow, to be precise. The sun was about to descend below the horizon and was so bright that it was blinding her. She shielded her eyes with one hand and slammed the car door shut with the other. Seeming hesitant, she took two steps towards the house. I tried to catch her eye by waving, hoping I could signal that I needed help without alerting Mikey to what I was doing, but she didn't notice me.

Mikey bounded towards her and blocked my view for a moment. She took a step back, body language nervous. I wondered why – was it because she suspected him, or because he was wearing a Christmas jumper outside of the festive season?

Mikey's voice rose through the air, loud and shrill, 'Hi, how can I help?'

He glanced back at the house, up at me as if warning me to stay silent.

Lori's voice was quiet. Too quiet for me to hear what she was saying. But of course, I knew exactly what she was saying – have you seen my husband? He's missing. Please help me find him. But if she was here, why weren't the police? It didn't make sense. Perhaps she sensed foul play; had always found Mikey strange. Either way, it didn't matter. I needed to make the most of this chance.

My heart roared. I raised my fist to the glass.

Mikey's hand moved to his pocket. He glanced back at me again and shook his head subtly. He turned back to his unwanted visitor and said loudly, 'Not seen him for ages. Sorry.'

She nodded. Her shoulders slumped and she began to turn towards her car.

I pulled back my fist to knock on the window, then stopped. What if he hurt her because of me?

No. Life's too short to get caught up in what ifs. Do something – quick – before she leaves!

Just then, Christmas music blasted through the house. Mikey and Lori looked at the cottage as one, Lori's eyebrows rising in surprise. Mikey was talking, gesturing animatedly back at the house. He even did a little jig.

Knowing Ethel had turned on the music, I cursed her silently, then opened my mouth wide against the window and screamed as loudly as I could, desperate to make myself heard above the cacophony blaring into the air. 'Help! Help me! He's kidnapped me!'

I smashed my fists against the window, making the glass quiver, but Lori's eyes were trained on Mikey. She couldn't hear me. She was nodding, agreeing with him, shaking his hand, turning back to her car, getting in, and driving away.

Chapter 32

Horror froze my throat. My chance had gone.

I stared at the room. I wasn't cuffed to anything. Mikey was out. A few minutes after Lori had left, he'd left too. I needed to take advantage of this opportunity before he came back.

I dashed back to the window and tried to open it; to my surprise, it responded, opening wide enough for me to slip through. The problem was that I was on the first floor. If I jumped I'd surely break my ankle or worse. What would Jacob do? *Think*.

I spun and headed for the bed. I ripped off the duvet and clawed off the bedsheet then twisted the thin material into rope. It was hard work with my hands cuffed and took me far longer than I wanted it to.

When it was done, I pushed the bed towards the window then climbed onto it and tied the sheet as tightly as I could around the iron post. I gave it a few hard tugs, checked outside; he wasn't back. Yet.

Sweating profusely, I picked up my makeshift rope and tossed it out of the window. If I climbed to the bottom of the rope before I let go, I'd be about three feet off the ground. Not too far to fall. If I sustained an injury there was zero chance I'd get away – unless…Mikey's Ranger was still parked out the front of the cottage. If he hadn't locked the front door, I could slip inside, find his car key, and drive away. Shit. I slapped my forehead. He kept his keys on the lanyard he wore around his neck. There could have been a spare key of course. The question was: should I waste time looking for it?

Realising I should already be outside, I swung my legs

over the windowsill. How long had Mikey been gone now? Ten, fifteen minutes? I didn't know how long it took to set fire to a car – not very long probably. Then again, he might have decided to drive quite far away to avoid suspicion landing on him.

I started to climb down the side of the house. Dusk had fallen and the air was yellow-grey and nippy. Acid churned in my stomach and my muscles protested. Fit people made things like this look so easy, but it was bloody hard.

It seemed to take me forever to reach the bottom of the sheet. When I did, every limb was trembling, my breaths coming in gasps. I counted to three in my head then dropped to the ground and rolled onto my side. I was fine. Shaky and out of breath but fine. I ran to the Ranger and tried the door; it opened. I scanned the interior, checked behind both sunshields. Nothing. Frustrated but not surprised, I ran back to the cottage and tried the front door; it too opened. I ran inside and checked the table in the hallway – nothing. I hesitated – should I give up looking for the car key and make a run for it on foot or keep hunting? I'd be more likely to get away if I could drive. I glanced back, certain for a second that I'd heard his car, but the beaten path that led to the house was empty.

I hurried down the hallway into the kitchen, which was a mess.

Frantically, I opened every drawer, looking for the 'odds and sods drawer' as Jacob and I called it – the one where you stuffed everything you thought you might need but rarely did.

Bingo! A drawer stuffed full of coins, old bills, a nail file…

I yanked out the drawer and tipped the contents onto the counter. A blast of HALLELUJAH played in my head as my fingers closed on the car key.

I whirled around, a stupid grin plastered on my face,

and barely had time to register what was happening before Ethel, her frail body quivering like a rabbit with myxomatosis, smashed me over the head with the fringe lamp. Pain exploded in my temple. I staggered to the side and fell against the fridge. She raised the lamp again, arms trembling like jelly cubes, and made to strike, but I blocked it, my arm taking the brunt. Reacting quickly, I tore it out of her hand, shoved her aside and ran for the front door, halting in my tracks halfway down the hallway.

The door was shut, and Mikey stood in front of it.

*

Mikey ran into the kitchen and seized my arms. He reeked of smoke. 'Why did you do that? Why did you hurt Nana?'

His eyes were wild. Tears soaked his cheeks. His nails dug into my skin so hard they drew blood.

'She hit me first,' I said, 'I was defending myself.'

'She was trying to leave us,' Ethel hissed. Blood oozed through the scarf around her neck onto her already blood-stained nightgown. She hobbled to the kitchen table, sat down heavily, glared at Mikey, and rasped, 'What the hell did you do? Where did you go? Who was out there? The commotion woke me up! I need answers. Now. And don't you dare lie to me. You know what happens to wicked boys who lie.'

He glanced at me, wide-eyed with panic.

'Look at me. Not her!' she said, snapping her fingers.

'I'm sorry, Nana, I-'

He was going to tell her about Simon. I couldn't let that happen. If Ethel knew he'd killed someone, she'd put two and two together and work out that staying here with me wasn't an option, because eventually the police would come knocking. She might tell him to kill me, or insist they move elsewhere. I couldn't let either of those things happen. Much as I hated this hell hole, if they moved, it would be much harder for the police to track me down.

I blurted, 'I tried to leave and he stopped me. We argued. He sent me back inside the cottage and told me to go up to my room while he went to get something from the car, but I didn't. I came in here instead. It's my fault. Mikey's done nothing wrong.'

Mikey bit his lip. We both watched Ethel. Her eyes narrowed to buttonholes, disappearing into her crepey skin like fleas.

'Don't just stand there!' she snapped, making us both jump. 'Go and fetch something to sort out this mess.' She waved at her bleeding neck.

Mikey nodded and dragged me out of the room into the living room where the equipment still stood on the flowery tray.

In a spiky voice, he said, 'You shouldn't have done that you know. She'll work out you're lying – she always does – and then we'll both be in trouble.'

He grabbed up the cotton pads and disinfectant then stopped and yanked me around to face him. 'I didn't mean to do it.' His lip quivered. Tears brimmed in his eyes. He suddenly looked so utterly bereft I was stumped for words.

'I liked Simon. He was nice to me. He didn't laugh or stare or tease. And he liked my jumper, the one I'm wearing today.'

I placed my hand on his hand and tried not to think about the fact that not long ago he'd used that very hand to kill a man. 'It was a mistake. One you won't make again. I know you panicked. I also know that you did it because Ethel will make you suffer if she finds out that anyone knows about me. But listen Mikey, you don't need to do what she says anymore. You're a grown man and you're strong. I know you think you love her, but -'

'I do love her. More than anyone else on the planet. She's the only one who's ever taken care of me.'

'By putting you in a well and burning you with

cigarettes?'

His larynx bobbed. He nodded slowly, though I could see the tiniest bit of confusion and unease settling behind his eyes. 'I'd be wicked if that hadn't happened. I needed to learn. I, I still do sometimes.' His voice was thick, slow with creeping uncertainty.

It gave me hope.

He led me out of the room, along the hallway and back into the kitchen. Ethel has taken it upon herself to unwrap both scarfs from her neck. My gorge rose as I took in the bleeding welt; the bloody flesh reminded me of a squashed tomato. Why I always thought of fruit and vegetables when I looked at body parts, I didn't know. First a potato and now a tomato – what next? An avocado?

'Fix it,' she said.

Mikey unlocked my cuffs and hovered by my side wringing his hands.

'I need to clean my hands first,' I said moving to the sink.

Ethel nodded, stare fixed on me as if I was a lamb about to bolt. 'Watch her, Mikey. She's a sly one.'

'I'm sure she won't try anything again, will you, Doc?'

I shook my head, picked up a wad of cotton pads, doused them in disinfectant and pressed them firmly to the wound. Ethel inhaled sharply.

'Wound dressing please,' I murmured.

Mikey passed me one and I taped it over the injury. Blood seeped through. I held my hand out for another and another and another. Finally, only the dark stain of blood was visible beneath the top dressing. I sighed with relief. I was drained and nauseous. Despite everything the thought of getting into bed in the Christmas room held a strong appeal.

'Thanks Doc,' Mikey said with a rare smile.

I glanced at Ethel, saw - to my surprise - a small smile lift her lips.

Mikey cuffed me to the radiator then carried her upstairs.

I slumped against the wall and exhaled. Outside the night was cold and black. I could see a slither of moon. I wondered what Jacob was doing. Was he looking for me? Had he steered the police in the direction of those men who'd messaged me on Instagram? Had they found any leads? He must be frantic with worry.

If he's still alive, he will be. What if Mikey killed him?

I shook my head, told myself not to go there. Mikey might have been a killer, but he wasn't a liar. At least, he wasn't a liar before I came along and corrupted him. Hysteria clutched at me, and I almost laughed.

Mikey strode into the room. He looked down at his feet and mumbled something.

'What?'

He looked up, rushed out the words, 'Nana says you're to go in the well.'

I staggered back. 'No Mikey, you can't. You don't have to do what she says. She'll never know. Just take me back to my room. You can cuff me to the railing again like before. I promise I won't try anything.'

'You need to be punished for hitting her and trying to run away…' his gaze grew distant. In a faint voice, he said, 'I tried to run away once when I was ten. She caught me. I was punished for that too.'

'What did she do to you?'

'She made me take a bath in hot water. Water so hot it burned.' He shivered and looked at me suddenly. 'I don't want to put you in the well.'

'Then don't. Be your own person. Make your own decisions.' I reached out but he drifted away to stare out at the back garden.

'It's my fault. It's all my fault,' he said.

'No it's not. It's her fault. She's abused you, Mikey. She's abused you your whole life.'

But it was as if he'd gone into a hypnotic trance. He turned, uncuffed me from the radiator, cuffed me again then carried me out of the room. In a distant voice, he murmured, 'Frank liked to go hunting. He shot rabbits. We still have his gun somewhere.'

I shivered at the idea, thanked God he hadn't decided to use that very gun when he's taken me from my house.

I expected Mikey to take me straight outside, but he took me upstairs and told me to go to the toilet and brush my teeth. My teeth chattered as I brushed, thoughts of going back into that well stabbing my mind like poison darts. There'd be no climbing out this time, he'd make sure of it.

I stared at my reflection, haunted by the fear etched into every muscle in my face. My head hurt from where Ethel had hit me and I was thirsty as hell. Worried he was going to keep me down there all night, I drank as much water as I could.

He opened the door as I was drying my mouth and took hold of my arms. I expected him to lead me back downstairs, but he didn't. He took me to the Christmas room, cuffed me to the bed and drifted to the doorway.

With his back to me, he whispered, 'Night night, Doc. I'm going to sleep in the well tonight. I deserve to, not you. But don't tell Nana, okay?'

'I won't.'

He opened the door.

'Mikey?'

He stopped, turned slightly. His shoulders were rounded in defeat.

'Thank you,' I said. After a second, I added, 'I'm proud of you.'

As soon as he locked the door, I burst into tears.

*

I scanned the dark room. Shadows played games with my mind; the wardrobe was Ethel, swollen to a black dragon, like Maleficent in Sleeping Beauty; the curtain was Simon come to haunt me for what I'd done. If I hadn't run away, Simon would still be alive.

A headache bloomed again, grinding my temples like a pepper mill.

I squeezed my eyes closed to shut out the room and tried to clutch onto the only thing I could – Mikey had sacrificed himself by going to the well. He'd gone instead of me. My heart fluttered with the tiniest bit of hope. He'd defied her, probably for the first time in a very long time. This meant progress. Immense progress. If he was starting to think for himself, there was a chance he would stay true to his word and let me go.

If you can keep her alive until Christmas.

My head pounded harder.

I stared at the hulking shadow in the corner of the room. Mikey's prided tree. I was taken on 1st September. How long had I been in this hell hole? It felt like a year. I'd lost track of the days. Jacob's birthday was in October. I'd booked tickets to a show. It was going to be a surprise.

Not anymore.

I jack-knifed, eyes wide. I'd completely forgotten to tell Mikey to check on Ethel in the night, and now he was down that bloody well so there was no way I could get his attention. She could die in the night. What if the pain made her throw up and she choked on her own sick? What if she tried to get out of bed and the dressings ripped off, exposing the injury to a world of bacteria? What if she bled to death?

Shit.

I lay back down, mind spinning, furious at myself for not realising this earlier. If she died, Mikey would be distraught, demented with irrational despair. In my mind, his hands were around my throat, knees digging into my ribs, face twisted with rage and grief.

Please, if there's a God up there, don't let that evil cow die tonight.

Chapter 33

The next day Mikey looked dreadful. I'd barely slept but I doubted he'd slept at all. He trudged into my room, deposited a bowl of Coco Pops on my lap and left without a word or a glance. I didn't have a chance to ask him if Ethel was still alive and kicking. My palms sweated as I pictured her corpse in the room next door; grey and stiff. I groaned inwardly. Though it wasn't real, the picture I'd conjured up would stick in my mind and torment me for ever. She was bad enough to look at when she was alive, let alone dead.

I listened to the muffled sound of the shower, desperate for one myself. My skin felt cold and grimy, clammy to the touch, and my hair stank of cigarette smoke.

With a shiver, I wondered what today would bring. If Ethel was still with us, I expected I'd be by her side all day. The idea filled me with dread, but it was better than being murdered.

The cereal was stale. I forced it down and drank the remaining milk, knowing I'd need my strength.

Voices mumbled from next door – thank God – she was alive.

I smiled grimly at the irony that the witch still breathing made me feel good.

Bizarrely, the munchkins scene from The Wizard of Oz popped into my mind. Their squealy voices sang *Ding dong the wicked witch is NOT dead!* I was Dorothy, but I'd failed to kill the witch, and no one was congratulating me for that failure apart from myself.

As a little girl, I'd adored the film, even the scary monkeys, loving the thrill of fear they sent into my heart.

Now I knew I'd never be able to watch the film again without thinking about Ethel. I closed my eyes and imagined her being crushed by a house. It made me feel slightly better.

A few minutes later Mikey entered the room. For once, he smelled clean. Bags hung under his eyes though, aging him about ten years.

'Thank you,' I said, meaning it.

'For what?'

'Taking my place.'

He shrugged and leaned over to uncuff my wrist. Averting his gaze, he murmured, 'Remember, don't say anything to Nana.'

'I won't. I promise. You can trust me, Mikey. You know that don't you?'

He stared directly at me. The skin below his left eye twitched. 'Nana's in a lot of pain.'

I stood up, switching into character. 'Of course. I'll come right away.' I picked up my white lab coat and pulled it on. I'd slept in my clothes; Mikey had forgotten to let me change and I'd felt too tired to ask.

The heating hadn't come on yet and there was a chill in the air. Hugging the coat around myself, I walked ahead of him out of the room, turned right and entered the gorgon's cave.

Mikey had opened the curtains to reveal a drab morning. Ethel sat up in bed, watching me. She might have been alive, but she could have passed for dead. Her skin was a sickly yellow colour, her lips tinged purple. She shifted and coughed. Phlegm rattled in her throat.

'Water,' she hissed.

Mikey lunged forward and handed her the yellow cup. I noticed the fringe lamp she'd attacked me with had been returned to its rightful place. For a second, I considered ripping it out of its socket and smashing Mikey over the back of the head with it. But the moment passed; he straightened and moved away.

'How are you feeling today, Ethel?' I said.

'Awful. Get on with it and give me morphine.'

I caught Mikey's shocked expression; I think he was surprised she was showing me – Doctor Sparks – so little respect.

'That's to be expected, I'm afraid,' I said. I injected her with her third dose of morphine and mentally crossed my fingers, hoping I wasn't giving her an overdose.

'Now,' I said, feeling sick, 'I need to take a look at the wound and clean it out properly.'

Ethel nodded.

I turned to look at Mikey. 'Please can you boil some water and bring it up? Oh, and do you have a thermometer? I'd like to check the patient's temperature. Also, do you think you could turn the heating on? I don't want her getting too cold.'

Mikey's chest inflated with pride – he liked feeling important. 'Yes, right away, Doctor.'

With a bounce in his step, he turned to go, and my heart leaped. He hadn't cuffed me again, and I didn't think there was a lock on Ethel's door.

'Stop,' Ethel said.

Mikey spun around, face full of fear. 'Sorry, Nana. Did I do something wrong?'

She curled a gnarly finger and beckoned him over.

He swallowed and slunk towards the bed. I stood back, tummy churning.

She curled her finger repeatedly until he lowered his face to hers. In a tone sharp enough to cut ice, she said, 'Don't you think you're forgetting something?'

'No – uh – no, Nana. I don't think so. I'm being good. I'm doing what Doctor Sparks told me. I'm helping to make you better.'

There was a long silence.

I glanced at the open door. My body tingled with

adrenaline. Should I make a break for it?

No. The front door will be locked, and he's got the key around his neck. Now's not the right time.

There's never a right time. Do it.

Still, I edged away from the bed.

'Stay there,' she snapped, flinty stare locked on me.

I froze.

Mikey's head whipped from me to her.

'You were going to leave her in the room with me without the handcuffs on, weren't you?' she was whispering now, fixed on Mikey.

'I'm sorry. I didn't think. I just wanted to help you feel better. I -'

Her hand moved whip-fast, slapping him across the face.

He gasped and darted backwards.

'How can you be so stupid?' she hissed. 'After all I taught you. You make me sick.'

She turned her face away. Mikey didn't move for a few seconds. I watched his back rise and fall.

Finally, he murmured, 'I'm sorry Nana. I'll do better. I promise.'

He grabbed my arm and pulled me roughly towards the bed. I tried to catch his eye, but he wouldn't look at me. A tear rolled down his red cheek as he cuffed me to the iron railing behind her head.

He left the room, leaving me to glare down at my nemesis. Ethel slowly turned her head and opened her eyes. Her lips curled into a smile. 'See? He'll never go against me. Never.'

I wouldn't give her the satisfaction of a response. Inside, my heart burned. I fell into a daydream where I climbed on top of her frail body and choked her to death with my knee whilst stabbing her with the needle, over and over again until her body was a bloody mess. The fantasy stopped being satisfying when it played on and Mikey ran screaming into the room, threw the boiling water on my head then pushed me onto the floor and crushed my windpipe with his bare hands.

'How was your night?' she said with a smirk.

Now was the time to lie convincingly. I cleared my throat. 'What do you think?'

She smiled wider. Nodded as if pleased. 'Wicked girls need to be punished too. It's the only way they learn.'

'Were you punished as a child?'

She snorted and looked away. 'On the contrary, I was worshipped by my parents.' A slight frown drew her eyebrows together. 'Until they died, of course.'

'How did they die?' I half-expected her to say she killed them.

'My father found out she was having an affair, so he beat her to death. Then he hung himself.'

She spoke matter-of-factly but her jaw tightened.

'I'm sorry.'

Her eyes snapped to mine. 'There's nothing to feel sorry for. She was a fool and so was he. They deserved what they got.'

'You can't really believe that?'

'Don't you dare try to tell me what I can and can't believe.'

Though she hadn't touched me, I felt like I'd been slapped too. She closed her eyes. Multiple eyelid folds drooped over the rim of her pale eyelashes. Every inch of her skin sagged, and age spots littered her face like brown stains. I watched her and wondered what had happened after her parents died. Had she grown up in foster care? Been adopted? Been taken in by a relative?

'Your parents were too soft on you,' she said.

'Shut up.'

'Why? Can't accept the truth? That's why you're so pathetic, so weak. Your mother should have made you strong. Instead, she's turned you into a coward.'

'Shut up.'

'Or what? What exactly are you going to do about it?' She grinned revealing gaping black holes and sharp, yellow teeth, 'You don't even see your parents anymore, isn't that right? They disowned you because you spurned them and turned your back on everything they've ever done for you. You're a stupid, pathetic, spineless excuse for a daughter. You let them down. Decided to be selfish and pursue your own desires above theirs, despite the years of sacrifice they made for you. And choosing not to see them when they're still alive to be seen? I can't think of anything worse. You ought to be ashamed of yourself.'

How did she know that? Had Mikey found out and told the old harridan? How long had he been stalking her? Reporting back to Ethel?

Guilt surfaced, pricking my heart like thorns. All those years lost. I'd been so stubborn, so angry and unforgiving. I should have reached out years ago, apologised for lying. Maybe then we'd have been able to patch things up. I should have taken Mum's call, or at least listened to her voicemail. But now it was too late.

I looked up through stinging tears. 'Please, just let me go.'

'See? Even now, you're begging,' she turned and dragged on the cigarette, mouth curled in disgust. 'You're pathetic. Almost as pathetic as him.' She gestured to the door.

'You're wrong. You're to blame for him being like this. You've turned your grandson into a freak -'

Her hand shot out and slapped my cheek. I recoiled, hand to my face, skin burning, despair flooding my brain. There was no reasoning with her. Nothing I could do or say would make her see sense. Arguing was a lost cause. She'd chosen me and she was never going to let me go.

'Why did it have to be me?' I said in a small voice I hated myself for.

Ethel smiled slyly, dragged more poison into her lungs. She exhaled into my face, making me think of manure rolled in ash. Her gaze hardened.

'Because, my dear, you're pretty, dumb and shallow, just what I need.'

'You're evil.'

Her eyes narrowed and she peered over her glasses at me. In a low, steely voice, she said, 'I'd be careful what you say to me, Missy.'

'You've ruined Mikey's life,' I said.

'Shut your trap. I saved him. That's got nothing whatsoever to do with me. It's not my fault he's such a mindless simpleton.' She started coughing. Tears ran down her face, but her cold glare never left me.

Mikey trudged into the room looking worried.

'She sleeps in the well again tonight,' Ethel rasped, stabbing a finger at me.

I darted a terrified glance at Mikey, who jerked to a stop. He frowned and glanced back at me. I gave a subtle head shake and he stayed quiet.

He placed the bowl of water on her bedside table and murmured, 'Yes, Nana.'

'The water needs to cool,' I said, trying to speak normally, 'I need a shower before I clean out the wound to ensure I'm as sterile as possible.'

Mikey sought permission from Ethel. She gave a sharp nod then closed her eyes. 'Don't be too long, Doctor Sparks.'

Mikey took off the handcuffs and led me to the bathroom. I opened the door and he followed me in.

I raised my eyebrows in question as he uncuffed me.

'What did you do to make her mad?' he said.

'Nothing.'

'You must have done something. I don't want to put you in the well, but I don't want to go in there either.' He clamped his hands on either side of his head and paced the small space.

'Try to stay calm. Listen, you don't need to do either of those things. If we stick to the same story – that you put me in the well – she'll never know the truth.'

'But – but -'

'Neither of us deserve to go down there,' I said, putting my hand on his arm. 'You're doing such a good job of helping me to take care of her, and I'm doing my very best to make her better. She's just in pain so she's taking it out on you.'

'It's different being in the well now I'm big. It hurts more,' he whispered.

'I know. And it's not normal for you to be put down there. You need to stand up for yourself. Say no.'

He shook his head and looked at me as if I was crazy. 'No-one says no to Nana. Even Frank didn't say no to Nana.'

'Who was Frank?' I sat on the corner of the bath.

Mikey leaned against the sink. A faraway look took hold of him. 'Frank was my Grandpapa. He died when I was six. He was kind, and he did everything Nana said. I remember he took me fishing on my birthday and I caught one! He was so proud of me. When we got home, Nana said it was too small and made him throw it away.'

'How did he die, Mikey?'

A fleeting terror flashed in his face. 'No. No. No. You mustn't ask me that. We never talk about that.'

Before I could say anything, he pushed past me and dashed out of the room.

Chapter 34

This family gets more messed up by the second.

How the hell do I get out of here?

You don't. That's not in Ethel's grand plan.

What was her plan? She didn't want Mikey to let me go. Obviously, she knew I'd go straight to the police, but it was more than that – she wanted me to stay for him. But to what end? Did she want me to look after him once she was gone? Be his pretend girlfriend?

A wave of horror engulfed me. I dug my fists into my cheeks and took deep breaths. *Don't think about it. Think about something else. Be strong. Be brave.*

I thought about the heat of the water on my skin. The slippery feel of shower gel. The fact that I wasn't cuffed or gagged. Things could be worse. I could be dog-tied or down in that well. They could be starving or torturing me. As it was, I was relatively unharmed. Untouched. But for how long?

I shook my head as a stream of violent scenes crashed through my mind.

Still, light sparked in the darkness. I just needed to cling on to it. The police must be on the case. They'd be doing the rounds, questioning everyone in the neighbourhood. This mountain was sparsely populated, so the cottage must stick out like a sore thumb. They'd have to come knocking soon. And they'd come in a pair. Two police officers versus Mikey. It wasn't like he had a gun or anything. He wasn't James Bond or Jack Reacher. He was a twenty-five-year-old homebody. He might be a lot stronger than me, and he might have been able to incapacitate Jacob, but he was no match for two, highly trained officers. If I screamed for help, he'd be outnumbered. They'd take him down and rescue me. I just had to keep my wits about me. Wait. Be patient. Play it safe. Keep the gorgon alive a little longer. Continue to earn Mikey's trust. Keep him calm.

My heart settled. I rinsed my hair and reluctantly turned off the shower. Mikey had left a fresh pair of jeans and another monstrously fluffy jumper on the toilet seat for me. He must have crept in while my back was turned. Goosebumps erupted on my skin as I imagined his pale wandering eyes.

I threw on the clothes, brushed my teeth and braced myself.

'Ready?' Mikey said.

'Yes.'

He opened the door and beamed. 'You look great!'

He took me back to Ethel's bedroom where I donned the lab coat.

Ethel's stare chilled my veins. 'Took you long enough.'

I ignored her and began to peel off the top dressing. She winced but stayed quiet. Behind me, Mikey hovered and chewed the sleeve of his Santa jumper.

'How many Christmas jumpers have you got?' I said, peeling off the second dressing. Anything was better than thinking about the thing I was about to see – even talking to Mikey.

'Seven. One for each day of the week!'

Ethel rolled her eyes and hacked up phlegm. She flinched as the next dressing ripped off a strand of hair. I forced back a smile. She was as ugly on the outside as she was on the inside. Nothing more than a vessel of evil that fed on the pain and suffering of others. I wanted to kill her; but I couldn't. The fact was agonising.

'I love Christmas too. Why do you love it so much, Mikey?' I glanced over my shoulder. Peeled off the second last dressing.

Mikey's eyes gleamed. 'I don't know. I just do. I love

everything about it. I love the songs and the decorations and the tree. It makes me happy.'

'Me too,' I said enthusiastically, giving him a broad smile.

For a moment, we grinned at each other.

Ethel slapped my arm hard enough to hurt. 'Get on with it.'

A frown knitted Mikey's brow and he pursed his lips.

I was tempted to rip off the last dressing, just for the pleasure of it, but I played the good doctor and carefully pried it away, moistening the dried blood and skin to help it come off painlessly.

My mouth turned to liquid when I saw the wound. It was bloody and raw. I couldn't see any pus or sign of infection and it didn't smell bad. Relief lightened the pressure in my chest.

'It's beginning to heal,' I said. 'Now I'm going to wash it out with the sterile water. Ready? This might hurt a bit.'

Ethel nodded and shut her eyes.

Nausea uncurled like an eel and slithered onto my tongue.

Keep it together Rachel. You're Doctor Sparks remember, surgeon extraordinaire.

I dunked a handful of cotton pads into the bowl of cooled water, took a calming breath then dabbed at the wound quickly, nose crinkled in disgust.

Ethel's eyes shot open. She hissed, 'Can't you do it any gentler than that!'

'I'm sure Doctor Sparks is doing it as gently as she can,' Mikey murmured.

She glared at him and he recoiled as if bitten. I gave the wound a second wipe then whacked on another two dressings, hoping I hadn't done more damage than good. Mikey exhaled and patted my shoulder. I managed not to flinch at his touch and smiled up at him. 'All done.'

'Thank you so much Doc,' Mikey said. He moved to the

bed and leaned over. 'How are you feeling Nana?'

'How do you think I'm feeling?'

He jerked back and slipped his thumb into his mouth.

'Take that out this instant or you'll go to the well tonight instead.'

Mikey yanked out his thumb and hid his hand behind his back.

'Pathetic boy-child,' she hissed.

I grabbed the thermometer and stuck it in her mouth before she could have another go at him. When it beeped, I pulled it out and checked. 'It's normal. That's good.'

Ethel grunted and rolled over, turning her back to us. 'Take her to her room then come back. I want a word with you.'

I held out my hands. Mikey hesitated before cuffing me. I think he was starting to think the cuffs were unnecessary. My heart sang at the idea. If I could get him to let his guard down, I might be able to escape.

*

I was woken by something touching my face. I opened my eyes and stared up at Mikey. He smiled down. 'Hi, sleepyhead.'

Trying to hide how freaked out I was, I scooted into a sitting position and pressed my back against the railing in a futile effort to widen the gap between us. The handcuff rattled. He looked brighter and happier. He absently stroked the fluffy Santa on his jumper. His other hand rested an inch from my waist.

'How long have I been asleep?' I said.

'A while. You look like a baby when you're sleeping.'

I suppressed a shudder. How long had he been in here with me? Watching me? My skin crawled with a thousand fuzzy-legged spiders. He was sitting on the bed so close our hips almost touched. The second he looked beyond me, I inched away.

'You're such a brilliant Doctor,' he said. He hesitated, smoothed back his hair, and stared deeply into my eyes, 'And you're even more pretty in person.'

'Thanks Mikey,' I smiled, jaw clenched. 'How was she feeling when you left her?'

'Not that bad I don't think. She's pleased with you, even though she doesn't say it. And I know she likes you. I like you too.'

He reached forward and poked me on the nose. His cheeks flushed bright red like Bashful from *Snow White and the Seven Dwarves*, and a sick jolt of realisation gripped my spine; I was in some hellish fairy tale – Ethel was the evil queen – I was the innocent princess and Mikey was the huntsman sent to cut out my heart.

'Do you like me?' The words rushed out of him. His gaze was so intense I had to look away.

'Of course I like you. You're a good person Mikey. The way you went to the well instead of me was so selfless and brave. Listen, don't go to the well tonight. She'll never know.'

He beamed. Tucked his stringy orange hair behind his ear. 'Nana says we'd be great together.'

Ice crystals pierced my skin. 'We might have been, in another life, but I'm married, Mikey. You know that.'

He scowled. 'To that cheating dickhead, Doctor Sparks!'

I thought about correcting him – telling him that that was just in the show, that in real life Jacob was the most loyal man I knew – but stopped myself. If I contradicted his delusional belief that I was a real doctor and actually managed to convince him that I was Rachel Brown, the actress, he might lose the plot and take it out on me. The whole reason he'd brought me here was because he'd been under the impression that I was a proper surgeon who could treat his beloved nana. His entire world would implode if he knew the truth. And then all hell would break loose.

Shit. Think.

'He doesn't deserve you or need you. We need you. Nana needs you.'

He jerked to his feet and paced the room.

'Calm down.'

'I should've killed him when I had the chance.' He whirled around, eyes crazed, 'I could go back. Finish the job. That way he'll never hurt you again!'

'No!' I raised my voice so much it halted him in his tracks.

'Why not?'

'You're not a killer, Mikey. And he may have been unfaithful, but he doesn't deserve to die.'

'You're wrong.' His face fell. He dropped onto the end of the bed and put his head in his hands. 'I am a killer. You know I am.'

'You didn't mean to kill Simon. If you drive off back to my house and kill J – Doctor Sparks – you will be a real killer. A murderer. Planning to kill someone and then doing it is completely different to doing it in self-defence.'

He went completely still.

Silence swallowed the room. I stared at his frozen back. Had my words sunk in? If they hadn't and it came to it, I'd stab him a hundred times to stop him going after Jacob. I wouldn't even care what happened to me. There was no way I was letting him kill my husband.

In a small, shaky voice, he said, 'I'm not good enough for you either. I'm not good enough for anyone.'

'That's not true. One day you'll meet someone and fall in love. Someone your age who's single.'

He looked around at me, eyes wet. A frown furrowed his forehead. His pale eyes seemed to scour mine. 'But… that won't be good enough.'

'What do you mean?'

He walked over to me and perched on the mattress.

After a brief hesitation, he reached out and laid his clammy hand on top of mine. 'Nana said it has to be you.'

Chapter 35

No one deserves this.

I stared at the one-handed Santa and screamed at the top of my lungs, incoherent sounds that formed no meaning and made no sense. My throat grew hoarse and sore, but I continued screaming, eyes streaming, chest burning, head fit to bursting. I felt wild and displaced, as though someone had sucked my soul out of my body and put it elsewhere. I wasn't me in that moment; I was a thing possessed. I was helpless. Free-falling into a pit of feelings that at once consumed and tortured me. I felt like nothing could make me stop – that I could go on screaming forever, but eventually time and exhaustion won out, and I went silent and hid my head in my knees. My head throbbed with the quiet and the awful knowledge that I'd lost control – given in to fear and self-pity and despair. My tears evolved into sobs; I felt like I was burning up, and the rage resurfaced, hot and heavy as singed earth. I picked up the pillow next to me and threw it at the door, then pushed over both bedside tables, sending them crashing to the carpet. I turned and smashed my free fist into my pillow repeatedly until exhaustion took over again and I collapsed, half-curled into the foetal position, my cuffed wrist quivering with pain from where I'd carelessly yanked it against the hard metal.

A creak made me open my eyes.

Ethel stood in the doorway, leaning against the wall. She looked more like a witch than ever: sharp nose, beady eyes, matted hair against ashen skin. The blood-stained nightdress hung off her skeletal frame, emphasizing how small and bony she was. She inched towards the bed, one foot sliding in front of the other, eyes fixed on mine. Deep down I was horrified that she'd seen me like this, but I couldn't find the energy to move, so remained curled in on myself on my side, hand stretched above me awkwardly.

She moved liked a snail, but her eyes were wickedly sharp. When she reached the bed, she lowered herself onto the end of the mattress. If I reached out with my legs, I could kick her. Shove her onto the floor. But what was the point? It wouldn't achieve anything but to enrage the beast. I was trapped here for as long as she wanted.

Numbness absorbed my mind, swaddling it in a woollen blanket. I was spent. There was no energy left to care.

I closed my eyes to shut her out, but my ears couldn't silence her hideous voice.

'Hush little baby, don't say a word,
Papa's gonna buy you a mockingbird.
And if that mockingbird won't sing,
Papa's gonna buy you a diamond ring.
And if that diamond ring turns to brass,
Papa's gonna buy you a looking glass.
And if that looking glass gets broke,
Papa's gonna buy you a billy goat.
And if that billy goat won't pull,
Papa's gonna buy you a cart and bull.
And if that cart and bull turn over,
Papa's gonna buy you a dog named Rover.
And if that dog named Rover won't bark,
Papa's gonna buy you a horse and cart.
And if that horse and cart fall down,
You'll still be the sweetest little baby in town!'

There was moment's stillness where only her rasping breaths punctuated the quiet.

Finally, she murmured, 'You can't fool me, girl. I know you're awake.'

I kept my eyes closed. Tried to deepen my breathing.

'Fine. You go on pretending if you want but listen

carefully. Mikey is going to try to win you over. He's going to woo you, and you're going to let him. You're going to let him in completely, if you know what I mean. And you're going to make him believe you like him. Really like him. Make him happy and give me what I want, and I'll think about making your life more…pleasant.'

I opened my eyes. She smirked.

'What is it you want?' I said.

'Can't you guess?' Her gaze dropped to my middle. She looked up. Her eyes pierced mine. 'I want a great-grandchild of course. Someone to carry on the family name.'

I raised my chin, heart pounding. 'There's no way I'm doing that.'

'Oh, I think you will.'

She turned her back on me and began to shuffle out of the room.

'Nothing will make me do that. Ever,' I said.

She looked over her shoulder, her eyes ice-cold. 'If you don't, you'll live to regret it.'

'Why? There's nothing more you can do to me. You've already taken me away from everything and everyone I love.'

She shrugged and moved out of sight. 'Have it your way,' her voice was thin but sharp, cutting through the air like glass. 'If you don't cooperate, I'll tell Mikey to go back to your house and kill your husband. And what a dreadful shame that would be, don't you think?'

'There's no way he'd get away with it. The police will be keeping an eye on my house, just in case…'

She darted back into the room, moving with speed I didn't think her capable of. I jumped.

Slowly, crawling her fingers along the iron railing at the end of the bed, she approached my legs. Level with my knees, she stopped and peered down over her glasses at me, skin crinkling at the corners so severely her skin looked as though it had been carved into with a knife. I looked at the loose skin on her throat, thought about turkeys, and how good it would be to see her roast on Christmas Day.

'Just in case, what exactly?' she said, 'In case you come crawling back?' She coughed out a laugh. Her eyes gleamed. 'In about six months, they'll call off the search. No one will be looking for you then, so you might as well accept that this is your new life, for the rest of your days, however long I decide that may be.'

I didn't believe her for a second – they'd keep looking for me for at least a year, and Jacob – if he was still alive – would never stop searching for me, and yet the threat hung in the air around me like rotten meat in a knacker's yard. Her words wormed into my stomach, turning and churning what I'd always known but been afraid to fully accept; when I'd served my use, she'd order Mikey to kill me.

I looked away, desperate to hide the tears that stung my eyes.

'Don't say I didn't warn you,' she taunted, waggling her finger in front of my face.

'Leave me alone.'

'Now that's no way to talk to the great grandmother of your first baby, is it, Missy?'

First baby?

I looked at her.

She grinned, revealing her black and yellow smile. Like a box of dominoes, and just as unstable.

'Oh yes, dear. I'll be wanting lots of lovely babies to fill this house, so you'd better get cracking, don't you think?'

I stared at her open-mouthed, unable to conceal my horror.

'There, there, dear. You're young. You've got a decent pair of hips on you. You ought to be able to produce at least five babes before your time is up.' She stopped smiling and dropped a garment on my lap.

I stared down at a pale-yellow cardigan, tiny and perfect

and terrifying in its implications.

'Why on earth do you want that?' I said.

She looked at me as if I was simple. 'Family is everything. Babies die. The more you have the more likely one will live.'

'What do you mean babies die? Is that what happened to you?'

Ethel looked towards the window, drifted through the red-tinted light towards the curtains. With her back to me, she murmured, 'Babies die. It happens all the time. I need my family name to carry on,' she glanced around at me, her eyes bright with mania, 'forever.'

'But why? Why's that so important to you?'

She frowned and shuffled back towards the bed, her slippers whispering on the carpet. Tilting her head strangely, she said, 'Because it is. That's why.'

I shook my head, unable to think of anything to say.

She gave me a tight smile. 'Oh, and I've already decided on names. If it's a girl, Harriet.'

'Wasn't Harriet your daughter's name?'

Eyes glazed, seeming not to have heard my question, Ethel patted my hand, pushed hair out of my face with surprisingly gentle fingers, and hobbled out of the room singing *Hush Little Baby* in an eerie rasp that made the hairs on my skin stand on end.

*

Giving me a worried look, Mikey put my pillow back on the bed and righted the bedside tables. He placed a chicken and mushroom Pot Noodle on my lap and handed me a spoon. I murmured thanks and began to eat. He hovered beside the bed and watched me. I pretended not to notice and tried to concentrate on the food. His leg jigged up and down, and he kept opening his mouth then shutting it, as if there was something he wanted to say but couldn't bring himself to say it. I kept my eyes down and made noises to suggest I was enjoying the bland noodles. He smiled with pleasure and puffed out his chest, pleased with himself. Still, he didn't speak. Neither did I.

I had almost finished the pot, when the silence was broken by the rumble of an engine. Our eyes met. I opened my mouth to scream, and Mikey clamped his palm over my lips, eyes wild.

'Don't make a sound,' he whispered.

With one hand around my mouth, he ripped off his belt. I tried to struggle, but his fingers dug into my jaw so fiercely I feared he'd break the bone.

'Don't move,' he said.

Quick as a whip, he wrapped the belt around my head twice, tying it in two knots at the back to gag me. The belt indented my cheeks, painful but not cutting. I shook my head frantically and begged with my eyes, but he ignored me and ran to the window. He was still wearing his Christmas pug pyjamas. Pulling back the curtains an inch, he peered outside and gasped.

He looked round at me, strode across the room, slipped his thumb into his mouth. 'It's the police! What shall I say?'

I tried to speak but it was impossible. I moaned as loudly as I could, and he frowned hard at me. 'Don't do that. If they hear you -'

Three loud knocks came.

'Shit!' Mikey shot across the room to the wardrobe, dug a dusty CD player out, plugged it in and hit play. Classical music belted into the room.

He pressed his finger to his lips and gave me a warning look, then bounded out of the room, locking the door behind him.

I immediately tried to untie the belt, but it was too tight.

Moaning as loudly as I could, I stood on the bed and tried to see through the narrow gap in the curtains, but nothing was visible except for pale grey sky.

If the police were here, this was my chance.

I looked around the room, heart pummelling my ribs like a boxer's fists. My gaze fell on the bedside table.

I crawled across the bed and used my free arm to heave the table onto the mattress. Once there, I pushed it closer to the railing and used both hands to manoeuvre it into my arms, then threw it as hard as I could onto the floor. It made a loud thud. I froze and listened, waiting for the sound of steps to pound the stairs, but all I could hear was classical music belting out. I needed to destroy the CD player so they could hear me. Mikey had put it on the floor next to the other bedside table. I hurried to the other side of the bed, got on all fours and reached out. My fingers remained inches from the silver machine. I couldn't reach it properly. Frantically, I scanned the room and racked my brain.

Mikey's porn magazines!

I scrambled over to the other side of the bed, stretched out on my belly, reached for the bedside table I'd chucked on the floor and yanked open the drawer. Desperately, I pulled out a magazine, shuffled back onto the bed and rolled it into a cylinder. I crawled back across the bed and reached out with the magazine, holding it at the very tip. Tongue pinched between my teeth, I stretched my arm and upper body as far as the cuff would allow and managed to slide the magazine underneath the wire. I pulled but the CD player stayed put.

I heard a very muffled rumble of voices below. I groaned as loudly as I could, swivelled around and slammed my heels into the wall behind the iron railing. I stopped and listened. The voices seemed to have stopped. Tchaikovsky's *Dance of the Little Swans* attacked my eardrums. I strained, desperate to hear footsteps plodding up the stairs, but nothing sounded from outside the room. I smashed my feet into the wall again. Listened. Nothing.

Turning back to the CD player, I reached out again with

the magazine and slid it under the wire. Tugged. The machine moved closer.

I pulled again and again and again, inch by inch, and at last, it was in reach. I lunged for the buttons and jabbed stop. Silence swallowed the room and hummed in my ears. I started to reach for the other bedside table, hoping to throw it on the floor to create another thud, and froze as the unmistakable sound of two car doors slamming met my ears.

No!

I moaned as loudly as I could, rolled onto my back and smashed my feet into the wall above the bed, but the engine started, and the car rumbled away. It was too late. The police had gone.

Chapter 36

Mikey showered me with gifts. At first, they were innocent; a scented candle, a small crystal vase filled with fake flowers, a hideous black velvet choker with a silver heart, six Mills and Boon romances, a cheap box of chocolates and a pink Christmas jumper that he insisted I wear every day. They all came from charity shops. After a while, the musty scent disappeared, blending with my own. The jumper was pale pink with a snowflake in the centre. As Christmas jumpers went, it could have been worse. I thanked him for each present and dutifully admired the choker before he put it around my neck. It felt like a dog collar – another symbol of entrapment and possession. My skin goosed when his eel fingers touched me.

My days were spent in my room for the most part. I forced myself to run on the spot and do two hundred star jumps every day. It was tricky being handcuffed to the bed but just about manageable. If, somehow, I got the chance to run, I didn't want my lack of fitness to be my downfall. I also did yoga on the bed, keen to keep my body supple and strong, and lessen the crippling muscle stiffness and soreness that set in if I stayed still for too long.

If I hadn't had the books, I'd have died of boredom. I read all six Mills and Boons then pulled *Tom's Midnight Garden* out of the bedside table and read that twice. I couldn't help seeing a similarity between how Willy's mother treated him and how Ethel treated Mikey. It made me wonder if that was why Mikey treasured the story so much. The pages were worn thin, the spine as creased as hundred-year-old bark. Maybe, even though he knew Willy was made up, he found solace in the idea that he wasn't the only little boy in the world being neglected and abused.

I spent hours staring sightlessly at the plastic tree worrying about Jacob.

Mikey let me out of the Christmas room every three hours or so to check on Ethel, who grew smugger by the day. Unfortunately, I'd not managed to give her an infection or make her ill. Sometimes I let my mind drift to the wonderful idea that the tumour would grow back fast, bigger and deadlier than before, or that the disease would spread throughout her entire body and deaden her mind until she was nothing but a vegetable with no voice left to use on bending Mikey to her will, but it seemed as if she was going to make it to Christmas. The festive deadline no longer held any hope; she wasn't going to allow Mikey to let me go. She wanted a great-grandchild and was going to do everything in her power to get one.

I now thought it would be better for me if she died. I could be there for Mikey in his grief; persuade him to let me go. There was a slight chance he'd lash out in anger and blame me for her death, but I didn't think he'd go so far as to kill me. These romantic overtures might have been encouraged by Ethel, but he'd softened with me. He was beginning to trust me. Let his guard down a little. Over the last week, he'd forgotten to lock the door three times. Each time, I'd battled with the cuff to no avail. It was the bane of my existence, almost as infuriating as the hag next door. She lived in the bedroom now and coughed incessantly day and night. Often, I lay there trying to sleep, imagining her choking on her own phlegm. Sadly, it hadn't happened yet. Mikey was still giving her cigarettes, so there was hope.

Every day, I heard the mumble of their voices in the room next door, and knew she was working on him, steering his mind towards evil.

One day when he came in to see me after speaking to her, he was flushed and slightly sheepish, and his eyes kept flitting from my lips to my chest. I crossed my arms. He wrung his hands and perched on the mattress. Opened his mouth and closed it. Stood up, stared down at me. Confusion and something that looked worryingly like excitement tussled in his pale eyes.

'Nana says it's time,' he said. His voice was hopeful. It was as if he was willing me to nod my head excitedly and welcome him with open arms.

I played dumb. 'Time for what?'

He yanked something out of his pocket and thrust it at me. I didn't want to look but couldn't stop myself.

Oh my God.

I stared in horror at the black lace thong dangling from his fingers.

'I got it from Ann Summers,' he said nervously. It still had the tag on it.

'What's it for?' I couldn't believe I sounded so calm.

'For,' he bit his lip, pushed it into my hand, 'for you. Nana said you'd like it. That it would make you feel, um, sexy.'

I imagined throttling Ethel with the thong. Pictured her lips turning blue.

'I can, er, leave the room, while you put it on…'

I sat up straighter, picked up the offensive garment and dropped it on the bedside table. His eyes followed. A frown I'd grown to fear pinched his eyebrows.

'What's wrong? Don't you like it?'

'It's not that. It's just that…look, Mikey, do you really want to do this? It's not that I don't like you, but I don't feel about you that way.' I thought about mentioning Jacob, but fear eclipsed my words. I didn't want Mikey to decide he needed Jacob out of the way.

'I – uh,' he plonked down on the mattress and scrunched up his face. 'I don't know what I want.'

'You're a good person, Mikey. You need to understand something important, and that's that I don't want this. I don't want us to be any more than friends, and if you try to,' I swallowed a lump of panic, 'have sex with me, you'll be doing it against my wishes.' I considered telling him that even if we did have sex, I wouldn't conceive, but if that got back to Ethel, what would she do? If she thought I couldn't have a baby, her entire plan was shot. I'd be of no use anymore. She'd have to persuade Mikey to find someone else and get rid of me.

'Nana said you'd say something like that, but she says you do want me really. You're just playing hard to get. She says that's what girls do when they like someone.'

I shook my head. 'No. She's wrong. That's not true.'

'But…why don't you want me? What's wrong with me?'

'Nothing's wrong with you. It's just…I'm older than you and -'

His head snapped up. That manic gleam surfaced. 'I don't care that you're older than me! I like it. I like you.' He blushed scarlet.

'I like you too, but I don't want to have sex with you.'

He looked like he'd been slapped. Hurt flashed in his eyes. He tugged at the sleeve of his Christmas jumper, stood up and darted away. From the doorway, frowning deeply, he stared at me. He shook his head, stamped his foot and left, slamming the door behind him.

I shook from head to toe. Slowly, I uncurled my fists.

Voices erupted from next door. Ethel screamed, 'DON'T BE SUCH A BLOODY COWARD.'

Mikey reappeared in the doorway, chest heaving, eyes wet. 'Nana says I must do it. She says she wants a baby and this is the only way. I have to make her happy.'

He advanced slowly, eyes darting everywhere.

'Screw her, Mikey. Screw everything she's ever told you. She's a bully and a brute. She's abused you your entire life. And I know she did something bad to Frank. She's not right in the head. You need to trust your instincts. If you don't want to do this, don't. Don't let her control you. If you do this, you'll not only be a murderer, but you'll be also a rapist. You don't want that on your conscience, and if you really like me and want to be friends, you won't take advantage of me like this. Haven't I done right by you? I've operated on your nana and saved her life. I've kept your secrets. I've done everything I can to make you feel good. If you do this, you'll never forgive yourself.'

He stopped. Tears rolled over his lashes. He looked utterly helpless. 'But Nana wants -'

'Screw that! What do you want? It's time to put yourself first. Think about your own happiness. Come on. Sit down and let's talk about it. What do you want out of life? What will make you happy?'

But he was far away, turned inward, listening to that dark voice. His eyes narrowed and he jabbed a finger at me. 'You can't say those things. You don't know her. She took me in after my mother left me. She took care of me. She lets me have my Christmas room, and my music in December. She even used to get a tree and put it in the living room. And she'd cook a roast turkey with all the trimmings and buy me a present.'

'But did she love you? Did she give you cuddles? Did she hold you when you cried?'

His eye twitched. He shook his head as if trying to shut out my words, but I carried on. 'Or did she hurt you? Burn you? Force you to sleep in a cold, damp well?'

'She had to. I didn't give her a choice. I was wicked. I needed to learn…'

'No Mikey. What she did was wrong. What she's doing now is wrong. Hell, it's more than wrong. It's evil!'

I was crying now. He was too.

His shoulders slumped. His chest heaved and he buried his face in his hands.

'Come here,' I said softly.

He peeked between his fingers, looking so like a child it would've broken my heart had I not known what he was capable of.

He walked over and sat on the bed. I pulled him into a hug and held him, and he sobbed, tears dampening my jumper. He smelled of sweat and garlic. The urge to push him away dug in, but I fought it and rubbed his back.

'It's okay, Mikey. It's okay. I'm here. I'll never hurt you like she has.'

He cried for what felt like an hour. At last, he pulled back. His face was puffy, eyes red and swollen. He smiled and wiped his nose on his sleeve. He stared deeply into my eyes. 'I think I love you, Elouise.'

With shaking fingers, he unlocked my wrist from the cuff and gave me a weepy smile.

I stared open-mouthed as he strode out of the room and locked the door.

Chapter 37

Mikey hovered outside the bathroom humming *Silent Night.*

I dressed quickly and went to the toilet. Stared at the toilet paper in my hand.

There's no blood. Again.

Could that mean?

No. It's impossible. Doctor Somerton said…

Almost impossible. Not entirely.

I dropped the paper in the toilet. Stood on trembly legs, flushed, drifted to the mirror above the bathroom sink, and stared at myself. My hand floated to my stomach as if pulled by a puppet master.

Jacob and I had sex when I was ovulating, right before my appointment with Doctor Somerton. *And you still haven't started your period.*

You've been here, in this godforsaken hell hole, for over two months.

It could be the stress. Lots of women's periods stop when they're stressed.

I looked at my breasts. They were sore and larger than normal, had been like that for a while. I'd thought it was just because my period was due, but it was overdue now. For the second time since I'd been here. And I'd felt extra tired these last few weeks. I'd put it down to everything that I was going through, but I'd also had a bit of cramping.

They're all pregnancy symptoms.

Two missed periods. Sore breasts. Fatigue. Cramping.

I must be about three months pregnant.

I looked down at my tummy. It looked slightly bigger than normal. Was I showing?

A beat of excitement was crushed by fear. I sank to the

floor and stared at the wall. I couldn't bring a baby into this. Jacob's baby. The baby we'd been trying to conceive for so long. Ethel would take her or him from me and bring it up as her own. She'd allow me access to feed the baby and would probably insist I did all the dirty work like changing nappies, but she wouldn't let me close to the baby other than that, because she wouldn't want us to bond. I could imagine it all; the abject terror whenever my baby was taken away from me; the misery when I wasn't allowed to hold him or her when they cried. Would she burn my baby if it didn't stop crying? Force Mikey to put it in the well when it was naughty?

Blood thumped in my temples. I wouldn't let that happen. There was no way on earth any baby of mine was suffering what Mikey had. No way I was bringing an innocent being into the world only to be caged and tortured.

Mikey knocked on the door. Opened it. 'Ready yet?'

He had a stupid grin on his face. I wanted to slap it away. Beat him until he couldn't smile again.

A puzzled frown replaced the smile. 'What's wrong?'

'Nothing.' I pushed past him and headed back to my room.

He followed me and hovered in the doorway looking lost. 'Have I done something wrong?'

I ignored him, got under the covers and rolled onto my side.

'I'll just finish the breakfast then,' he said, 'and get you some paper and a pencil for your book list.'

I waited for him to cross the room and cuff me to the bed, but he didn't. He backed out, shut the door and locked it. I shot up and reached for the crystal vase, heart hammering. That would do more damage than Mikey's pathetic little snow globe.

*

I waited next to the wall. When he opened the door, I was going to smash the vase into his face as hard as I could. He'd expect me to be sitting on the bed, so it would take him a couple of seconds to register I wasn't there. His confusion would make him falter. That was when I'd strike. If I hit him hard enough, I might be able to knock him unconscious. If he was unconscious, I'd be able to pull the lanyard off his neck and grab his house and car keys.

My hands were sweaty. I'd pulled on my trainers and a second fluffy jumper, ready to run. It was December and I was on a mountain. I didn't know how cold it was outside, but even with the heating on, the house was a bit chilly. If I didn't manage to knock him out, I'd need to make a run for it again.

I imagined running down the mountain with him coming after me and cold sweat erupted under my armpits. Mikey was faster than me, but if I managed to catch him in the eye with the vase, or bust up his nose, the pain might slow him down. I might have been three months pregnant, but I'd been doing my exercise, keeping fit. If he was in agony, I might be able to outrun him. Last time when I'd escaped, he'd been fighting fit. This time would be different. I considered smashing Mikey in the face until I was sure he wouldn't be able to come after me. That would be the only sure-fire way to incapacitate him, but that meant being able to hit him hard enough to make him fall to the ground. He was a lot taller than me, but if I reached up and hit him high, I should catch him right and knock him out. It would rely on Mikey not noticing me until it was too late. What if he came in and immediately sensed where I was?

Don't worry about that. He won't. Just hit him the second he steps through the doorway.

I pushed damp hair behind my ear and listened for footsteps on the stairs, but Christmas music was still blaring through the house. I was surprised Ethel allowed him to have it on so loud. I thought about her for a moment. I wasn't worried about her stopping me. If she heard a scuffle, she might try to come out of her room to investigate, but I could easily overpower her. I'd take great pleasure in pushing her down the stairs if I needed to. I wouldn't even hesitate.

I raised my arms above my head. Every muscle shook. I clenched my jaw and told myself I could do this. I was a strong, powerful woman defending her unborn baby. If I didn't do this, my baby would either die in childbirth or suffer for its entire life. Even if Ethel died the week the baby was born, Mikey wouldn't be able to give my baby the safe, secure, loving environment she or he deserved. He might even decide to punish the baby in the same way Ethel had punished him. There was no way he'd send the child to school. It would be too risky. He'd force me to home-school the child, turning the poor little dot into a hermit just like him. Knowing my luck, the evil old witch would live another decade at least. With her whispering orders in Mikey's ear, my baby escaping cruelty was highly unlikely.

That was, of course, if my baby even survived. I couldn't imagine Mikey taking me to a hospital to give birth. Ethel would probably feed him another set of lies, telling him that doctors could deliver their own babies, that going to hospital was a ridiculous idea. And, deep down, Mikey must have known that taking me to hospital was risky. He didn't want to get caught - he'd taken as many precautions as possible to prevent that happening. He liked his freedom. Enjoyed his little shopping expeditions to charity shops. Apart from getting praise from his nana and me, that was the only thing that seemed to give him joy. It was sad. And sick. I was sick of feeling sorry for him, trying to understand him. He was a freak and a coward. He needed to man-up and get a life. He might have had an awful upbringing but lots of other people had too, and they didn't do this.

Another horrific idea stabbed. What if I died giving birth but my baby survived?

Don't think about it.

Without me there to try to steer Mikey on the right course, who knew what terrible things would happen.

Don't think about it.

I blinked back tears and focused on the future, and what it would hold when I made it out of here. I calculated when our baby would be born. If I was three months now and it was the first of December, I'd be due around the first week of June. A summer baby, just like me.

No longer able to hold the position, I lowered my arms and rolled my shoulders. I put my ear to the wall and listened intently. There was a sound beneath the music – a soft thud. And another. Was he coming?

Heart in my mouth, I raised the vase.

Chapter 38

I maintained my vigil by the door for hours but Mikey never came. In the end, exhaustion pulled me towards the desk.

I tried to stay awake all night, terrified Mikey would come to see me - passionate words streaming from his lips, unspeakable thoughts roving behind his pale eyes - but I eventually fell asleep with my head on the table, drool dripping onto the pine surface beside the discarded vase.

In the early hours of the morning with the first glow of sun creeping through the curtains, *All I Want for Christmas Is You* smashed through the silence. The music was so loud that the air vibrated. My head snapped up. Groggy from sleep, I reached for the vase and knocked it off the table. It rolled across the carpet but didn't break. Frantically, I stood, smashing my knees on the desk. I lunged for it, but the damn thing was out of reach. I pushed back the chair so that I could move to grab my weapon, but Mikey slipped into the room holding a chocolate advent calendar, a stupid smile stretching his lips. Cursing my stupidity, I perched on the edge of the bed, fingers itching with the desire to grab the crystal bludgeon off the floor and smash it into his face.

He'd dressed and showered, but his eyelids were puffy and red. When he beamed at me, his eyes held a slightly crazed look. 'Like it?'

It was a Disney princess one. When I was five, I'd adored all things Disney. For Christmas that year, Mum and Dad had given me a Disney princess bike. Dad had spent hours and hours teaching me to ride. I was a slow learner, but he'd been patient and loving, the perfect father. Mum had made us sandwiches and brought them out front, so we didn't need to go inside. She'd watched him teach me with a big, proud smile on her face.

Up until the age of about twelve, I'd thought of them as perfect. They were my heroes. Everything they did and said was gospel. My mum and dad were the best parents in the world, and no one could tell me any different. But when I started to talk about being an actress and going to drama school, they'd shown their true colours. Instead of supporting me, they'd belittled the idea and dismissed my dream as if it meant nothing. But it had meant everything to me. They pushed me into studying psychology and tried to steer me away from what I wanted, but I fought back and went my own way. Back then, I'd been brave and strong-willed. Where had that version of me gone? I wanted her back. I needed her to help me get out of here.

Jacob loves Disney too. His favourite's The Lion King.

A brutal hand crushed my heart. I stared through Mikey as he positioned the calendar on the desk opposite the bed, opened number 1, bounded across the room and slipped a chocolate snowman in my mouth. I almost spat it out but reminded myself to play nice. With dead eyes and a tasteless tongue, I forced down the chocolate, anger spiralling, red-eyed and deadly as the devil. I glanced at the tree. Pictured myself ramming plastic needles into the soft yolk of his eye.

As if sensing my rage he darted backwards, hovering too far away for me to reach him. 'Only twenty-four days until Christmas Day! You'll have to make a list of what you want.'

I said nothing.

'What's that? Another jumper?' he said brightly, acting like I'd spoken.

But I couldn't speak.

He scratched his head. 'No? Okay. Maybe you'd like some more books. They're cheap in the charity shop. Only

£1 for six Mills and Boon stories!'

I turned away from him.

'Or what about Goosebumps? I love Goosebumps...Oh, I know! That's a great idea. I'll bring you up a piece of paper and a pencil when I fetch breakfast and you can write a list of things you want.'

He pulled me off the bed. I moved heavily, as if drugged.

Excitedly, he said, 'We're having a full English today, so you need to shower quick or the sausages'll burn.'

He steered me onto the landing, and guided me into the bathroom whistling along to *Santa Baby.*

I showered and dressed, anger burning in my chest like acid.

As soon as Mikey locked me in the Christmas prison, I picked up the crystal vase once more and waited for his return.

Chapter 39

It felt like hours had passed and he still hadn't come back.

I lowered the vase and rolled my shoulders again. The knots in my muscles crunched. I stretched my neck one way then the other and looked over my shoulder at the curtains. They were tightly closed. A tingle ran down my spine – was that the sound of an engine? Was it Mikey's car or had someone else come? I felt pulled towards the elves as if Santa himself was calling me. Was someone out there or was I imagining it? The music was loud – *Silver Bells* was on now - but I could have sworn I'd heard a car. Mikey had said the sausages would burn if he didn't get to them quickly. Did that mean they had burned and he was having to cook new ones or was he busy doing other things like toasting and buttering the bread? He cooked a full English every couple of weeks or so and seemed to take a lot of pride in it. It was the only meal he made from scratch. Everything else was a pop-in-the-oven or microwave kind of deal. Sometimes he added peas, carrots or broccoli on the side, all of which were clearly boiled from frozen. Cooking wasn't his thing unless it was a full English.

Maybe he's burned the sausages and run out of them, so he's driven to the shop to buy more. The sound I heard could be him leaving or coming back.

I looked at the curtains again. Hesitated. I wanted to go over to the window and pull them open, just to see, but if I moved and Mikey came back, my chance to attack would be lost.

What if someone's out there?

Unlikely.

But what if…

My stomach churned. I bit my lip. Indecision locked me in a vise. I put my ear to the wall, tried to hear through the blare of Frank Sinatra's voice. Tears sprang to my eyes. *I'll be home for Christmas* was Jacob's favourite Christmas song. I began to crumble. My heart throbbed like an infected sore.

'Fuck it.'

I shot over to the locked window, held my breath and whipped back the elf curtains. The sky was a blink away from white, primed to snow. My breath misted the glass and I rubbed it clear and stared open-mouthed, unable to believe the mirage before me, because there was a DPD van parked out front. A stumpy woman with short blue hair climbed out of the van looking down at her phone. In her right hand she held a medium-sized parcel. My pulse skipped and I hammered my fist against the window, but she didn't look up. I bashed harder, screamed 'HELP', trying to raise my voice above bloody Frank Sinatra, and beat the glass so hard my hands shrieked in protest, but still, she didn't look up...why couldn't she hear me? Was she deaf? I scanned her face desperately and it was then that I noticed she had earphones in. I screamed again, mouth flush against the window, but she disappeared. I stopped screaming and stared at the van. If only I could get to it…

Music blasted through the house. Frank was finished. Now it was Nat King Cole's turn.

The sound of knocking drew my attention to the bedroom door, and Ethel's voice hissed into the room, 'Be quiet girl, or suffer the consequences.'

I bit back a retort, knowing there was no time to engage with her, and even less point. She was clearly terrified that the DPD woman was going to realise something weird was going on and try to help me. The fact that the hag was rattled gave me hope. Ignoring more hissed orders, I decided on a plan: when the delivery lady headed back towards the van, I'd throw the chair at the window. The noise ought to get her attention.

I rushed over to the desk, placed the vase down, seized the chair, carried it over to the window and raised it to my shoulder. It was light but sturdy. I stood with my feet hip-width apart and focused on the van. Any second now she ought to appear. Any second…

BAM! There she was, striding back to the van with a swing in her hips.

I threw the chair directly at the window. It smacked into the glass and a great thud penetrated the Christmas music. The driver glanced up at me, and did a double-take. I screamed HELP as loud as I could. She froze, eyes locked on mine. Horror and understanding widened her eyes and her brown eyebrows shot up into her blue fringe. She was quick. One look at my crazed expression and she'd clocked everything. Relief bloomed in my chest as her gaze flicked away from mine towards the front door. After a split second's hesitation, she turned and ran towards the van. Despite her stocky build, she was fast. She reached the van and yanked open the door. Instead of climbing inside, she stayed on the ground and reached in. What was she doing?

Please let her be dialling 999. Please, God, please. Or grabbing an axe. That would do the trick.

Mikey flew into view, hunched over, long legs moving fast. In both hands he held a frying pan. He raced towards her, pan raised; and she spun around with a can of something in her hand and sprayed it at his face. The pan hit the earth, his hands moved to his eyes, and he stumbled backwards, bent at the waist. The DPD lady looked up at me and gave a quick nod. Eyes on Mikey, who was on his knees, hands clasped around his face, she strode forward and smashed her elbow into his temple. He fell onto his side and curled into a ball. She delivered a kick to his ribs, watched him for second, then hurried towards the house.

I watched Mikey writhing around on the ground and prayed he was too hurt to get up. Either he was being a drama queen, or he was in real pain. Hopefully it was the latter. The woman looked like she'd kicked him pretty hard. She might have cracked a rib or two. Anything to slow him down was good. If he got on his feet, he wouldn't be so easy to fight. The DPD driver looked even shorter than me. The way she'd attacked suggested she had some sort of combat training, kickboxing perhaps, but Mikey was strong and fast and at least a foot taller than her. I doubted she'd be able to beat him once he recovered from her kick to the ribs. Also, wasn't it true that madness overrode pain? Was that a myth I'd picked up – an old wives' tale - or something I'd learned during my psychology course? I couldn't remember. For now, at least, he remained on the ground hugging his knees to his chest. I couldn't see his face but imagined tears ran from his reddened eyes. The thought gave me a zing of sadistic pleasure. The more pain he was in, the less threat he posed and the more likely it was that I would escape, but it was also nice to imagine him in pain. After everything he'd put me through, he deserved a little comeuppance.

A moment later, the muffled thud of racing steps met my ears. I ran to the door. The woman was already trying to open it.

'It's locked,' I shouted. 'The key's on a lanyard around his neck. Have you called the police?'

'There's no reception up here,' she shouted back. 'I'll go get the key. What's your name? I'm Bethan.'

'Rachel Brown.'

'The missing actress? Oh shit. Right, don't worry Rachel. I'm getting you out of here. Just hold on. I'll be right back.'

'No – wait!'

'What?'

'There's an old woman here too.'

'Oh, okay. Back in a sec.'

Abruptly the Christmas music cut out.

I realised I hadn't told the driver that the old woman in

the house was dangerous. I screamed, 'She's with him!'

Muffled voices came from the room next door. The voices moved onto the landing.

Ethel rasped, 'He's crazy! He's kept us here for months. Please help us.'

'Don't worry. I'll get you out. Wait here a moment. I'll just get the key to let Rachel out then I'll help you down the stairs.' It was Bethan.

'Oh, thank you so much.'

'Don't listen to her!' I screamed.

'What? Why?' Bethan said.

'She's gone mad,' Ethel said, 'she's not well. Go, get the keys then come back for us.'

'No! She's danger-'

There was a gasp then the sound of something falling down the stairs.

Silence flooded the cottage.

The slow creak of descending footsteps pierced the air.

'What's going on?' I shouted.

No one answered.

My pulse slammed in my throat. I knew what had happened but didn't want to accept it. Ethel had pushed the driver down the stairs. I pictured Bethan lying at the bottom of the steps, neck twisted. If she was dead, all hope was lost.

The stairs continued to creak as Ethel descended. How was she walking? She had to be in agony, and yet, once again, when disaster struck, the evil hag found the strength to get up and hurt others.

I listened hard, praying she'd lose her footing, fall, and crack her head so badly that her rotten brain burst out of her skull like a smashed piñata.

But of course that didn't happen.

After another three creaks, silence swooped down again, heavy and toxic as a nuclear bomb. I imagined the wrathful shrew leaning over, checking the woman's pulse, smiling when there wasn't one. My mind raced as I attempted to draw something positive from what had happened. If Bethan had been marking her progress with her deliveries and she didn't check in after this house, would someone investigate? Would DPD send someone out to the cottage? Would they call the police when they couldn't get in touch with her? How long would they leave it before they followed up on her disappearance? She'd probably marked Mikey's parcel as delivered when she'd first gone to the front door, but when she didn't deliver the next parcel, her line manager would be concerned and follow it up. If her line manager was any good at his or her job, surely they'd chase up an answer as quickly as possible. When they couldn't get in touch with the driver, they'd have to alert the police.

A shriek rang out. It sounded like Ethel.

I dashed to the window to see the driver limp into view. She froze and stared at the ground.

Mikey had gone.

Chapter 40

Snowflakes drifted down settling on Bethan's head and speckling the ground like Chicken Pox spots. She pushed back her fringe and looked up at me through the feathery air. Confusion pinched her forehead, adding years to her age. She couldn't have been much more than twenty-five. Too young to go through something like this, to be haunted for the rest of her life – if she survives.

At least she's still alive.

She is, for now.

I shrugged back and squinted through the snow, frantically trying to see where Mikey had gone. Could he still be out there somewhere waiting for the perfect moment to attack Bethan? I watched as she scanned the front of the cottage. She looked calm, but the set of her shoulders spoke volumes. I didn't know this woman, but terror was an easy thing to spot. Her spine was as stiff as a steel rod, every sense alert and twitching. Slowly, she walked towards her van, eyes on the can of pepper spray that she'd dropped earlier.

Be careful, Bethan. He could be anywhere.

No he couldn't. There's nowhere to hide.

There weren't any trees or buildings out the front of the cottage. No sheds or fences or upturned wheelbarrows. The ground was rock, soil, grass and moss, nothing more. The only objects out there were the two vehicles. Unless…

He could have gone around the back of the cottage through the back door and hidden in the kitchen. He could have gone to get a knife or something else equally terrifying. He might have even entered via the front door once Bethan had disappeared upstairs. He could have easily hidden in the living room or the dining room, biding his time until the right opportunity presented itself to get the upper hand and take Bethan by surprise.

I found myself wishing Bethan had knocked him unconscious before she'd left him or, better still, killed him. I didn't feel guilty at the wish, just regretful. If Bethan had killed Mikey, neither of us would be in danger right now – all of this would be over.

Bethan leaned over and picked up the pepper spray. She stood and peered around the open space, eyeing Mikey's car for a few seconds before turning her attention to the cottage. The snow grew heavier, settling on both vehicles and whitening Bethan's hair and shoulders. She was shivering now – from fear and cold I guessed. She shielded her eyes from the downfall and met mine. I tried to work out what she should do next – if Mikey was in the cottage, which seemed likely, she couldn't risk going back inside. But that meant she'd have to hightail it away in the van and leave me here. While she was gone, any number of things could happen. Ethel – if she was still alive that was – might decide it was time for Mikey to kill me before it was too late and the police rolled up. Would Mikey be able to kill me? He'd just confessed his undying love for me…was he so fickle that he could go from loving me to killing me in a heartbeat?

Yes.

No.

He won't have a choice. She'll force him. She always does.

Everyone has a choice.

Bethan raised a hand and waved at me. I shrugged again, indicating I had no clue as to his whereabouts.

She nodded grimly then turned towards the van.

I watched her, all hope deflating, wishing she'd pull out a gun and go inside and shoot him dead then get the key and let me out, but knowing that was never going to happen.

Bethan hurried around the front of the vehicle heading for the driver's side.

Something – a shadow – moved behind the windscreen.

He's in the van.

The realisation flew into my mind like a murder of crows, stabbing and jabbing and tearing with violent need. I banged my fists against the window and Bethan turned her face back towards mine. After a slight delay, she raised her hand to shield her eyes, brows up in question, mouth stretched into an O.

'HE'S IN THE VAN!' I screamed.

With no music to drown out my voice, my words travelled to her, but they were too late.

Mikey leapt out of the van and threw himself on top of her. Bethan fell to her knees, neck bent, and Mikey wrapped his arms around her throat and began to squeeze.

Déjà vu enveloped my brain as echoes of Simon's death swallowed all else. I was helpless once more, unable to help her. I couldn't let another person die because of me, but there was nothing I could do except watch and pray Mikey was going to slip up or Bethan was going to fight back.

Bethan wasn't going to go down without a fight; somehow, she twisted round and caught Mikey in the side of the head with her elbow. The hit loosened his grip enough for her to flip him over onto his back. He landed in the settling snow with a thud I could hear through the window. Wind knocked out of him, he barely had time to bring his knees up to his chest in protection before Bethan was staggering to her feet and landing a series of kicks to his torso. After the fifth kick, Mikey stopped writhing and Bethan paused for a breath, hands on hips. She looked like she was struggling for breath. Bent a little at the waist, she reached into her jeans and pulled out a small blue inhaler and took two puffs, eyes never leaving Mikey. He was still conscious, but not making any attempt to get up. I half-wanted her to carry on kicking him until she was certain he posed no more threat, but she seemed satisfied that he was out of action.

She lowered herself to her haunches, staying a foot away from him, and held the can of pepper spray up. In a loud, firm voice, she said, 'If you move an inch, I'll use this again.'

Mikey nodded, eyes wide and scared. His cheeks were wet, from snow or tears or both I couldn't be sure, but he seemed to be in a lot of pain.

She nodded sharply, gave me a quick smile, then placed the pepper spray beside her on the ground and said, 'Give me the lanyard. Now.'

Slowly, Mikey uncurled and pulled the lanyard over his head.

This was actually happening. Bethan was going to save me. I was getting out of here. Me and my baby were getting out of here.

Blurry-eyed, I focused on Bethan, who shifted so that her back faced me. Still on her haunches, she removed the lanyard strap from the key ring and instructed Mikey to crawl towards her van. He did so immediately, cheeks wet, breathing laboured. Once next to the door, Bethan tied the strap around the side mirror then tied the other end around Mikey's wrist binding him to the car. It was a clever idea. Mikey made no move to argue or fight back. It was as if the will had been knocked out of him, as if he'd accepted defeat. Relief made me weak; now that he posed no threat, Bethan could come back inside the cottage and unlock the bedroom door without any fear that he'd come after her.

After checking that there was no way Mikey could untie the knots with one hand, Bethan turned around and gave me a thumbs-up. I waved back, urging her to hurry. I thought about how I'd ever repay her for her courage; wondered if I could petition for her to receive the George Cross, knew that would never be enough. Nothing would ever come close to showing her how much she'd done for me, this complete stranger who'd risked everything for me without a second's hesitation.

Bethan hurried towards the house and vanished from view. I watched Mikey for a moment, suddenly afraid he was going to untie himself and run after her, but he remained on his knees tied to the side mirror, head bowed.

Feeling sorry for yourself Mikey? Now you know how it feels.

A hard beat of hatred hit. For a second, I wanted to kick him now, when he was down, scream in his face, tell him what he'd put me through, make him suffer. But there was something so pitiful about him now, so vulnerable and childlike, that I knew even if I had the chance to do that, I wouldn't be able to go through with it. The courts would make sure he was punished for this and treated for whatever mental health issues haunted him. Ethel would pay too. I was glad now that I'd managed to keep her alive; she'd live to suffer for her crimes, though I doubted she'd ever suffer as much as Mikey had at her hands.

My neck snapped down towards the floor as a bang sounded. The bang was so loud it felt as if it had taken place in the bedroom. Panic flooded my system, killing all relief. There was no mistaking that sound for anything else: it had come from a gun.

A blur of movement caught my eye and I looked out of the window to see Bethan running towards the van. Mikey's head was up, trained on the front of the cottage. He wasn't looking at Bethan but past her, at something else, and he looked shocked but pleased.

Another shot rang out and Ethel hobbled into view holding a shotgun. The huge weapon wobbled in her grasp, making her sway and teeter to the side.

Bethan ran for the van, heading for the driver's side. She slipped and fell to her hands and knees.

Ethel stopped walking, hauled the gun to her shoulder, took aim and fired for a third time. She staggered backward and somehow managed to remain standing. The bullet skimmed Bethan's right arm and she cried out and rolled onto her side. Blood soaked through her grey jumper and puddled on the ground beside her.

'GET UP! RUN!' I screamed.

Bethan scrambled to her feet and lurched towards the driver's door. Ethel lowered the gun and hobbled after her, dragging it by her side like a dead leg. Her skeletal face was as white as the snow, and shiny with sickness.

As Bethan slammed the door shut, Ethel raised the gun. Her arms shook from the weapon's weight, yet she crowed with victory and held the gun aloft, madness gifting her a devilish strength that defied rhyme or reason.

The van's engine roared to life and Bethan began to reverse, dragging Mikey backwards along the ground, his legs flipping out in front of his body, flailing madly. He reached up and clung on to the side mirror with his free hand as the van reversed faster, swerving side to side. Ethel fired again and the bullet shattered the windscreen, spraying chips of glass over the bonnet. Blood splattered Bethan's face: but she remained upright, growing smaller as the van continued its chaotic retreat. Ethel let the gun drop to her side. Her body heaved. Mikey grappled with the side mirror, shouting words I couldn't make out, his face contorted with fear and pain, and then suddenly, the mirror snapped off the car and he thudded to the ground and lay in a twisted heap.

Had Bethan been shot? It was impossible to tell.

The van was now about fifty metres back from the cottage, but instead of speeding up, it was slowing down. Ethel dragged the gun by her side and limped steadily towards the van, which was grinding to a halt. She wore only her white nightgown, a brown cardigan and slippers. Dirt and blood mussed her long, straggly hair. She looked like a walking corpse, a zombie trudging after the living.

That's if Bethan's even still alive…

The van rolled to a stop, engine humming. Glass

sprinkled the bonnet like crystals. Snow continued to fall like frozen tears.

I pressed my nose to the window and tried to see if Bethan was moving, but all I could make out was a smudge of blue hair above the shattered windscreen. Ethel limped on, possessed by inhuman strength, undeterred by her injuries or the weight of the gun, which must have pulled savagely on her neck wound. Was she numb from the cold? Able to carry on because she could no longer feel any pain? Or was she indeed a thing possessed by the devil, her rotten soul replaced by a heinous core of rage and hate able to vivify the dying?

I didn't know. All I knew what that Bethan had to be alive. She had to fight.

There was movement – slow but definite behind the wheel. The driver's door opened and Bethan staggered into view clutching her cheek. Scarlet bloomed between her fingers. Either she'd been shot in the face or glass had cut her; I prayed it was the latter. She managed three steps then dropped to all fours on the ice-cold snow. She rolled onto her back, hand still held to her cheek, chest heaving, face turned towards Ethel, who continued her slow advance, gun drawing a narrow path in the snow behind her like the road to hell.

Blood streamed from Bethan's cheek and puddled on the ground melting into the snow and turning it to red slush.

'GET UP! BETHAN, GET UP!' I screamed. I pounded my palms against the window, useless as ever, unable to do anything but watch.

The snow stopped as Ethel stopped a foot away from Bethan's body. Mikey's head moved in their direction. He was still alive. Was Bethan?

Bethan lay as still as the dead. Her chest wasn't rising and falling anymore.

With difficulty, Ethel lifted the gun to her shoulder. Her

body trembled, but she held the gun aloft and aimed the nozzle at Bethan's face.

She fired.

Chapter 41

I closed my eyes, turned and vomited on the carpet. My insides heaved and I wretched, but nothing more came out. Watching had been a mistake. I should have looked away, but horror and respect stole all sense and kept me glued to the end. Bethan didn't deserve to be alone when she died. By watching, I'd accompanied her in some small way. Total bullshit, but it made the horror slightly less acute.

I risked a glance. Flesh scattered the snow like crushed red velvet cake. It looked like the scene of a massacre.

Ethel let the gun drop to the ground. Her shoulders were rounded, body quivering. She looked up directly at me. A slow smile stretched her lips. I couldn't make out the expression in her eyes and was glad because I knew it would reek of victory. She'd beaten Bethan, ruined my chances of escape, killed her enemy, taken her down despite her own ill health and age. To her, Bethan was no more than an ant she'd crushed beneath her heel. She wouldn't feel remorse or guilt for murdering the heroic young woman; she'd feel only relief and delight that she'd triumphed against the odds; that she'd won, and Bethan had lost. Ethel wasn't the sort of person who did guilt. She didn't have a conscience. What she'd done just now wouldn't keep her up at night. It wouldn't give her cold sweats or drive her insane. She was already insane. Only an utterly unhinged person would allow an untrained doctor to remove a tumour from their neck to play into a lie designed to control someone else; it was warped and totally crazy. She was mad, and completely amoral. The most dangerous sort of monster because she didn't feel empathy. She was someone who would do anything they could to come out on top and get what they wanted, no matter how deranged those wants were. She didn't care who she hurt as long as her selfish needs were met.

It's my fault they're dead. First Simon, now Bethan. Who's next?

And where are the police! Why the hell haven't they worked it out by now?

She was barking orders at Mikey, limping towards him through the snow, gun abandoned beside the body, lying on the snow like an amputated limb.

To my horror, a crow landed on Bethan's chest and began to peck at what remained of her face. My gorge rose again. I breathed through it; tried to calm myself with thoughts of my baby. Stress could damage the foetus; I wasn't sure exactly how, but I knew it was true. There was no way of avoiding stress, but if I could fixate on something else, it might help.

Focus on revenge. On killing the murderous bitch. On all the things you'll do to her when you get the chance.

Mikey dragged himself up. He was clearly in great pain, movements slow and laboured, face as white as the snow around him. His clothes were wet-through, Christmas jumper sticking to his torso like a second skin. He was shivering too and hugging himself for warmth.

Ethel continued to bark instructions at him. He nodded glumly, head down. Body concave as if every inch hurt, he trudged towards the body, taking care to avoid the flesh scattered the ground like lumps of Play Doh. Sensing his presence, the crow fluttered away soaring high like a black omen against the sky, taking a piece of Bethan with it in its beak.

Ethel turned to watch Mikey. She stabbed her finger at the body then at him then at the van as she fired order after order. Mikey said nothing. He nodded and wiped his eyes. I wondered if he was crying. Every time she yelled a command he flinched. He couldn't look at the body. When he reached Bethan's feet, he bent over, turned his face to the side and vomited. Ethel shook her head bitterly and clapped her hands in mock applause then barked more orders, her words indistinct but her tone sharp and shrill in the cold air, reaching me through the distance and glass well enough to send shivers down my back. It was almost as if she was in her element; controlling him like a puppet master; jerking his strings to her own sick tune, imposing order upon the chaos she'd wreaked.

Mikey wiped his hand with his sleeve, sucked a few lungfuls of air then took hold of Bethan's feet. He made sure to keep chin raised, eyes up. He began to drag her around the back of the van taking a careful route to avoid the bloody debris. He stopped to catch his breath, hands on his hips, chest heaving, and she barked at him again. He jumped and grabbed her feet and managed to pull off her boot. For a second, he looked at it blankly in his hand. She screeched and he dropped the boot, seized her feet again and dragged her around the back. He disappeared. I pictured him hauling the body into the cargo area, heaving her body onto the packages that lay inside, her blood staining them scarlet. He reappeared shaking so badly he stumbled and fell to one knee. Ethel screamed and jabbed her finger. He trudged forward, picked up the boot and returned to the rear of the vehicle.

He smeared sweat from his forehead and spoke to her. She hooked a finger and he approached slowly, head bowed like a shameful pupil. She slapped him across the face then stabbed her finger into his chest and ranted some more. He nodded, wiped his eyes then returned to the back of the van. He came back holding Bethan's key ring.

Ethel clapped mockingly once more.

She stood back and watched as he got in behind the wheel and started the engine. He reversed the van a few metres then turned and drove off. He hadn't taken any petrol with him this time, so I wondered what he was planning to do with the van. Drive it off the mountain?

Hide it in some woods? How long would it take before it was recovered?

Snow fell once more, this time so thickly it obscured Ethel from view. I prayed she'd freeze to death out there, that her heart would give out and she'd drop dead and turn to ice, but several minutes later I heard the front door slam. The stairs creaked as she ascended very slowly. I half-expected her to boast about her victory or scream murder at me when she reached the landing, but I heard the creak of her bedroom door as she entered her room and the wheeze of her mattress as she lay down. Though she hadn't spoken to me, I knew she wouldn't let it go. Soon she'd come to deliver my punishment. I just hoped that punishment didn't involve sleeping in the well in the snow.

Exhausted and too weary to stand, I made my way to the bed and sat down with my head in my hands. The smell of sick filled the room bringing bile to my throat. My temples pounded savagely, and my ears roared. I stared at the door, tried to think of a way out of this mess. Nothing came. I placed my hand on my stomach, tried to focus on saving my baby.

Maybe the sound of the gun travelled. Maybe someone heard the shots. Called the police. Maybe they're on the way here right now.

A creak pierced the silence. My head shot up as a voice croaked through the door, 'If you don't make me a baby soon, you're next.'

*

A taxi dropped Mikey off after dark. Snow had blanketed the mountain, hiding what remained of the incident. I ran to the window and watched him trudge towards the cottage with his hands deep in his pockets, backlit by the driver's lights. He still wore the same clothes as earlier, but they looked dry. Had the driver noticed anything strange – seen any blood on Mikey? All I could do was pray that they had.

I screamed and smashed on the window but the taxi rolled away.

Mikey paused beneath my window and glanced up at me. I hesitated, then raised my hand in greeting. He didn't smile or wave back. He hung his head. He looked completely defeated, miserable and broken. The worst I'd seen him.

I heard the front door open and shut. Heard the click of the lock. Then nothing for a while.

I sat on the bed, legs jigging.

After a while, the stairs creaked. Ethel's voice came, 'Get me a ciggy, boy, then we need to discuss important matters.'

He went back down the stairs moving slowly.

I willed him to grow a backbone, but as always he obeyed her, returning a minute later and disappearing into her room. I dashed to the wall and tried to make out their words. Ethel was doing all of the talking while Mikey remained muter than I'd ever known him.

'You need to take her, boy. There's no time to waste. I'm dying and I need to see my great-grandchild on this earth before I pass. I will see him or her before I die. Not tonight while you're still recovering from what that blue-haired bitch did to you, but tomorrow, after you've showered. Oh yes, it's important to make yourself clean and presentable, and remember to brush your teeth. Things like that make a difference. Now, you need to be prepared for her to make a fuss. She'll likely play hard to get, like I told you before, but you can't take no for an answer. You must do this. There's no two ways about it. Understand?'

It was as if she was speaking more loudly than normal to make sure I heard every horrific word. She sounded excited. And desperate.

Amid the surging dread, I found an iota of hope. Was she so desperate because she could feel her body failing? Was the cancer digging in its claws?

I listened for Mikey's response, but he didn't utter a single word. I pictured him nodding, desperate as ever to please her.

Chills exploded on my skin as I imagined him touching me.

I hadn't eaten anything all day, but I wasn't hungry. I felt sick again, so sick and faint I had to lie down. Unable to go to the bathroom, I'd had to twist off the ceramic Santa's head and pee in that. Turned out it was some sort of grotesque cookie jar.

Now, in the red-tinted light of my prison, I picked up the crystal vase, realising there was only one way to protect myself and my unborn child from the horror that tomorrow would bring.

Chapter 42

Mikey didn't come to see me that night. It was almost as if he'd forgotten I existed, though of course I knew he hadn't – not after the talking to Ethel had given him. I'd listened to him make his way to the bathroom then head to his bedroom. Within seconds I heard him snoring. Ethel coughed away all night. Both sounds drilled into my skull making sleep impossible. My mind ran in circles with vision after vision of me attempting to fight Mikey, and him easily fighting me off and raping me. I couldn't stop imagining the pain that it would involve and worrying that the act would kill my baby. At three months along – if I was right that was – the chances of miscarriage were low, but such a brutal attack was bound to affect my pregnancy in some way. How could it not? Could a baby that immature survive such a traumatic event? Could I, after everything I'd been through? Would I fall to pieces? Would my mind finally shatter and fracture into a thousand shards like Mikey's had?

I tried to tell myself that I should just let it happen. Let him do it. If I let him, surely it would be less painful, less traumatic.

That's a load of crap. You know you won't be able to do that anyway. You'll fight back. You won't be able to stop yourself.

If, though, by some miracle, my original plan worked and I managed to knock him unconscious with the vase before he even touched me, I could escape unharmed. Everything would be okay, but only if I could pull off the ambush unscathed.

And what are the chances of you managing that? You're small and weak and pregnant.

I gnawed my already raw nail. Shook my head. Mikey was hurt. Bethan had beaten him badly, which meant he was weaker than normal, more vulnerable to attack. Maybe, if I hit him in his ribs where she'd kicked him, instead of his head, I'd stand more chance of incapacitating him.

Maybe you could reason with him? He says he loves you. Play on that.

I pulled the covers up around my shoulders and hugged my knees trying to quell the shaking that had possessed my body. There was a small chance Mikey could be persuaded not to hurt me, but that chance was so small I didn't think it was worth the risk. He was still under her control. Nothing I did or said would change that…unless…maybe I could tell him I loved him too, but that I wasn't ready for us to 'make love' yet. That I wanted it to be special, to happen at the right time under the right circumstances.

Indecision churned my guts to butter.

I didn't know what to do. All I knew was that I had to do something. Morning was rising. Outside the snow was still falling. The police weren't coming.

It wouldn't be long until Mikey came knocking.

Chapter 43

The lock clicked and my spine tingled. I held the vase next to my right shoulder in both hands, teeth gritted, waiting. After a few seconds, the knob rotated and the door swung outwards, but Mikey didn't appear. My arms shook and my heart rammed itself against my ribs. I waited.

Mikey's leg appeared. The edge of a tray followed, then his chest. I brought the vase crashing into his chest above the tray; it was the best I could do. Aim for the bastard's heart – I'd wanted to go for his ribs, but the tray was in the way.

He cried out and shot backwards, dropping the tray. The full makings of an English fry up fell to the carpet blending with the stench of stale vomit and urine.

Mikey charged forward as I brought the vase in for another attack – this time aiming for his face. The vase connected with his jaw, and he gasped but kept moving towards me, propelling me backwards by my shoulders.

The backs of my knees connected with the iron railing sending pain spiralling through my legs, and I fell onto my back with him on top of me, crushing my legs against the metal end of the bed. I screamed as agony sliced through my muscles and then - despite everything - even with the glint of rage, confusion and hurt in his face - he rolled onto his side and hoisted my whole body onto the bed so that my legs weren't being crushed against the iron end. With a grunt, he straddled me and hooked his brown-socked feet under my shins, holding me down by my shoulders.

'What did you do that for? I was only bringing you breakfast!'

His eyes glistened. He sniffed and I realised he was

crying. He frowned as if deeply hurt and shook his head at me. 'You shouldn't have done that.'

'I – I'm sorry. I thought -'

'Now I'll have to start all over again,' he said, looking back at the food splattering the carpet.

'I'll have to go out and get more sausages.'

He pulled the cuffs out of his pocket, and I writhed beneath him, 'No! Please don't, Mikey. I can't bear those things.'

'I believed I could trust you but Nana's right. I can't. You just want to hurt me like everyone else.'

'That's not true. I only did it because I thought you were going to try to hurt me.'

His jaw dropped. 'I'd never hurt you. I love you.' He smiled sheepishly. His cheeks flushed. Dark shadows ringed his pale eyes. He looked younger than ever.

'Oh. Good. Because last night I thought I heard her saying something to you about -'

Mikey's eyes clouded and he looked away and muttered, 'I need to go to the shop now. I'm sorry, Doc, but I have to cuff you. It's the only way, especially after,' he swallowed thickly, his gaze darting to mine and away again towards the window, 'after what happened yesterday.'

He snapped the cuff onto my wrist and attached the other end to the iron railing behind my head. My hopes curdled and died.

'You mean, after what she did to that poor lady,' I said, lowering my voice and willing him to look at me.

His eyes glazed over. In a thin voice, he said, 'Yes. That was…bad. But Nana didn't have a choice. She -'

'Everyone has a choice.'

He looked at me, sunk his teeth into his lip so hard it turned white. Red streaked the whites of his eyes. Beneath the scent of mint lay a bitter, metallic smell. He'd brushed his teeth, but it hadn't done much good. He smelled soapy from the shower but under that there was a sickly stink too, an even nastier smell than that of the stale vomit that lay on the carpet beneath the bedroom window. It was as if nothing could make him clean.

'Her name was Bethan,' I said softly. 'She was a nice young woman, and Ethel killed her just because she was trying to help me.'

'I don't know what you mean. Nana was trying to protect me. That – that – blue-haired bitch was trying to kill me!'

'That's not true, Mikey, and you know it.'

He met my eye. A frown gripped the space between his brows and anger twisted his face into something unrecognisable. 'All I know is Nana wants what's best for me. For us. And she's right. She's always right.'

'No, Mikey. Think for yourself. Was she right to shoot Bethan in the face? Was she right to burn you with cigarettes? Was she right to scald you in the bath? Was she right to put you down a well? In what world is any of that right? The right thing would have been to make you sit on a naughty step when you misbehaved. Or send you to your bedroom for a bit. Hurting you was wrong.'

'But her mother hurt her to make her good. That's why…that's why…'

Confusion masked his features. He slipped his thumb into his mouth and began to hum *Silent Night.*

'Mikey? Mikey! Listen to me -'

But he was gone, his mind in another place, lost to its infinite demons. He climbed off me and moved trance-like to the door where he proceeded to pick up the spilled breakfast items and return them to the tray.

He paused at the door and whispered, 'I must get more sausages,' then carried the tray out of the room and locked the door behind him, leaving me alone to dwell on my catastrophic failure and its likely consequences.

Chapter 44

Mikey returned about an hour later. With a spring in his step and a secret smile, he placed the breakfast tray on the bedside table and perched on the bed then forked up some baked beans and held them to my mouth.

'I can feed myself,' I said between gulps of orange juice. I hadn't drunk anything since the previous morning and at that moment nothing had ever tasted so good.

He wrinkled his nose and lowered the fork to the plate. 'What's that smell?'

My mouth popped open. I couldn't believe he'd only just noticed. 'I was sick yesterday after seeing what Ethel did to poor Bethan. Oh, and I had to pee in Santa.'

His Adam's apple bobbed, and he darted up and away from the bed towards the wardrobe. Wrinkling his nose, he picked up the ceramic cookie jar. Holding it away from himself as if it contained poison, he hurried to the door and glanced back at me, an embarrassed flush crawling down his neck. 'Back in a jiffy.'

He opened, shut and locked the door in double-quick speed. I listened to him hotfoot it to the bathroom.

I crammed as much breakfast down my throat as I could, hoping I'd be able to finish it before he came back and insisted on feeding me.

He was obviously trying to be romantic, and the thought made me feel sick. I pushed the idea away and shovelled egg and sausage into my mouth, chewing quickly. I was hungrier than I'd thought, ravenous now that the food was in front of me. This baby needed food.

I had almost finished when he came back carrying a bucket of steaming water, wearing marigolds. He didn't bother to shut or lock the door. He dashed over to the window, crinkled his nose and got down on his knees where he scrubbed and scrubbed for ages, muttering something under his breath. When he was done, he stood, pulled out the lanyard, found the right key and unlocked the window, opening it a couple of inches.

Icy air blasted into the room. Outside, six inches of snow blanketed the mountain, and giant flakes continued to fall. It was as pretty as a postcard. Beautiful but deadly.

'What did you do with Bethan and the van?' I said.

His back stiffened. After a long pause, he murmured, 'Hid them.'

He glanced around; chin raised a notch as if proud of himself. 'I wiped down the steering wheel and door, just like Nana told me to. Don't worry, I won't get caught.'

'Where did you hide them?'

'The woods.'

By now the van would be covered with snow. The trees around it would be covered by snow too. What were the chances of anyone discovering it any time soon?

Zilch. No one's going out in this weather anyway. It's too dangerous.

He retrieved the bucket and practically ran out of the room.

I hastily finished the breakfast and orange juice.

A few minutes later, he returned, forehead shiny, something hidden behind his back. The fact he was beaming from ear to ear made warning bells blare in my head.

'I'm desperate for the toilet,' I said.

Disappointment shadowed his face, but he recovered quickly. With a grin, he said, 'Close your eyes for a sec.'

I sighed and did as I was told, bladder burning.

'You can open them now.'

I looked. Both hands were visible. One reached into his jumper for the handcuff key. He leaned over me and uncuffed me from the bed, and I fought the urge to headbutt him, knowing it would never be enough.

Coward.

Shut. Up.

Mikey steered me out of the room, close to my back, his body odour rife now that he'd worked up a sweat cleaning the carpet. We both jumped at the sight of Ethel standing in her bedroom doorway leaning against the wall. Her face was pale and sweaty. Clumps of hair stuck to her hollow cheeks. She looked like a living corpse. Pleasure rippled through me. She'd exerted herself too much yesterday.

Please, God, let her drop down dead. Let her die.

'I need a ciggy. Now.'

'Yes, Nana. Right away. Doctor Sparks just needs to use the bathroom -'

'Now.'

Mikey jumped. She turned and hobbled back into her room. Mikey pushed me in front of him after her. The room reeked of cigarettes and sickness. Mikey pushed me down to sit on the edge of the bed then helped Ethel back into bed and covered her with a blanket.

She glared at him, eyes glassy. 'What took you so long?'

'Are you in a lot of pain, Ethel?' I said.

She eyed me suspiciously but nodded. 'Yes. My neck feels like it's on fire.'

The wound didn't appear to be seeping. I'd covered it with a fresh wound dressing two days ago and the bandage was still white and clean-looking.

'Would you like some morphine?' I said.

I'd offered her morphine every day ever since I realised she'd be better off dead, but she always refused, saying paracetamol would be enough. It was possible she was onto me. If I had the chance to give her morphine again, I wanted to stab her in the eye with the needle or give her an overdose. Mikey might get mad and kill me, but I didn't think he would want to lose me too. Being alone was something he feared more than anything else. And besides, he loved me – or at least he thought he did. If push came to shove, I had to believe he wouldn't kill me.

But he might. You can't risk it.

My eye found the bottle of morphine and syringe. They were on her chest of drawers.

'Paracetamol will do nicely,' she said dryly, following my gaze.

I nodded and dutifully removed two tablets from the packet on her bedside table. Why she couldn't do that herself was a mystery to me. For some reason, she seemed keen to maintain the façade of me being a real doctor.

Once she'd taken the pills, Mikey handed her a cigarette and lit it.

'You know those things'll kill you,' I said. The words were out before I could stop them.

She looked at me sharply, eyes narrowed to pinheads. With a slow smile, she turned her focus to Mikey and patted his hand. 'So, when are the happy couple going to try for their first baby?'

Mikey blushed scarlet and mumbled something into his penguin jumper. My stomach clenched.

'Speak up, boy. We can't hear you,' she snapped.

'I said, um, soon.'

She nodded and gave me a wicked smile. 'Good. That's what I like to hear. Now off you go you two lovebirds. I'm looking forward to hearing all about it later, Mikey.'

Mikey swallowed and darted a worried glance at me. He seized my arm and pulled me to my feet, hurrying us out of the room and shutting the door before she could say anything else. For the millionth time, I was furious at myself. I could have attacked her. I was only a foot away. If I had any guts, I could have launched myself at her face, jabbed my nails in her eyes. I didn't need the needle to do serious damage…

But Mikey would have hurt you. Maybe even killed you.

He wouldn't kill me. He thinks he loves me.

You're wrong. He's insane. He's killed two people. Of course he'll kill you. He won't even hesitate.

It was a constant battle. A constant question – to attack or not to attack? Will he or won't he kill you if you kill her?

I imagined squeezing the life out of her; how close I was, how she could be dead right now. Next time I'd do it. Next time I'd make a move. I just had to find the perfect moment.

Mikey opened the bathroom door and jostled me inside. I shut the door behind me and hurried to the toilet. Relief spread through my lower half. Now that I was pregnant, I felt like I needed to pee constantly, and I'd been holding this one in for ever.

I went very still. Sniffed. Shook my head at myself. For a second, I'd smelt Jacob. His aftershave, his smell.

I sighed heavily, wondering if I'd finally lost it. The stress and madness was making me imagine things. It was bad for the baby but there was nothing I could do to make things better.

Fresh clothes were already hanging over the edge of the bath. I moved them onto the toilet lid then took a long shower, hoping Mikey wouldn't rush me. Beneath the water, I tried to work out what he'd been hiding behind his back. More sexy lingerie? A present of some kind? It was small enough to fit in his pocket whatever it was.

I looked down at my stomach and a jolt of shock hit: my belly was slightly distended, rounder, bigger. I was beginning to show. This was real. It wasn't a figment of my warped imagination. I was pregnant with Jacob's baby.

Thinking about Jacob made my resolve harden. I was getting our baby out of this alive if it was the last thing I did. A second later, I felt myself begin to crumble as images of sexual assault attacked my mind. I felt breakfast swirling in the pit of my stomach. Turning off the shower,

I sat down in the wet bathtub and hung my head between my knees.

Breathe, Rachel. You're okay. Everything's going to be okay.

But panic was rising, taking over.

Mikey's voice rang out and my head shot up. 'Everything okay in there, Doc? I'm wai-ting!' He sang the last word like he was the happiest man alive.

I wanted to throttle him. I wanted to kill them both.

Is it possible to strangle someone with tinsel?

Stop. Stay calm. Keep it together.

With an almighty effort, I dried myself off, and picked up the pale pink jumper he'd put out for me. Underneath it lay the lacy black thong. It was the only underwear there. With a sinking feeling, I pulled it on. It felt scratchy and unnatural against my skin, totally wrong. Jaw clenched, body shaking, I yanked on the jumper, jeans and heart-covered socks then brushed my teeth, taking longer than necessary, making the most of every single second away from him. The clock was ticking. Ethel had applied more pressure. Mikey was going to have to make a move soon, and I was going to go through hell.

Chapter 45

Back in the bedroom, Mikey cuffed me to the bed then told me to close my eyes.

He was trembling, beyond excited. His body wagged like a puppy's, and he couldn't sit still.

With a noxious lump in my throat, I closed my eyes and waited.

'Hold out your hand,' he yipped.

I held out my left hand, palm up.

'Hold it the other way,' he said.

I turned my hand over and tried to stop it shaking.

'Ready?' he said.

I said nothing.

'Aren't you excited for your present?' He was wounded now. I pictured him pouting. Scared his sulk would escalate to anger, I nodded.

'Good! Right…' A clammy hand took hold of mine. I flinched at his touch. 'Doctor Elouise Sparks, will you marry me?'

I opened my eyes to see him sliding an engagement ring onto my finger. I looked up at his face. He was grinning from ear to ear, but a slight worry creased his brow. His eyes were sparkling yet manic. He looked from the ring to my face then back again.

'Well? What do you say?'

He'd slid the ring on top of my other wedding and engagement rings without seeming to notice or care. I thought about pointing that out, and telling him that I was already married, but behind his smile, darkness was brewing; I sensed it in the shift in his posture, and the way he tilted his head and eyed me like I was a puzzle to be solved.

'If we're engaged, we can have, um, we can do it.' He mumbled the last two words into his collar bone and looked up at me, cheeks rosy as Bashful's. I wanted to slap him. Slap away his delusions until there was nothing left but a pulpy mess.

I cleared my throat. Forced a smile that felt more like a grimace. 'Do you really love me that way, Mikey?'

He frowned and nodded. 'I – er – yes.'

'What do you love about me?'

He raised his eyes as if searching for the answer inside his warped brain. Finally, tightening his grip on my hand and looking directly into my eyes, he said, 'I love your face. And your eyes. And your, um…' He glanced down at my chest, blushed and looked up quickly.

'So you find me physically attractive. But what do you love about me?' I pulled my hand out of his sweaty grasp and poked my thumb at my heart.

After a moment, his eyes lit up. 'I love the way you can keep secrets!'

An idea sparked in my brain, and I grabbed onto it with both hands and pounced. Leaning forward, I patted his knee and whispered, 'Like the secret about how you accidentally killed Simon?'

He swallowed thickly but nodded, eyes wet. 'I don't like to think about that.'

'No. I know you don't. Sorry. But let's think about this. Who are we working hard to keep this secret from?'

'Nana.'

'OK. Good. And why are we keeping that secret from Nana?'

'Because we don't want her to get cross and punish me?'

'Exactly. What other secret are we keeping from her?'

He frowned then wiggled with pride. 'I know! We're keeping it secret that I didn't put you down the well when she told me to.'

'Yes! And why are we keeping that a secret, Mikey?'

'Because…because I didn't want you to go down there again, because it's not nice and I, well, I care about you.'

'Yes. Now, what's the last secret we're keeping?'

'That I didn't sleep down the well the second time she told me to.'

'And why aren't we telling her that?'

He raised his thumb to his mouth but scratched his head instead of slipping it between his lips. As if struggling to process his thoughts, he said, 'Because I don't want to go down there anymore.'

'And because making you go down there is wrong,' I added firmly, patting his knee, and nodding, eyes locked on his.

Mikey mirrored my nod. 'Yes. Because it's…wrong.'

'And do you think it's right to marry me because she told you to?'

He frowned heavily and yanked on his hair. 'But I think I love you…'

'Think carefully before you answer this. Do you think about me every waking moment? Would you die for me? Because that's what real love is.'

'I – I'm not sure. No. I don't think so. I think about Christmas every second of every day, so I guess I love that more than you.' His eyes dropped to the gold band on my finger. His lower lip wobbled, and he looked up at me. A tear hovered in the corner of his left eye. 'But if we're not married, you won't do it with me, and that's what needs to happen.'

'That's what she says needs to happen, but what do you want to happen? And is she right to force us to do something we don't want to do?'

He smiled shyly and glanced up at me through his long, orange lashes, 'But I do want to do it with you. I've never done it before, and I think you're really pretty.'

My heart thumped. He rested his hand on top of mine on his knee. I fought the urge to rip it away. 'Well, I don't want to do it so it's wrong to force me, isn't it?'

'I don't want to force you to do anything.'

'Good. You agree it's wrong of her to tell you to have sex with me?'

His larynx bobbed and he scratched a piece of sleep out of his eye and flicked it onto the carpet. He didn't say anything, only stared at the iron railing behind me, a frown lying thickly behind his gaze.

'Ethel always tells you to do something because it suits her, not because it suits you. Why does she want you to have sex with me Mikey? What's in it for her?'

He glanced up at me, shock dropping his jaw and widening his eyes, as if he couldn't believe I understood the woman so well. 'She wants a baby.' He whispered the word 'baby' as if it was a sinful thing.

'Do you want a baby?'

He shook his head. 'I don't know anything about babies. I'm worried I'd hurt it.'

'Well, I have a secret that we can keep that will mean we don't have to do anything we don't feel ready to do, but which will also give her what she wants.'

He perked up and smiled excitedly. 'What secret?'

It seemed secrets were fun to him now.

'I'm already pregnant.'

He jumped as if he'd been shot and jerked to his feet. 'What? How?'

'That doesn't matter,' I said, frightened of the anger and confusion darkening his stare, 'all that matters is that I'm going to have a baby. We can tell Ethel that we had sex and I'm pregnant. It'll make her happy, but we'll keep the rest a secret.'

I smiled manically and nodded, trying to express that this was the best idea in the whole world. But he began to pace the space beside the bed, shaking his head and muttering indecipherable sentences.

'Mikey?'

He turned his head at my voice but his eyes were gone. In a distant voice, he said, 'I need to think about this. I need to think. Secrets aren't always good, you know. I don't want to be a wicked boy. Wicked boys get punished.'

Then he was gone – striding out of the room and locking the door without a glance or word.

*

It was long past lunch, I guessed nearing dinnertime. Outside snow was falling again, the sky a sallow-grey that reminded me of hospital corridors. In the snowstorm and lowering light, the cottage seemed more remote than ever, trapped within mounds of snow and ice, hidden too well from prying eyes and wondering feet. I realised I'd recently gained another enemy. The snow was a profound, unpredictable force that continued to smother all hope of escape as it swamped the mountain and swallowed the earth. Even if I did somehow manage to flee the confines of the cottage, I wouldn't get far. Mikey's car would need to be dug out of the snow before it could be driven anywhere, and I doubted I'd have time to find a shovel and dig, unless of course Mikey and the witch were already dead.

He'd been gone for ages, where to I didn't know. There hadn't been any noise next door so at least he hadn't gone to see Ethel, and he hadn't left the house. I would have heard the engine, and besides, he wasn't driving anywhere in this weather.

Unfortunately, he was back.

'Lie on your back and take off your jumper,' Mikey said.

He stood in the doorway with his hands on his hips. His jaw was clenched, and his temple twitched. Behind him the landing light was off, plunging his face in shadow.

I tensed. His voice held an authoritarian edge I'd never

known before. I couldn't make out his expression, but sensed danger. Suddenly, the metal cuff felt even tighter on my wrist, my situation the worst it had ever been. Despite the icy chill in the air, the room felt too hot.

'I said, lie on your back and take off your jumper.' His voice was hard and deep, deeper than before. It was as if he'd been possessed by an older man.

'Why?' I said, trying to keep the wobble out of my voice.

'Because I said so.'

He stepped into the bedroom, shut and locked the door behind him. Turning to face me, he looked down at my body, expression hard and unreadable, hands once more on his hips, a pose I imagined a younger Ethel would have adopted whenever she felt called upon to punish little Mikey Bell.

I tried to read his face, but it was impossible. The Mikey I'd grown to know was gone. In his place was an imposter whose intentions I couldn't work out. There was no vulnerability here, no weakness, only self-assuredness and control.

'I'm not going to tell you again.'

I wore no bra underneath the pink jumper.

My body began to shake uncontrollably, but I shuffled down the bed and lay on my back. With difficulty I pulled off the jumper using my free hand. Once it was off, my skin goosed and my nipples – which were larger and darker than normal - went erect. The jumper remained bunched up on the cuff above my right arm. I covered my breasts with my left arm and met his gaze. His eyes raked my torso, moving from my chest down to my abdomen where his gaze rested.

He took a step towards the bed then stopped and leaned over, staring intently at my stomach.

A huge gust of relief swept through me as I realised what he was doing: he was looking for a bump, checking to see whether I was lying or not about the baby.

'You can see a slight bump there -'

He glared at me, and I shut up, heart pounding.

He drew nearer to the bed never moving his gaze from the small protrusion, and I prayed he could see it, that he believed I was telling the truth. I peered down at myself. I wasn't imagining the slight distension of my belly, was I? It was obvious to other people too, wasn't it? It had to be. If Mikey – or whoever this person was who'd taken his place – didn't believe I was pregnant, he might decide to follow through with Ethel's instructions and take me by force.

For what felt like an hour, he remained leaning over me, so close I could smell the sourness of his breath and feel its heat against my skin. Any second I expected him to touch me, to feel his slippery eel fingers move up my stomach onto my breasts.

I remained as still as a statue.

His breath was hot against my skin. So close I could feel its moisture.

Chills coursed through my body, and I trembled like glass in an earthquake, feeling like I would break any second, wondering how I hadn't broken yet.

Finally, he walked away. I opened my eyes to see him at the door watching me. He shook his head suddenly, making me jump. A wide smile broke out on his face transforming him back into the Mikey I knew. In an excited voice, eyes glazed, he said, 'Yes! You're telling the truth.'

His eyes centred and focused on me. He blew me a kiss and grinned. 'I knew you wouldn't lie to me, Doc. I knew I could trust you. Isn't this exciting? Nana's going to be so pleased. I can't wait to tell her the good news.'

'Wait! Mikey, you can't tell her I'm pregnant yet.'

His face fell. 'Why not? I want to tell her now.'

Because she needs to think we've only just had sex. If that's the case, I won't know I'm pregnant for another two weeks or so when I miss my next period.'

‘Oh.’ His foot tapped. ‘OK.’

‘Promise me you won’t say anything yet?’

He kicked the end of the bed softly but nodded. ‘I promise.’

‘Great. I’ll let you know the second you can tell her, OK?’

A small smile lifted the corner of his mouth and he bounded over to me and gave me a hug. I stiffened in his arms. Luckily, he didn’t seem to notice.

Pulling back so that our noses were an inch apart, he said, ‘I’ll go get supper ready. Oh, and is there anything else you need to help with our baby?’

My stomach clenched at the word ‘our’, but I smiled and said, ‘I’ll need to start taking folic acid and pregnancy vitamins. Can you get me a pregnancy bra too please? Oh, and some maternity clothes. Perhaps you could get them when the snow’s melted?’ He liked to feel useful. It gave him an iota of the self-worth he was so greatly lacking.

‘Of course! Great. Gosh, I can’t wait to tell Nana! She’s going to be so pleased.’ He skipped out of the room, not bothering to close or lock the door.

A minute later Christmas music blasted through the house. Doris Day, one of my favourite female singers of all time, sang *Let it Snow! Let it Snow! Let it Snow!* I pushed myself up into a sitting position and tried not to think about what could have happened to me if Mikey’s inner demon hadn’t thought I was telling the truth.

Chapter 46

After lights out, when Mikey had taken himself off to bed, I heard movement on the landing. I lay in the darkness, heart hurtling along at a rip-roaring pace, fearing the worst. Had Mikey changed his mind? Had his evil internal voice won out and persuaded him that I was lying about being pregnant? Was he coming back to force himself on me after all?

But when the lock clicked and the door opened, the landing light revealed Ethel's scrawny, hunched silhouette, her body black against the harsh brightness. Dangling from her fingertips was Mikey's lanyard. She must have crept into his room and taken it. For a long time, she remained in the doorway regarding me in silence. Only her wheezy breaths pierced the quiet heaviness of the night. It was too dark for me to see her face. Mikey had drawn the elf curtains closed and clouds obscured the moon making the room pitch black.

I closed my eyes and pretended to be asleep, hoping she'd go away, but she stayed put. I could feel her decaying body hovering in the doorway souring the stale air with its sickness. She hacked out a cough and I listened, half-pleased and half-disgusted. How long did the vile battle-ax have left? Weeks? Months? I prayed she was dead before the baby was born. Surely the cancer was metastasising by now, or something fatal like sepsis would wipe her out soon after Christmas Day.

My breath hitched and panic skewered all else - what would happen when I went into labour? If Ethel was still alive, there was no way she'd allow Mikey to take me to hospital. She'd force him to help me or make me give birth all alone. As long as the baby survived, she wouldn't care what happened to me. She probably hoped I'd die during the process. With me out of the way, she could take complete control of the baby.

A creak made me flinch.

'I know you're awake,' she rasped.

I opened my eyes and shifted into a seated position, desperate to get this over with and get her gone. 'What do you want?'

She shuffled towards the bed, moving at a snail's pace, breathing heavily. 'I want to talk to you.'

She perched on the far corner of the bed. Now that she was closer, with the landing light casting a glow, I could make out her face. She was smiling but her eyes were narrow. The smell of urine wafted towards me. When she spoke, a foul, manure-like smell tainted the air.

'How was it?' she said.

I knew what she was referring to. I readied myself to lie. Told myself to sound more distraught than I felt, which wouldn't be hard. I hugged my knees to my chest and shook my head. 'I don't want to talk about it.'

'I don't care. I need to hear how it went. Did he inject you with his seed?'

I winced at her language and nodded, looking down at my knees.

'Did it hurt?' Her voice was strange; softer, more human.

'Yes.' I looked up. Met her eyes. Sniffed.

'And you didn't go to the toilet afterwards?'

'No. Mikey didn't give me the option.'

She nodded, a small smile on her lips. 'That's good. We wouldn't want you to get rid of the seed now, would we?'

I swallowed and looked away.

For a long time, she was quiet. Her eyes never left my face. Finally, she sighed and said, 'I know that can't have been easy for you, but sometimes the most important things are the hardest. I never would have had my daughter had I not done what you've just done. In time, you'll be glad you did this.'

'What – were you forced too?'

She raised her chin and stared at the wall. 'Yes. But it was for the best. If I hadn't had my daughter, she wouldn't have had Mikey and I wouldn't have him here today to look after me. Everything works out for the best in the end.'

It was a bizarre sort of logic, but I knew better than to question it. Instead, I said, 'I have a good feeling that it worked.'

Her face snapped around and her eyes thinned to black slits. 'How on earth would you know that?'

Shit. Think of something.

I remembered a friend saying she'd felt a zing of electricity one of the times she and her husband had tried for a baby and hey presto, she'd fallen pregnant. It was the only idea I had.

'I felt something strange, like a spark, when he, you know.'

She shuffled up the bed and grabbed my wrist in an iron grip. 'You'd better not be lying to me, Rachel. You know how much I hate filthy liars.'

'I'm not lying. I promise. I thought you'd be pleased.'

'Did he make you bleed?' she said suddenly, releasing my wrist.

Oh God.

She stood and hobbled towards the front door where she reached up and flicked on the bedroom light. I blinked away the brightness. She began to shuffle back towards me, and panic clogged my throat. There wasn't any blood because he hadn't touched me. Was she going to look? Could I persuade her he'd been gentle and that I hadn't fought, which was why there wasn't any blood?

'He's a large lad, is Mikey,' she said, her insinuation disgustingly clear. 'So was the father of my daughter, so I know there should be blood.'

She shuffled back towards the bed, and I tensed, knowing full well there was no blood to see down there. Frantically, I blurted, 'He was gentle, and I was too scared to fight. I let it happen.'

'I don't believe you,' she snarled.

She stood beside the bed, nostrils flaring, chest heaving, eyes pinpricks in the saggy skin of her face. 'Pull back the cover.'

'Why?'

'You know full well why!'

'What was your daughter's name?' I said, desperate to distract her.

Ethel's face went slack and, for a moment, she looked vulnerable and small. In a thin voice, she said, 'Harriet. Her name was Harriet. She died in a car crash when Mikey was six. She left him in the house on another one of her booze runs and crashed her car into a tree.'

'I'm sorry. Mikey told me she left him.'

She focused on me, eyes hard and glittering. 'It was better he thought that. Easier to hate her, easier to move on and accept me as his new mother that way.'

'Do you love Mikey?'

She scowled, and I regretted the question. Ignoring me, she said, 'Pull back the cover so I can see you.'

'What happened to Frank?' I blurted.

Her face turned purple. The loose skin around her jaw quivered as she stabbed her finger into my chest, brought her face close to mine and spat, 'Don't you ever say his name! Ever!'

'You killed him, didn't you?'

Her eyes went apoplectic, bulging from her skull like glass marbles. She raised a hand to slap me and I grabbed her wrist before she could strike and smashed my forehead into her nose. She cried out and her face whipped backwards. I held her wrist tightly to stop her falling off the bed and snatched the lanyard out of her other hand. Realisation widened her eyes, and she reached forward and tried to get it back, blood streaming from her nose, eyes watering, mouth foaming with rage. Letting go of her wrist, I looped the lanyard strap around her neck, pulled tight, and began to choke her, pushing my knee into her side to create more tension.

The strap cut into her skin, and she flailed at it with gnarled fingers, eyes wide, mouth open, spit rattling in her throat like cyanide. Her legs kicked out, but she was weaker than me, older and riddled with cancer - no match for my strength or fury.

Anger flooded my system as I continued to choke her. Echoes of everything she'd said and done to me over the last three months spun around my mind like a whorl of barbed wire, stabbing and tearing at me, urging me to squeeze tighter.

All the while, I kept darting glances at the doorway, fearful Mikey would appear any second, but the opening remained empty, a bright rectangle of light symbolising freedom.

Ethel kicked out a foot and managed to catch the bedside table. The small lamp and snow globe fell to the ground with thunderous thuds. I tensed and froze, and she reached around. Twisting and hissing like Medusa, she scratched her nail down my cheek. Warm liquid trickled off my face onto my leg. Gritting my teeth, I kneed her back more forcefully and retightened my chokehold. She clawed at my fingers and tore my skin, but I pulled harder, arms shaking from the effort, determined not to loosen my grip again.

After another minute or so, she stopped struggling and went limp. Her eyes were gone. Blank and staring, milky and bloodshot. Chilling, even in death.

Shaking violently, I pulled the strap over her head, lowered her back onto the bed, and scrambled to find the handcuff key, listening all the time for any movement coming from Mikey's bedroom or the landing. For now, all was quiet.

I slotted the key into the tiny mechanism. When the metal clicked open, the relief was insane. I ripped my wrist out of the cuff and got off the bed.

I hesitated next to the bed. Ethel remained on her back on top of the mattress, eyes closed, feet dangling off the edge.

I watched for a second to check she was definitely dead. There was no movement. No hint of life left in the wicked witch.

I had no time left. Mikey could wake up any second.

A muffled groan broke the silence. It was a sound unlike I'd ever heard before – an odd noise, like a mournful, desperate moan. I wondered if Mikey was having a nightmare, or if he'd fallen out of bed. Either way, I needed to get moving.

I glanced at the tree, dashed over, yanked out the fairy light plug, dragged the plastic monstrosity over to the bed and heaved it on top of her. Dust tickled my nose. I stared at my artwork. Ethel's feet stuck out from under the tree, like the Wicked Witch of the East. I smiled.

Why did you do that?

For good measure.

You're losing it.

I don't care.

I hurried to the door, fingers tight and sweaty on the lanyard strap.

Chapter 47

I've got the keys! I've got the keys!

The mantra played on repeat in my head, my inner voice hysterical. I took one more look at Ethel then peered around the jamb at the landing. To get to the stairs I needed to pass Mikey's room. Knowing the landing light might wake him, I raised my hand and fumbled around on the wall outside my room, found the light switch and flicked it off, plummeting the house into solid darkness and immediately wondering whether that had been the right thing to do, because now I was blind, with only my memory and hands to guide me. I'd been along this landing, down the stairs and past the front door many times in the last three months, but had never navigated it blind.

A different kind of hysteria bubbled up in my lungs and I found myself breathing erratically and too loudly. I looped the lanyard around my neck and stepped out onto the landing, closing my mouth and trying to focus on breathing through my nose. My legs shook as I crept out of the room. With my left hand on the wall for guidance, I tiptoed across the thin carpet, aware I was only wearing socks. Soon I would be outside in the snow and my feet would be freezing, but there was no way in hell I was going back into that Christmas room to fetch some shoes. I could imagine Ethel rising from the dead, her skeletal hand wrapping itself in my hair; I pictured her screaming, Mikey running into the room, pinning me to the bed, cuffing me up again, and her ordering him to punish me.

That wasn't going to happen. She was dead. There was no way I was ever setting foot in that festive lair again.

I took a step and the floor creaked. Chills flared along

the back of my neck, and I froze. My heartbeat pulsed angrily in my throat, as if barking at me to slow down, take my time. The urge to sprint past Ethel's and then Mikey's room was overwhelming.

Take it slowly. Don't panic. Don't rush. You need to be as quiet as a mouse.

The Christmas poem threatened to erupt in my head. I crushed it with thoughts of freedom, trying not to fret about the elephant in my escape plan: the snow. Once I reached the car, what then?

Think about it when you get there. Now move.

I took another step. No creak. Relief was a warm balm on my chest. Another step and another. A creak, so loud it seemed to rock the cottage. I froze, heart somersaulting.

I had just reached level with Mikey's bedroom. I couldn't tell if his door was open or shut, it was that dark.

I took another step, my fingers curled around the banister, shifting closer to the stairs and away from the bedroom. A mattress squealed. My eyes widened and the hairs on my arms goosed. I stayed as still as stone and listened. There was another squeal, a grunt and then the sound of snoring – and nothing had ever sounded so good. He must have been heavily asleep. I almost melted with relief.

I crept past his bedroom and tiptoed past the end of the landing opposite the bathroom, hand sweaty on the banister. At the top of the stairs, I thought about trying something clever, like sliding down the banister Mary Poppins-style; that would mean no floorboard creaks that might give me away, but an image of me losing my balance and falling off the banister and breaking my wrist crumpled that idea and tossed it in the bin. I wasn't a gymnast or a stunt artist; who was I kidding? I was a pregnant woman who liked to do a bit of yoga in her spare time. The chances of me gliding accident-free down the banister like some sort of superhero amounted to zero.

Rolling my eyes at the idea, I turned to face the banister and gripped it with both hands, then began to descend, placing each foot on the step as close to the banister as possible. The middle of the steps creaked more than the outer edges. I knew this but couldn't remember how I knew it. One of those useless facts you accumulate through life. Except now it wasn't useless; now, it was golden.

The problem was the rule wasn't gospel.

On the fifth step down, an almighty creak screeched through the night, cutting the silence in half like a guillotine through someone's neck. I stayed stock-still. The air was cold but sweat dripped into my eye. An itch ticked my nose, but I didn't move to scratch it.

After a few more seconds, I felt safe enough to keep moving.

I had to fight the urge to sprint the rest of the way down. Finally, I made it to the ground floor of the cottage. I allowed myself a tremulous smile and felt my way to the front door.

This is it! Freedom!

But the house was so dark that I couldn‘t locate the right key without trying them all and I didn't have time to waste. I felt my way into the living room, fumbled across the sofa and found the lamp. I hesitated, sucked in a sharp breath then switched on the light. The room burst into colour and sweat trickled down the neck of my pink pyjamas. I looked down at the keys, trying to work out which one belonged to the front door. There were three that could have worked. I turned and began to run out of the room and caught my knee on Ethel's table, knocking her ash tray to the carpet. It landed with a dull thud. I flinched and looked up at the ceiling, certain I'd heard movement above. I waited for the sound of Mikey's voice or thundering feet, but all was silent except for the ticking of the clock.

With a shiver, I crossed the room and dashed to the

front door. My hands were shaking so much that it took me several tries to get my first attempt into the keyhole. It refused to go in all the way. I swapped it for the second key. Fumbled with it, slotted it in. Bingo.

I turned the key and the lock clicked. Peels from heaven rang down and I grinned. I took the lanyard off my neck, leaving the key in the door, grabbed Mikey's blue anorak off the coat hook and yanked it on. I spotted a scarf and pulled that on too, winding it around my neck three times. Then I slipped my feet into Mikey's boots. They were about five sizes too big, but better than nothing. I turned the key again, opened the door, removed the key and stepped outside. I was immediately hit by air so cold I thought I might freeze to death on the spot. The snow had stopped, and the temperature had plummeted turning the mountain to a wasteland of ice.

Now that I was outside, the moon made itself known, a curved blade in the blackened sky, tinting the land charcoal.

The expanse before me was quiet and still, suffocated by darkness and hardened snow. Not a breath of wind stirred, which seemed odd given I was on a mountain.

If I'd thought the cottage remote before, it was nothing to how I thought about it now. Everything looked so bleak and barren, so utterly alien that I felt like I'd been transported to a different planet. I may as well have been, I was so far from human life.

In my head, Ethel and Mikey didn't classify as human. Once upon a time he had been an innocent little boy full of hope and love, but Ethel's cruelty had stolen his humanity from him, and turned him into a monster.

My breath fogged in the ice-cold air and my nose began to tingle. I closed the door behind me and locked it. An immediate wave of relief rushed my senses, and I didn't delay; I swivelled and set off through eight inches of hard snow, crunching my way towards the Ranger.

Progress was tortuously slow, every inhalation painfully

cold. Each step had half of my leg plunging into the ice, crisp, wet snow slipping into Mikey's boots and soaking my socks. It was an effort to heave my foot back out and take the next step. Within three steps, I was panting from the exertion and my toes were stinging. I buried my fingers in the long sleeves of Mikey's anorak, despising the sour smell of breath that clung to the blue material. Memories stirred of that horrid night, the night Mikey had beaten Jacob and taken me from my home. I dug deeper, determined to keep going. I was getting my baby and myself out of here. Now. With Jacob in my mind's eye, I crumped on through the snow – one more step – two more steps - three - using my arms to push me forward, every breath an effort, my body seeming impossibly heavy. The car never seemed to get closer; it felt like a mirage in the desert, a fantasy I would never reach.

After three more steps and only two feet from the Ranger, fearing I'd pass out if I didn't rest for a moment, I stopped and put my hand in my pocket. My fingers brushed icy metal. I closed them around the small, thin object and pulled out a small torch. I grinned, knowing such a tool couldn't have come at a better time. My discovery spurred me on, and I reached the car door and used the torchlight to find the car key and slot it into the door. It worked.

I had to battle with the door to open it. Once behind the wheel, I jammed the key into the ignition and started the engine, relieved out of my head when it grumbled to life, my breath fogging in front of my face. Turning on the light, I found the heating dial and turned it on full. It blasted out cold, damp-smelling air and I silently told it to hurry and warm up quickly. The windscreen wipers refused to move because the screen was thick with compacted snow.

I dug around in the car looking for de-icer and found some in the glove compartment. Thanking my lucky stars, I got out of the vehicle and stamped my way around to the bonnet where I brushed off as much snow as possible. It was hard work, the snow stubbornly set on the glass, the final layer a rigid crust. Once I'd removed some of it, I sprayed the screen with the de-icer then did the same to the driver's and passenger's windows. I didn't bother with the back window – there wasn't any time to waste. I slipped behind the wheel again, shut the door and put the Ranger in first gear. The heater was producing tepid air now that barely cut the surface of the car's icy interior. I held my breath, pressed the accelerator, but the wheels didn't respond at all.

Oh God.

The car continued to rumble, mocking me. Hot mist plumed into the night air. The engine was alive, but the wheels were to all intents and purposes dead. Blocked in by too many inches of undamaged snow.

I climbed back out of the car and began to kick snow away from the front wheel, aiming to create a two metre-length path of snow-less ground, hoping that once the Ranger got a bit of traction and speed it would plough the rest of the way forward through the snow and whiz me out of here. White powder sprayed the air. Clods and crumbs flew and fell. I kept kicking. Clearing a pathway in front of each wheel was my only idea. I feared it might not work, but the urge to leave as fast as possible overrode everything else. I didn't have time to come up with another plan or create a longer path and I didn't have a shovel. There was probably one in the house or garden shed but I wasn't going back there. I'd rather hike down the mountain in the ice and snow than return to the cottage. But driving away from here was my best, fastest and safest bet. I would have to use my feet.

I glanced back at the cottage, neck tingling, suddenly certain I'd heard something, but the cottage remained a silent bulk in the darkness. I hadn't turned off the living room lamp so light glowed softly behind the downstairs curtains but upstairs remained pitch black. The rumbling engine and my frantic breathing were all the sound I could hear. Otherwise, the night remained still and undisturbed.

I turned back to the job at hand. Kicking the snow was too slow, so I got down on all fours and burrowed away like a dog digging for a bone. My fingers were numb, and the cold had seeped into my bones, but I kept going until I could see earth. I pushed myself to my feet and stomped over to the front passenger wheel, knelt, and attacked the snow there, body quivering, teeth chattering, knees wet and freezing. Mikey's anorak wasn't especially thick, and my cotton pyjamas offered little warmth against the icy air. Fears of pneumonia swept through my mind, but I kept going, my movements generating much-needed heat; heat that I hoped would keep my baby warm enough to stay alive.

I heard something then. A blood-curdling wail.

I looked back at the house to see Mikey plunging through the snow towards me with something large in his hand.

Chapter 48

I stamped past the bonnet, rounded the car and dived in behind the wheel. A glance told me Mikey was a foot from the boot. I slammed the door shut and jabbed on the central locking just as he lunged for the door. He hammered his fists against the window, eyes red and glassy, hair wild. Rage consumed him.

'NANA'S DEAD. SHE'S DEAD. YOU KILLED HER! AND YOU MOVED MY TREE!' He was sobbing and screaming at the same time, smashing his fists so hard against the glass I worried he'd break it. In his right hand he gripped a long-handled axe.

'YOU'RE NOT LEAVING ME. GET OUT. GET OUT NOW OR I'LL USE THIS.'

He stood back and raised the axe, eyes glinting madly, snot streaming out of his nose onto his lips.

I stamped on the accelerator and the Ranger lurched forward then stopped. *Oh no. Oh no, no, no, no – this can't be happening.*

Mikey ran to catch up and rounded the bonnet, standing between me and the stretch of snow-covered terrain behind him. The headlights made him raise his left hand to shield his eyes, but he never lowered the axe. He bared his teeth, chest rising and falling heavily and advanced on the windscreen. I knew what he was going to do, so I put the car in reverse and shot backwards two metres. The Ranger stopped again. Mikey continued to advance, and I accelerated and slammed the car into him, knocking him backwards off his feet. But the car stopped again, refusing to travel further because of the wretched snow. For a second, I thought I'd killed him, but then he was getting up and advancing again, not even limping; I'd only hit him at about five miles per hour and it had barely left a bruise.

I reversed again as he swung at the windscreen. The axe missed by an inch and the Ranger lurched backwards, again stopping. This time, Mikey didn't advance. He smeared sweat from his forehead and held his ground, daring me to try driving at him again, axe held ready in case I did.

'YOU NEED TO BE PUNISHED FOR WHAT YOU'VE DONE,' he screamed.

'Get out of the way!' I shrieked back, slamming my hand on the horn.

'NO.'

I looked down at the two metres of tramped-down snow in front of the car. Now that I'd driven over it twice, would I be able to gain enough speed to plough through the untouched snow? The Ranger was giving off a lot of heat, melting the snow around it. Exhaust fumes plumed in the air around us. I wanted to plough into him again, but if he brought the axe down at the right moment, he could shatter the windscreen and possibly split open my face along with it. Indecision locked me in chains.

Not knowing what to do but knowing the longer the car had to melt the ice, the better, I blurted, 'I didn't think she was dead. Her chest was moving when I left the room. She was breathing. Did you check her pulse?'

Uncertainty flickered in his eyes. 'Um, yes, I mean, no. But she looked dead.'

Little lost Mikey surfaced. My heart leapt with hope.

He sniffed. 'Do you really think she's not dead?'

I nodded. 'When I left, she was breathing. I'm certain of it.'

'Really?' Hope came to life in his eyes, and for a fleeting second pity swooped down on me.

'Yes. Go and see her. She probably needs a ciggy,' I said, forcing a laugh.

He lowered the axe and nodded, eyes shining. 'Yes. I'll do that. Okay. Don't worry, I'll be right back.'

He tramped through the snow past the bonnet and straight past my window. The axe swung by his side now and a hopeful smile pulled at his cheeks. It was as if all of his earlier distress had been wiped away by a giant, invisible hand.

I watched him disappear into the cottage in the rearview mirror with inexpressible relief surging through me. As soon as he was out of sight, I inched the Ranger forward. When it met resistance, it refused to go any further, so I reversed a little, then drove forward slowly, hoping to break through the compacted snow little by little. I kept checking the mirror, fearing that Mikey could come storming out any minute, but the cottage remained still.

Progress was minute and painful, but I was making small inroads into the snow. An idea suddenly sprang to my mind; the land ahead was flat for only about ten feet before it began to slope down. If I could clear those ten feet for the wheels, maybe gravity would do the rest. But how could I clear those ten feet? I glanced at the rear-view mirror. No Mikey.

I exhaled shakily then climbed through the space between the driver and passenger seats into the back and flicked on the back light then peered over the seats into the boot. Hallelujah! There was a pack of extra-long matches and two orange plastic fuel cans. Praying they still contained something, I pulled one over, beaming when liquid swished inside. I held my breath and opened the lid. It looked to be about two thirds full. I checked the other can but that was empty. I grabbed the pack of matches and shoved them in the anorak pocket.

I looked out of the back window at the cottage. It remained quiet as the dead. How long would it take for him to realise she was dead?

Leaving the engine running, I unlocked the doors and

climbed out of the car, lugging the petrol can with me, hoping lit fuel melted snow. Science wasn't my forte. I didn't have a clue. All I could do was attempt to set the snow on fire and hope for the best.

I moved round to the front right wheel as fast as possible. Reaching the section of untrampled snow, I poured a ten-step trail of gasoline onto the ground in front of the Ranger. Arms straining, I hurried back to the front passenger wheel and did the same, running out of gas about a step earlier than I had on the other side. I grabbed the packet out of my pocket and frantically pulled out a match. I tried to light it twice and failed. My fingers were numb, and I dropped the matchstick. Cursing, I pulled out another and attempted to light it. On the third attempt, it caught, and I bent over and dropped it onto the gas trail. The entire trail burst into flame for about two seconds, then went out. The snow had melted a little but not enough. I did it again, managing to light it on the first attempt this time, and dropped the stick onto the path. The same thing happened. Another inch or so of snow melted. I looked back at the cottage, spine prickling, but Mikey wasn't anywhere to be seen.

Exhaling unsteadily, I lit the path again and again until only about four inches of snow remained. Hoping it would be enough I ran over to the other trail. It took me another three attempts to light the match. I repeated the same thing, over and over again. When about four inches of snow was left, I turned to go back to the car and jumped.

Mikey was in the Ranger sitting behind the wheel.

Chapter 49

I froze and stared, too horrified to move.

Mikey sat in the driver's seat. He'd turned off the headlights but kept on the inner light meaning we could both see each other.

He wants to see me. He wants to watch me die.

There was no sanity or mercy in his gaze, only cold, concrete hatred.

I thought of wolves and blood, and helpless maidens in distress.

Mikey was the wolf, and I was Little Red Riding Hood, but there was no huntsman to save me.

His eyes were on fire.

All the better to see you with, my dear.

I met his glare and tried to arrange my features into some semblance of anger to mask the tearing terror. I couldn't let him sense any weakness. I needed to pretend I wasn't afraid, act like I didn't know he was about to kill me.

Behind the wheel, his face glowed as white and round as a clown's. I thought about Stephen King's *IT*, wondered for a surreal beat if all of this was in my head, if I was the mad one rather than him. Mirror mirror on the wall, who's the maddest clown of all?

Random words kept jutting into my head, destroying all logical thought.

Soon it'll be you, Rachel. You'll be lying spread-eagled on the snow, blood turning the ground red.

I shook my head against its chaos and tried to think.

This was happening. It was real. I hadn't cleared a path and driven away from here and escaped. I'd failed, again.

It's not too late to save yourself.

And how exactly are you going to do that? He's in the car, engine humming, about to mow you down. You'll be dead quicker than he can say 'silent night'. In a moment, your heart will be as silent as the stars. And just as dead.

Mikey's eyes burned into mine. He was a wolf out for blood. Nothing was going to sway or stop him.

Above us, the moon hovered like a poised scythe, the sky black and dense, the snow on either side of the Ranger solid and unbroken; the opposite to me.

Shaking uncontrollably, I took a step back, raised my hand to my brow and shouted, 'Is she OK?'

My voice wobbled, as jellified as my legs, but I knew he'd heard me. I knew she wasn't OK. The wicked witch was dead. Unfortunately, Mikey's rage wasn't. It was alive and rampant.

I stepped back again and nearly fell over. Breathing hard, I placed my hand on my stomach in a desperate attempt to protect my baby.

He made the engine growl. His face twitched, and he lowered his head like a bull about to charge.

I held out my hands and began to back off the trail, out of the car's path, inching away, sensing sudden movement would make him attack.

The engine revved again, and Mikey's knuckles whitened on the steering wheel. Fumes barrelled into the air.

'Mikey, think about what you're doing. You don't want this.'

'You don't know what I want!' he screamed, white-lipped and shaking, 'No one does! No one ever has and no one ever will.'

He revved the engine again.

His eyes closed for a second and then he hunched over the wheel.

It was then that I knew for certain he was going to do it.

I leapt back as he drove forward. The Ranger sped towards me, and the corner of the bonnet caught my leg and knocked me to the ground. Pain speared my knee, and I watched helplessly as he stopped the car and climbed out, axe in hand.

I scrabbled backward on my bottom and tried to get to my feet, but my leg buckled under my weight, and I fell back down. Mikey advanced, swinging the axe by his side. I pulled the torch out of my pocket, switched it on and aimed it at his face.

'Please, Mikey, don't,' I said.

He stopped a foot away sneering down at me. Gone was little lost boy Mikey. In its place was that inner demon, the older man, the vindictive, cruel ego that a lifetime of Ethel's brutality had created.

'Mikey, I'm sorry about what happened to your nana. I really am, but I'm pregnant. An innocent baby is growing inside me. I couldn't stay here. Ethel hurt you when you were little. I knew she was going to hurt my baby and I couldn't let that happen.'

He began to hum *Rocking Around the Christmas Tree*, his eyes somewhere above my head, the axe passing from hand to hand. Without looking at me, he said, 'You killed her. You deserve to be punished now. I knew I couldn't trust you. You're bad, just like the rest of them.'

'The rest of who, Mikey?' I said, desperate to keep him talking.

His eyes locked on mine, and he crouched down in front of me. 'Everyone – me, my mother,' he hesitated, and uncertainty flickered before he whispered, 'Frank…'

'Your mother didn't abandon you, Mikey. She was killed in a car crash. Ethel told me.'

His eyes widened then thinned into a scowl. 'You're lying.'

'It's true. I promise. If you look it up on the internet, I'm sure you'll find evidence. A newspaper article or something. She lied to you to make you easier to control. Everything she's ever done to you has been about control and power. And what about Frank? What happened to him? She did something to him, didn't she? Something bad.'

A shudder seized his shoulders. He cast wildly about then, haunted and scared-looking, face pinched, and looked at me, some of the certainty gone.

Hope burst through my fear. 'Tell me about it Mikey. Tell me what happened.'

He rubbed his head aggressively with both hands. 'I can't. She made me promise.'

'She's gone, Mikey,' I whispered, 'She can't hurt you anymore.'

He looked up at me through tears. His chin wobbled and he whispered back, 'I need her.'

'You need to be safe and happy and free. She never would have allowed that. Think about what she did to Frank.'

He flinched at the name and jerked to his feet. Staring through me, he spoke in a hushed tone, words quick, hands wringing. 'I'm not sure I can. I'm not allowed to talk about it.'

'It's OK, Mikey. You can tell me everything. She's not here to punish you anymore.'

He stopped pacing and clasped his hands together in front of his heart, almost as if praying. In a small voice, he said, 'One day, Fr-Frank, well - one day – when I was about six years old - we were all in the kitchen and Nana was cooking a full English breakfast, and I accidentally spilled my drink and she turned and burned me with the pan, and Frank – I remember it like it was yesterday – he slammed his hands down on the kitchen table and shouted 'THAT'S ENOUGH!' His voice was so loud and scary that it made her jump. I'd never seen her look so shocked. Frank said he'd leave her if she ever laid a hand on me again. She nodded and turned back to the oven and Frank went back to his paper and I wanted to give Frank the biggest hug in the world, and then…then…' His lower lip trembled, and he dropped the axe, sank to his haunches and rocked back and forth, slipping his thumb into his mouth.

'What happened?' I said, placing the torch on the ground and leaning towards him.

Mikey's eyes widened with horror as they met mine; I could tell he wasn't seeing me; he was seeing that dreadful day, a day he'd tried so hard to forget.

'What did she do, Mikey?'

'She-she-she spun around and smashed the pan into his face. He fell off his chair and tried to protect himself with his hands. He was begging her to stop, and I was crying and trying to pull her off, but she wouldn't stop. She just kept hitting and hitting and hitting him until he was dead.'

He exhaled a long, shuddery breath and slipped his thumb back into his mouth. He carried on rocking, rocking and sucking, rocking and sucking. I shuffled on my bottom closer to him, eyes trained on his face, sure he was going to reach out suddenly and grab me by my throat, but he was gone.

'What happened next, Mikey?'

He didn't seem to hear me.

I inched my way closer, leg screaming in pain. Closer and closer until we were mere centimetres apart.

I opened my arms. 'Do you want a hug?'

He looked up at me, hope and confusion tussling, then nodded and bowed his head. I shifted onto my uninjured side and wrapped my right arm around his back. With my left arm, I reached behind him and crawled my fingers up the axe as close to the metal blade as possible. He let out a long, shaky sigh and began to cry. I raised the axe into the air. My arm shook with the weight of it. I hugged him closer with my right arm, felt him quivering against me. I remembered everything he'd done to me, everything he'd made me do. Tears ran down my cheeks. I tried to push them back. My arm shook. I remembered his scars, his horror. Thought about what could have happened to my baby because of him and his need for love.

I have to do this. He's given you no other choice.

You always have a choice.

'I'm sorry,' he mumbled the words into my neck. His breath caught at my nose, sour and rank.

The axe hung in the air, urging me to let it fall. I looked at the blade. Saw Ethel's ghost smiling back at me blackly.

I lay the axe on the snow, eased myself back and took his face in my hands. Looking into his eyes, I said, 'We're going to get in the car now, and I'm going to drive us out of here.'

He looked back sadly. His voice sounded small and impossibly young. 'Are we going to the police station?'

I hesitated, surprised he was so aware of what was happening and worried he would change and attack me again, but he lowered his eyes to his hands and nodded. When he looked up there was sad acceptance in his gaze, and a bit of relief.

'You're freezing,' I said, 'let's go.' I made myself sound less afraid than I felt.

I began to struggle to my feet, and he rushed to help me. He took most of my weight and side by side we walked over to the car.

'I think I can drive,' I said, frightened he'd offer.

He nodded again, slipped his thumb into his mouth, passed me the car key and trudged around to the passenger side.

My heart skipped a beat as a vision of him grabbing the wheel and steering us into a tree whipped and stuck.

'Mikey, I know this is a lot to ask, but would you mind getting in the boot?'

Disappointment furrowed his brow. It was then I knew I'd made a mistake.

'No,' he said, eyes wild, 'I can't get in the boot. I won't.'

He edged away. I clicked the fob and unlocked the boot, a cold sweat returning in my armpits.

'Please, Mikey,' I said, inching towards the driver's door.

He shook his head. Sweat flew from his face. He'd gone very white.

'Why won't you get in the boot? I'm sorry but I'd feel safer that way, just in case…' I trailed off, not sure what to say – just in case you go mental on me…

'NO.' He stamped his foot and pouted, which would have been comical if not for the flaring of his nose and darkening of his eyes. 'I won't and you can't make me.'

Movement behind him caught my eye. I swallowed a gasp but couldn't stop my eyes betraying what I'd seen. Jacob was walking out of the house dressed in the pjyamas he'd been wearing the night Mikey had taken me. He was bent double, skin whiter than paper, but alive – gloriously, miraculously alive. But...what? Had my Jacob been here all this time?

For a second or two, I stared, unable to believe my husband was here. That I wasn't imagining him. Then Jacob looked into my eyes and nodded. Tears shone in his eyes and a tremulous smile touched his lips. Lips I never thought I would see again.

He put a finger to his mouth, and I gave the tiniest of nods back, heart singing. The future suddenly seemed like a rainbow-filled utopia, and the infinite black tunnel of before began to shrink in my mind, to be eradicated by joy and hope.

I allowed myself a brief moment to imagine the future, one in which Jacob and I and our baby were together. And I forgave my parents and let them back in to my life. I had been too stubborn. It was time to let it go, and be a proper family again.

But that would only happen if we could escape the mountain with our lives. Mikey was watching me, begging with his eyes for me not to force him to get inside the boot.

Behind Mikey, Jacob inched closer.

I looked at Mikey. Smiling at him, I said, 'That's okay. You can sit in the back instead.'

Relief flew out of him in one whoosh of breath and he clapped his hands.

Jacob edged towards the axe, which I'd left lying in the snow. The movement caught Mikey's periphery; he spun around and stared straight at Jacob. My husband's eyes were woozy and he'd lost a lot of weight. Had Mikey been keeping him drugged, sedating him all this time so he couldn't escape?

My heart jolted.

For a second, neither man moved, and then Jacob shot towards the axe and grabbed it up - but Mikey lunged forward and gripped his inner elbow, holding his arm high. Jacob's arm quivered with the effort of fighting back.

I darted forward and said, 'Stop. Jacob, stop. He's handing himself in.'

'I don't believe that for a second,' Jacob snarled back, his voice hoarse and rough, as if it hadn't been used for years.

'But -'

Jacob kicked Mikey in the stomach. Mikey cried out and doubled over, releasing his grip on Jacob's arm.

Jacob didn't hesitate; he swung the axe down directly onto Mikey's left shoulder. Mikey fell to the snow screaming. Blood splattered onto the snow, melting it to scarlet slush.

Jacob lunged forward, ripped the axe out of his shoulder and took aim at Mikey's head, but I ran forward and grabbed his quivering arm. 'No. Stop. It's over.'

My best friend shook his head at me. His lips were blue and trembly. 'It'll only be over when this bastard's dead.'

I shook my head and pushed down his arm. 'He's not in any state to put up a fight now. Look at him.'

Mikey writhed around in the snow, crying and hugging

himself, as helpless as a newborn baby, as helpless really as he'd always been.

'Why, Mikey? Why take Jacob too?' I said through gritted teeth.

'For you. He was for you,' he sobbed.

'What do you mean? '

'He was your Christmas present. I wanted to surprise you. Even though he's a liar and a cheat, I knew you wanted him. That he would be the perfect present. You always wanted him more than me.'

'But then what, Mikey? Were you going to keep us here forever?'

Mikey stopped writhing and shook his head. Snot ran from his nose like slime. 'I don't know. It would have been up to Nana.'

'Did she know he was here?' I said.

Mikey nodded. 'She was really angry with me when I told her, but I didn't have to go in the well that time. After a little bit, she thought it was funny.'

Funny? Even though the hag was dead, I wanted to grab some tinsel and wring her scrawny neck all over again.

Mikey buried his face in his hands. I looked away. I never wanted to speak to him again, couldn't bear the sight of him.

Jacob's gaze focused on mine.

'Have you been here all this time?' I said, thinking about the upstairs room I'd never been in. The one whose door was always shut. The odd sound I'd heard. Jacob's smell in the air that I thought I'd imagined.

He released a shuddery breath. 'No. Somehow he got into the house and took me – I don't know – it feels like decades but it must have been a couple of weeks ago. He's been injecting me with something, keeping me weak and helpless. He's given me protein shakes to drink. Kept me gagged. Most of the time I was so out of it I didn't know where I was. Sometimes I'd become aware of him helping me out of bed to go to the bathroom, but I was too weak to put up a fight.'

I shook my head, unable to believe Mikey had managed to hide him right under my nose, that Jacob had been so close all this time, that Mikey had lied so convincingly. Then again, he'd learnt to lie from the best. 'How did you get out of the room?'

'I think he got careless or maybe ran out of drugs. I woke up properly for the first time a while ago. After a bit, I was with it enough to get out of bed. When I tried the door, it was unlocked, so I came out.'

'Thank God he got careless.'

'He never hurt me,' Jacob said, preempting my next question. His eyes darkened and he glared around at Mikey. 'Has he touched you? Hurt you? If he has, I'll –'

'No. He hasn't touched me. That wasn't what he wanted. In fact none of this was really. It all came from his grandmother.'

Jacob's relief was palpable. After a moment, confusion flickered in his tired eyes. 'Who? There's been someone else here all this time?'

'Yes. Ethel. She's tortured him his whole life. Turned him into this monster. But she's dead now, thank God.'

Mikey was quiet now, eyes blank and staring, lying like a broken statue in the bloodied snow with his thumb tucked between his lips. Gone, possibly forever.

Jacob shook his head and wiped a tear off my cheek.

He choked out a brittle laugh. 'I must stink. I haven't had a wash since he took me.'

I held his hand and moved it to rest on the tiny miracle happening inside me. His eyes widened. He looked down, then up at my face, lips parted. 'Are you -'

I nodded. 'The baby's yours. *Ours*.'

'But…'

I threw my arms around his neck. Burying my nose in his shoulder, I said, 'I don't have a clue. All I know is we're going to have a baby and we're not going to call it Harriet.'

Jacob held me closer and I pushed my tummy against his shivering body. Between us, our little bump felt snug and secure. Safe. It was our first family cuddle. I smiled through my tears, thinking about how many more hugs there were to come, and how I was going to make sure my parents got to have their share. Life was too short and unpredictable to hold on to grudges. Between us, we'd wasted so much time. From now on, I was going to change that and give our baby the loving, unfractured family I'd had growing up. The sort of family Mikey had been denied, but so desperately needed.

Acknowledgements

Her No.1 Fan was inspired by Stephen King's *Misery*, so special thanks must go to this brilliant writer.

Thank you, as always, to my parents, Steve and Penny, and my husband, Tommy, who offered crucial ideas and spotted an embarrassing number of typos throughout the editing process.

Huge thanks to my dad (my secret no.1 fan), for spearheading the publishing side of things, giving me the time and energy to focus on the enjoyable stuff – writing!

Much gratitude goes to my superbly talented cover designer, Olly, at More Visual Ltd, and to my excellent beta readers, Cathryn Northfield and Veronika Jordan, for their invaluable feedback and positive comments.

I am incredibly grateful to everyone from ARC readers to bloggers, Instagrammers, and readers like you for supporting my writing journey and showing such enthusiasm and passion for my stories. My next book, *The Girl Who Heard Maggots*, is out in December 2024, so watch this space!

P.S. I would be ever so grateful if you could pop your review on Amazon and other social media sites when you get a spare moment. I love seeing your thoughts and it's such a huge help in spreading the word to other thriller fans.

ABOUT THE AUTHOR

Abby Davies was born in Macclesfield in 1984. She grew up in Bedfordshire in a seventeenth-century cottage near Flitton Moor and started writing thrillers when she was 7 years old.

After reading English Literature at Sheffield University and training to be an English teacher, she wrote novels in her free time and attained an MA in Creative Writing.

She was shortlisted for the Mslexia Novel Competition in 2018 and longlisted for the Blue Pencil Agency First Novel Award in 2019. Her debut *Mother Loves Me* was published by HarperCollins in 2020. *The Cult* came out in 2021. *Arrietty* was released in July 2023. *Her No.1 Fan* is her fourth novel.

She lives in Wiltshire with her husband, daughter and two crazy cocker spaniels.

Find out more about Abby and her books online at

www.abbydavies.com

Twitter: @Abby13Richards

Instagram: @abbydaviesauthor

Printed in Great Britain
by Amazon

28546221R00144